Carol's Image

The Fairfield Series

By

Maryann Jordan

Carol's Image
Copyright © 2014 Maryann Jordan
Print Edition

Cover Design by: Andrea Michelle, Artistry in Design
Editor: Shannon Brandee Eversoll

Print ISBN: 978-0-9916522-5-9

Dedication

I dedicate this book to the legions of teenagers who have sat across from me as I have counseled them over the past 20 years. To the ones that trusted me enough to tell me about their families, their fears, their hopes, their dreams. To the ones that discussed their depression, their anxieties, their disorders. To the ones I have held while they cried in grief. To the ones who hugged me for something as simple as listening to them. To those whose smiles have lit up my office and whose tears, I'll carry with me always. They have touched my life and I hope I have in some way touched theirs. Many of my students have long gone on to have families of their own. Some of my students have passed away. But always they are in my heart.

Chapter 1

Prologue

Carol (age five)

"Carol, how many times do I have to tell you to sit up straight? Your father will be here in a few minutes with his dinner guests, and I do not want to see your dress wrinkled. Do you hear me, young lady? Do not do anything to upset your father."

Carol, sitting as still as she could on the hard chair, tried not to wiggle. Her yellow blonde hair, curled tightly, hung in ringlets down her back. Her white, frilly dress felt itchy, but she knew not to complain.

"I'll be good, mama," she promised. Hoping against hope that her parents would notice how beautiful she looked, she sat as still as possible.

Hearing the front door open, she looked up expectantly as her father and his business associates came through the foyer. Sitting up, as pretty as possible, she smiled as they walked in front of her on their way to the dining room. Her father, leading the small group, walked by, ignoring his daughter completely. The smile leaving her face, Carol sat in the chair, not knowing if she could get down.

"Carol, come in here quickly," her mother admonished. Leading her into the dining room, she pointed to the corner chair that Carol was to occupy. Her mother leaned down, as though to kiss her daughter's cheek, but whispered instead. "Now eat carefully and don't spill a drop."

Carol, bored with the adult conversation, knew she needed to be quiet and not draw attention to herself. With nothing else to do, she concentrated on eating everything on her plate. Surely, that would make her parents happy.

After dinner, when Carol was up in her room, her nanny helped her out of her frilly, itchy dress.

"Were you a good girl at dinner, sweetums? Did you make your momma and daddy proud?" she asked, tickling Carol.

"I don't think they even noticed me," Carol admitted. "But I had chocolate cake for dessert," she continued with excitement.

Her nanny, clucking with frustration, helped Carol get into her pajamas and tucked her into bed. Carol was too young to understand, but her nanny knew that little Carol spent a lot of time trying to stay out of the line of fire with her parents. Mealtimes became a time for just eating as much as she could to remain out of the conversation. Looking down at Carol's sleeping, chubby little body, she said a prayer. *Lord, look out for this angel. She needs your love. She needs to feel love. She needs to find her own way and not just the image her parents have.*

Carol (age sixteen)

Running along the track at her high school, Carol continued long after the track practice had ended. *Just one more lap* she chanted to herself, mentally calculating the number of calories each lap would burn off.

Her body lean and toned, she forced her quivering legs to speed up around the last turn. Finishing the last lap, she slowed down, jogging around one more time as she slowly stretched her muscles.

"Hey Carol," came a shout from over by the field house.

3

Turning toward them, her long yellow pony-tail swinging behind her, she lifted her hand to shield her eyes from the sun. Several girls were standing next to the locker rooms, with a group of guys. One of the boys, the cutest of them all, was smiling at her, waving her over. *He is so cute. But his father owns the hardware store. Daddy would never approve.* Sighing, Carol walked over to her friends.

"We're heading out to go grab some food at the Hang Out. Wanna come?"

Carol carefully considered her answer. She loved the food at The Hang Out but knew the exact calorie count of every item on the menu. Weighing the pros and cons, she looked into the eyes of the cutest boy, staring back at her. Her parents would never miss her since they would be having one of their many dinner parties tonight. Breathing deeply, she knew she could be in control of the situation and have some fun.

"Sure, just let me change first," she replied.

Spending the next couple of hours at The Hang Out, Carol enjoyed herself more than she had in a long time. The group shared the pizzas, cheesy fries, milkshakes, and the cute boy even shared a hot fudge sundae with just her.

"Why haven't you hung out with us before?"

he asked, smiling over at her. "You're the prettiest girl in school and yet we almost never see you."

She looked down and mumbled, "Oh, my parents don't want me to go out much."

One of the girls in their group, hearing her comment, immediately began to prattle on about her parents never letting her do anything. Much to Carol's relief, the conversation quickly became a debate of whose parents were the worst.

As the group broke up and headed out to their cars, the cute boy asked, "So can I drive you home?"

"No thank you," she replied. "I've got my car here and have a few errands to run first."

They all said goodbye and Carol watched them as they drove away. Sliding back out of her car after the last of her friends left the parking lot, she quickly walked around to the back of the building. Glancing around carefully to make sure no one was around, she knelt in the grassy area and began to push her finger down into her mouth.

Forcefully gagging herself over and over, she began to feel the familiar feeling of her stomach churning. It did not take long for the vomiting to begin. Leaning over, she expelled everything she had eaten in the restaurant. She wiped her mouth with a practiced hand, standing in the process. Taking a shaky breath, she walked back to her car, smiling. *All those calories…gone.*

Driving home, she arrived while the dinner party was still in progress. Slipping through the back door, she headed up to her room, bypassing her parents. *It doesn't matter; they're just in there planning my future anyway.* Quietly making her way up the stairs, she walked through her bedroom and into her bathroom. Stripping to take a shower, she turned and viewed her reflection in the mirror. Blue eyes moving head to toe, she scanned her image. *What do I see? A bother. A disappointment. Not the son they wanted.* Perusing her figure, she continued to stare into the mirror, her image staring back. *A little roundness at her stomach. Thighs a little heavy.* Shaking her head, trying to get the images out of her mind, she turned to the shower. *What else is new?*

Chapter 2

(Ten years later)

"Hi, Tommy," came the giggling voice from the parking lot.

God, I hate being called Tommy. Especially by someone who giggles. Tom Rivers looked over at the woman standing next to her car, recognizing her as one of his past hook-ups. Bleach blonde with black roots. Tight dress. Lots of makeup. She had that look…the 'please won't you come over here so we can start something up again' look. *Not happening.* Tom threw up his hand in a half-hearted wave and kept walking, not breathing easy until he saw her drive off.

Shaking his head, he wondered how old a man needed to be to learn that some decisions were just plain dumb. And hooking up in his hometown when he was a detective was dumb. Tom had now taken a page from his police partner Jake's playbook – no hometown hookups—too risky when investigating crimes in the area. *And there are plenty of women in the next town over,* he thought while remembering last weekend's fun. *What was her name? Oh hell, it doesn't matter. It was great for one night.*

"Look out!" he heard someone scream, as the squeal of tires ended with a flash of pain and then blackness.

"Sir, sir…can you hear me?"

A voice. I hear a voice. Struggling to come out of the darkness, Tom painfully opened his eyes, a blurry vision of an angel leaning over him filled his sight. Yellow gold hair, waving all about, framing porcelain skin with faintly pink-tinged cheeks. Sky blue eyes, rosy mouth, perfect features. Everything else appeared fuzzy. But her face was clear. *I have died. Is this what angels look like?* "Are you an angel?" he asked, his voice slurring in confusion.

He felt her holding his hand, gently rubbing her other hand over his brow. He heard her soft voice, pulling him back from the darkness. "Stay with me. Keep your eyes on me. I'll help you."

Oh yeah, I'll stay with you. Forever.

The shrill sound of a siren encroached on her voice, and he wanted to rail against the intrusion. Slowly the blackness began to take over again, but he forced his eyes open one more time, searching for her face. Yeah, she was still there. Smiling down at him. Ethereal, beautiful, glowing. He knew she had to be an angel. There was no other explanation.

Tom's eyes opened slowly again, this time to harsh lights. Jerking his head to the right, he felt a flash of pain. Squinting his eyes, he willed the pain to lessen.

"What the hell you doing, getting hit by a car going into a fuckin' grocery store?"

Tom reopened his eyes, recognizing the voice of his childhood friend and partner, Jake Campbell. "Where is she?" he croaked out.

Jake's eyebrow raised in confusion. "Who?"

"The angel. She was there," Tom answered back, rubbing his hand over his face, trying to bring the room into focus.

"What is he talking about?" Rob MacDonald asked as he walked into the ER room. Rob and Jake were Tom's oldest friends. Having grown up on the same street, the three of them became best friends in preschool. They played high school football, then college football, then all three moved back to their hometown to settle as adults. Tom and Jake were detectives with the

Fairfield police department and Rob with the Fairfield fire department.

Smirking, Jake said, "He's asking for an angel."

Rob couldn't help but join in the harassment. "Well hell, Tom, if you find one, be sure to share her with us."

Struggling to sit up, Tom glared at his friends. "I'm telling you, she was there. I saw her. Jesus, I thought I'd died, and all I could think about was how great it was to be greeted by her." Wincing, he rubbed his head, feeling the knot on the back.

A nurse walked into the room, stopping short when she saw the three men in the small area, taking up all of the space. All three were over six feet tall, muscular, well built, and handsome. Seeing the immediate interest of the dark haired one with the panty-melting smile, she flashed her wedding ring as she walked over to Tom still on the bed. "The doctor says you have a concussion from hitting your head on the pavement. Other than that you're fine. You'll need someone to drive you home, and I have your discharge information for you here."

While Tom dealt with the nurse, Jake and Rob walked outside of the room to confer. Rob leaned up against the wall, looked over at Jake and asked, "What the hell happened?"

"According to bystanders, he was just walking across the parking lot and an elderly woman stepped on the gas instead of the brake. The car wasn't going fast, but it knocked him down and he slammed his head on the concrete."

"What about the angel he was talking about?" Rob asked.

Jake answered, "He must have been dreaming about his last date... or his dream date. Who the hell knows?" He laughed momentarily, then sobered. "But I gotta confess, he looked so serious when he was asking where she was like she should've been right there."

The nurse walked out of the room with Tom and he went to stand between his two friends. She looked at the wall of masculinity standing before her, feeling dwarfed. "Gentlemen, I trust you will see to your friend," she said with efficiency.

Rob, smiling as he turned on his charm, answered, "Yeah, I'm a paramedic."

Looking up, she smiled. "Keep your charm, mister," waving her wedding ring in his face again as she walked away.

Jake laughed, knowing that Rob would bang anything, anywhere. "That reputation is gonna kick your ass one day." Turning to Tom, he said, "Let's go, angel hunter. Gotta get you home."

Rob jogged off to get the car as Jake walked slower with Tom. Halfway down the hall, Tom stopped, turning toward his friend. "Jake, no shit man, she was there. I don't know if she was real or not, but she was there. And if she was real, I'm gonna find her." With that, the two friends walked out of the hospital.

Carol walked down the hall of the ER, her shift just starting and looked at the back of the men leaving the hospital. *Wow, this must be the day for hunks to be out in numbers.* Smiling to herself, she thought of the gorgeous man she assisted at the grocery store this afternoon. She noticed him as he was walking across the parking lot. *Who wouldn't have noticed him?* Tall, blond, gorgeous. He looked like a...Nordic God... or maybe a Viking standing on the bow of his ship. *God, I read too many romance novels.* He was just a man. Well...maybe the most handsome man she had ever laid eyes on, but just a man.

Seeing the car lurch toward him she screamed for him to look out, but it was too late. After he had hit his head on the pavement, she ran over to assist. He was unconscious, and while another bystander called 911, she tried to keep him awake. Holding his hand and rubbing his brow, she felt an electric current running through her. Something she hadn't felt in a long time. Well, maybe never.

What was it he asked? *Are you my angel?* Smiling to herself, Carol knew she could have stared into his blue eyes all afternoon, but as soon as the fire truck and ambulance arrived she quickly moved back. The tall, dark-haired fireman seemed to know the victim and immediately went to work on him, ascertaining his injuries. Knowing he was in good hands, Carol slipped away into the store. Now back at in the ER, she shook her head to clear her musings.

Hearing fast footsteps behind her, she barely had time to turn around before being grabbed from behind. "Hey beautiful," her friend Jon exclaimed.

Laughing, she pushed him off. "Jon, stop trying to scare me. Remember where we are. The last time you came up and scared me, Dr. Maklin was by the desk and threatened to report us."

"Oh, that troll has no idea how to have fun," Jon stated just as Sofia came up.

"Did you all see the three hunks in Bay 7? The ones that just left?" Sofia asked, lowering her voice so that no one else could overhear. "All three, over six feet tall, muscular, one blond, one light brown, one black haired. Oh. My. God. If it hadn't been for my wedding ring reminding me how much I love my husband, I might have jumped all three!"

Jon, never one to miss out on a great piece of male eye candy, just moaned. "Damn, I missed them. I was stuck in Bay 3 with an old lady swearing she was having a heart attack because she hit some man with her car."

Carol's eyes grew wide. "Was she having a heart attack?" She had been so wrapped up in helping the man on the ground, she never thought of the driver of the car.

"Oh hell, no. She just had a panic attack. But that means I missed the hunks," he complained.

Carol playfully punched him in the arm as she walked away. "Maybe next time you'll get lucky," she called over her shoulder.

"What about you, sweetheart? When are you going to get lucky?" Jon called out after her.

Turning back around to face her friends, she continued to walk backward, she just smiled and shrugged her shoulders. Giving a little wave, she headed back down the hall.

Jon and Sofia looked at each other, both sighing at the same time. Jon spoke softly,

"When I first met her, I thought that she just needed to get laid. Now I know, she just needs to be loved."

Giving his arm a squeeze before walking away, Sofia agreed, "Never has one so sweet needed to have someone love her just for her. One day, though, that handsome prince will come."

❧

Several evenings later Tom, Jake, and Rob met at Smokey's, the local bar. Walking in the three men caught the eyes of every woman there. Bill and Wendy Evans, the bar's owners and long-time friends with the handsome trio, looked over and waved.

Wendy, a knockout blonde, came over to their table bringing their beers. "Hey boys, how's everyone doing tonight?"

"Just water for me tonight, Wendy," Tom said ruefully. "Still under the doctor's orders."

"Oh, that's right. Bill said he heard you were hit by a car. Are you okay, honey?"

Before Tom could answer, Rob said, "Nah, he wasn't hit by a car. Some low-flying angel swooped in and knocked him on his ass."

Jake chuckled over his beer while Tom glared at his friend. "Fuck you, man."

A few more of their friends came in, from both the police and fire department.

Rob continued his taunting, "I was there, bro. I didn't see any blonde girl."

"I saw her," stated Chuck, one of the paramedics. Shoveling Smokey's famous chicken wings into his mouth, he was oblivious to the group's reaction.

The men looked over at him in stunned silence. Finally realizing that the table had grown quiet, he blushed under the immediate scrutiny of the others. "She was… th…there," he stammered. "With Tom."

"Who was there?" Rob asked. "I didn't see anyone."

"You were focused on Tom. But there was a girl there… holding his hand when we first came up. She was real cute. Blonde, tiny. Looked kinda like pictures of little fairy angels. I thought maybe you knew her until she disappeared."

Tom, leaned in closer to Chuck, piercing him with his look. "Where. Did. She. Go?"

Chuck, nervous from the intense glare from Tom, could only shrug. "I don't know, man. She just…disappeared."

"She couldn't have just disappeared," Jake growled. "If you saw her, she was real."

"I don't know where she went. She wasn't there when we loaded Tom into the ambulance."

"Damn," Tom exclaimed. "I knew she was real. You dickheads tried to convince me I dreamed that shit up."

Jake, always the voice of reason of the three, stated the obvious. "Tom, if she's real then that means you can find her. Someone at the store must have noticed her."

Rob, jumping into the conversation, added, "You've got the witness' names. One of them must have seen the girl."

Jake agreeing, turned to Tom, lifting his beer in a salute. "Tomorrow, you can start your angel hunt."

That night Tom dreamed once again of being visited by this girl. Leaning over him, her blonde tresses falling like a curtain around him, she placed a gentle kiss on his lips. Waking the next morning with a raging hard on, he headed to the shower to take care of himself. Picturing her image in front of him as he jerked off, he knew he had to find her. No other woman would do. No other woman had ever filled his mind as she did.

∞

Sitting in the police station at his desk, Tom looked at the witness report and read the statement from the man who dialed 911.

As I ran over to the man on the ground, another bystander was kneeling with him. She seemed to be checking his head and pulse. She told me to call 911. She talked to the victim for a few minutes, trying to get him to stay awake. The ambulance came and we all stood back.

Tossing the report down on the desk he looked over at Jake. Their desks were facing each other, and he noticed Jake staring at him.

"Did you find something?" Jake asked.

"Yeah, look," Tom replied as he pushed the report over to Jake.

"So she's real. Your girl is real."

Tom sat for a moment in silence, pondering his options before piercing Jake with his gaze. "Now to find her."

Tom spent the next two weeks tracking down every possible avenue, coming up empty. *I have an easier time catching criminals than I do finding this one woman.* Jake and Rob met him at the downtown diner one day for lunch.

"So what's the news?" Rob asked, winking at their cute waitress, giving her his famous smile.

"Jesus, would you stop pussy hunting long enough for us to have a conversation?" Tom complained.

"I remember when not too long ago you were only too happy to join me in pussy hunting. Ever since you've been looking for this girl, you've been no fun at all, man. Why don't we just go out, you find yourself some blonde and pound away until you get her out of your system?"

"Jesus, Rob. Do you hear yourself? One day you're gonna meet some nice girl and hate like hell that you've slept your way through Fairfield," Jake retorted.

"Tom, you don't even hang around your fuck-buddies. You might bang them for a while before moving on, but hell, you don't even take them out to dinner."

Tom brought his friends back to the matter at hand. "Rob, I'm not looking for a easy lay. This girl helped me. Hell, I don't know how to explain it. All I know is that I'm not interested in any other woman. I felt something when she touched me." Shaking his head, he looked up at Jake and Rob. "You guys can think I have lost my mind, but swear to God, that girl's in here," he said, rubbing his chest.

Rob stopped in mid-bite, staring at the man sitting across from him. Knowing him as well as anyone, he had never heard Tom speak of any woman as he was now. Cutting his eyes over to Jake, they shared a glance before Rob set his sandwich back down on his plate.

"Sorry, man. I honestly didn't know it was like that," Rob replied. "So, you can't find her anywhere?"

Tom shook his head. "No one at the grocery story remembers her ever shopping there. But the manager remembers seeing her that day."

Jake chuckled, looking over at Rob. "Yeah, you should have seen Tom when the manager recognized her. He was making rude comments about noticin' her sweet ass when Tom almost decked him."

Jake and Rob laughed, but Tom just cursed. "He's got no right to talk about her that way. I'd have beaten the shit out of him if Jake hadn't forced me outta the store."

Rob, shaking his head at this friend, stated, "You've got it bad, don't ya? I mean, you've really obsessed with this girl."

Knowing to anyone else his confession would sound foolish, he replied to his two best friends, "Yeah, I'm gonna find that girl. And when I do, she's mine."

Piercing him with his gaze, Jake retorted, "And what if she belongs to someone else. Or what if she isn't interested?"

Staring at his barely touched lunch, Tom just shook his head before a slow smile crept across his handsome face. "Then I just work harder to make sure I'm the man she needs."

Chapter 3

"Carol, how nice to see you again. How have you been?" Ronda Clark asked, ushering her into the comfortable office. The two women sat in deep leather chairs, facing each other.

Carol smiled over at the counselor that she had come to rely on over the past year. In her early forties, Ronda was the most approachable one that Carol had worked with. She had first sought counseling services when she had been a sophomore in college, striking out on her own. Her former counselor retired, leaving Ronda in charge of her clients. Nervous at first, Carol quickly came to value Ronda as a professional although it sometimes bordered more on friendship.

"I'm good," Carol replied but continued knowing Ronda would want to know what brought her in today. "I found myself wanting to watch my eating again. Not badly," she added quickly, "but I received an invitation from my parents last weekend, and it seemed to slam me back to standing in front of the mirror once again." She sighed. "Just when I think that I'll never do this again, something happens and all I see is someone unlovable, someone to be ignored."

Nodding in understanding, Ronda replied, "You know Carol, bulimia is something that you'll always deal with, but your recovery is going very well. Your self-image is so much healthier than when we first met."

Looking into Ronda's eyes, Carol sighed. "I know I'm a thousand times better. I almost never count calories anymore. When I exercise, it's only a modest amount. And I avoid scales like the plague! I haven't tried to throw up in years." Silent for a moment, she continued, "I handle stress in my job with little problem, but my parents…one letter from them and I feel like running off the lunch I ate earlier. Why is the hold still there?"

Ronda turned her gaze toward the beautiful woman sitting in front of her. Carol had the classic Hollywood looks that most women desperately want. Natural yellow blond hair, flowing over her shoulders. Porcelain complexion. Large, bright blue eyes. A petite, athletic figure that included soft, gentle curves. Dainty hands. Many women would be envious of all that beauty; most men would be admirers, wanting to claim her as their own. But Carol? Ronda knew when she looked in the mirror the image glaring back was not what everyone else saw.

"So tell me about this invitation?" she prodded.

Carol, leaning back in the comfortable chair, settled in. *How many hours over the past year have I spent in this chair? Talking. Listening. Learning.*

"My parents hold a charity event every year. It's a massive event, with hundreds of guests paying a lot of money for their dinner. It's really more about seeing who is there and being seen. My father makes sure that everyone knows his law firm is hosting the event. And you can be sure that the politicians are there to crawl up his butt," she said with rancor.

Ronda was silent, letting the comfortable pause give Carol the time to organize her thoughts.

Carol's gaze went to the window, overlooking a small garden with trees and flowers. She loved that view. It always seemed so peaceful. Taking another deep breath, she continued. "The first time I was allowed to make an appearance, I was sixteen. My dress was perfect, my hair and nails done, and my parents made sure to parade me around to everyone, announcing that I was the top of my class, sure to take over the law firm one day. There was such a cute young man there with his dad and he asked me to dance several times. He told me I was beautiful and I was thrilled to be seen with him."

"What happened?" Ronda asked.

"Oh, the typical. I overheard him tell one of his friends that my dad paid him to be my escort for the evening so that it looked like I had a date. My father didn't want to take a chance on me being a wallflower – that would never fit the image he wanted to present of his rising star daughter."

Silence followed. "Yeah," Carol ruefully said. "I went into the bathroom and gagged myself until I threw up the very expensive dinner." Suddenly, Carol burst into laughter. "Oh, Ronda, looking back it seems so dumb!

"I went back every year for the next three years until I was twenty. I continued to try to fit my parent's image of a very successful daughter; Valedictorian of my high school and making dean's list the first year in college. I managed to get through those meals without gagging myself, but I confess to running for miles the next day. I always hated trying to live up to their image!"

"So what happened the next year?"

"That's when everything changed!" Carol smiled at the memory. "I got horribly sick from food poisoning and ended up in the ER one night. I loved it. Oh, not being sick...but the ER. The nurses had such purpose. Jobs they loved. Jobs they were good at. The knowledge that when they went to work, they were changing lives, not just trying to get rich. That was when I saw myself."

Ronda looked at the sparkle that had returned to Carol's eyes. Smiling, she encouraged her to continue.

"When I was discharged, I went into the bathroom to get dressed and I looked into the mirror. I could see it. I could see myself in nursing scrubs, with my hair pulled back, and a stethoscope around my neck. Ronda, I could actually see it. Me, a nurse. For the first time, I was hopeful when I looked in the mirror."

"And that was what caused the career change...and the parental freeze began?"

"Freeze? More like a glacial iceberg!" Carol announced. "But yeah, you're right. I finally grew bold enough to change my major and managed to keep it a secret for two years. I worked a part-time job in the hospital as a nurse's aide, making money of my own. I saved it all so that I could afford a place to live when my parents finally found out."

"And when the blow up happened?"

"That's when I started seeing a counselor!" Carol retorted. "You know it wasn't easy, but the counselor at the University helped me finally see that my self-image was as warped as my parents. And for the past six years, I've been a work in progress!"

Ronda added, "A very successful work in progress, I must say! So, tell me about the invitation."

"There's not much to tell. I opened the invitation yesterday to the annual charity event – an event that I haven't been to in seven years. I barely speak to my parents after they made it very clear that I was a complete disappointment to them when they found out I was a nursing major instead of a pre-law major. My father's words… 'Carol, you're not living up to the image of our daughter. You're a complete disappointment.' Yep, I remember those words."

Looking back up at Ronda, she shrugged her delicate shoulders. "But why now? I have no idea why they are inviting me? I just know that I instantly felt like throwing up my lunch."

"But you didn't. You came here instead. You're continuing to choose healthy over an unhealthy, distorted image."

The acknowledgment flowed over her, settling in her dark corners. "You're right. I just have to keep telling myself when I look in the mirror, that I'm worthy."

"You mentioned last time that you thought you were ready for a relationship. So, have you met anyone special since we last spoke?"

"No," Carol admitted, but then found herself blushing and looking down at her clasped hands. "I have to confess that I met someone in passing that caught my attention, but nothing would ever come of it."

"Why do you say that?" Ronda wondered.

"We just met for a few minutes in rather unusual circumstances, so we haven't really officially met yet. But there was something about him that captured my attention. Well, besides the fact that he is gorgeous," she laughed.

"But when we touched, it was…I don't know…different." Her eyes sought Ronda's, searching for signs of disbelief, but the warm gaze looking back just held interest, not judgment. "I've never felt a spark before. But…then he was gone, and I'm sure I won't see him again." *But I can dream, can't I? And I have dreamed about him for a couple of weeks.* Sighing, she looked back at Ronda.

The two women continued to talk for a few more minutes until her time was finished. Giving Ronda a heartfelt hug, she left the counseling office as she had done so many times before...a little stronger, a little surer.

Chapter 4

The emergency room at Fairfield Hospital was finally having a lull after a busy evening. The graveyard shift was almost over, and the nurses gathered around the desk completing charts. The lights were harsh in the sterile environment and Carol found herself squinting to focus on the words she was writing. Tired of her long blonde hair hanging in her face as she leaned down, she pushed it behind her ears.

"Here, need this?" Sofia asked, handing her a protein power bar.

Carol took the much-needed nutrition, forcing herself to not look at the calories listed on the side.

Sofia noticed. "Still hard, isn't it sweetie?"

Carol looking at her friend's understanding face and agreed. "Yeah, but then it always will be. The desire to count calories going in and burning up…God, it still pulls at me sometimes. But as my counselor says, one day at a time."

Sofia patted Carol's shoulder as she walked

by. Carol unwrapped the bar and chewed appreciatively. The ER had been so busy for most of her shift she had missed her mid-shift snack. Having eaten the bar without checking the calories, she balled the wrapper up and made a shot into the trashcan.

"Score!" came a shout from behind her. Turning around, she almost ran into Jon.

"You scared me," she exclaimed.

Walking over, he hugged her. "How's it going tonight?"

"Busy earlier, but it's slowed down now. Aren't you here early? Your shift doesn't start for another two hours." She closed the last file and placed it in the stack on the nurse's desk.

"Yeah, but one of the nurses on the graveyard shift got a call; her kid is sick so I volunteered to get some overtime."

Their conversation was interrupted by a call concerning a policeman with a severe knife wound coming in. Running to her station near the door, she and her team were ready to accept the patient. The ambulance pulled up and Carol noticed a large number of policemen around.

The EMT began shouting out vitals as they transported the patient into the ER. The knife wound was in the abdomen, and he was rushed back to the ER bay, where triage began. She assisted the ER surgeon as he prepped the patient for surgery. When he was taken up to surgery, it was her duty to talk to the family in the waiting room. The wound was severe, and she knew that the operation would take several hours.

Looking down at her blood splattered clothing, she cleaned up and changed into fresh scrubs. Pushing her hair behind her ears again, she walked out to the waiting room.

Entering, she was overwhelmed by the number of policemen in the crowded room. While there were several women in uniform, the amount of testosterone in the room felt claustrophobic. "Family of James Whitten?" she called out.

Tom and his partner Jake raced into the ER, wanting to be there for James and his wife. James had been working with them on a robbery case, and they were close to making an arrest when the suspect pulled out a knife and stabbed James. Jake managed to disarm the suspect and he was in custody, but that did not make Tom feel any better. James was a rookie cop and a good one at that. Riding to the hospital, Tom berated himself for not seeing the knife.

"Damn, I knew something was up when that shithead acted so Goddamn calm as we entered his house."

Driving, Jake looked over at his partner. "Tom, you can't blame yourself. We were all following protocol. James entered first, and we couldn't see clearly into the room."

Tom was still angry as they pulled into the parking lot. How was he going to explain this to James' pregnant wife? As they were jogging up to the entrance of the ER, they saw the ambulance unloading James. Tom stopped in his tracks. His angel was leaning over James, talking to him as they went into the hospital.

Jake looked at him, eyebrow cocked in question.

"It's her. It's the girl I've been looking for."

Hurrying into the ER, James had already been taken back to treatment and the blonde nurse was nowhere to be seen, so they settled in the waiting room, making sure James' wife was cared for when she came. One of the firemen on the rescue team was Rob, who settled in a chair to wait with them.

After college, Rob settled into the life he had always wanted – working with his father, the fire chief. Jake had returned after the police academy when his father was diagnosed with cancer and then his mother became ill. Tom was the only one of the three who had moved away from Fairfield for a few years before discovering that being back home with his familiar friends was important. Following Jake to the police academy, he then returned to Fairfield also.

Rob had never outgrown his frat-boy ways of casual "fuck and run" as he liked to call them. Tom, another notorious one-night-stand man, decided several years ago that Jake was right about being a detective and casual sex in the same hometown was difficult. He managed to spend most weekends in a neighboring town, enjoying the nightlife and bar hookups there.

The ER doors opened. Tom's breath caught in his throat. She was walking through the doors.

A halo of thick, yellow blonde hair framed her porcelain face. Her body, hidden by hospital scrubs, was tiny, almost fragile. Her large, blue eyes widened as she scanned the room filled with policemen. As she called out James' name, her roving gaze settled, directing the bluest eyes he had ever seen just on him. The room appeared empty, leaving only the two of them. Her gaze never wavered from his.

Suddenly, he realized that James' wife had

approached her and her attention was diverted. Talking in soft tones, she began to usher James' wife away. Before re-entering the double doors leading away from him, she turned, piercing him with her gaze once again, a surprised look on her face. Tom smiled. He knew she was feeling it too. Whatever it was, he was not alone. She must have noticed his smile as she walked away because he saw her blush. *When was the last time you saw a woman blush? Too damn long.*

Jake looked over at his partner staring at the closed doors then caught Rob's gaze, both men smiling. Shaking his head, Jake wondered if Tom even knew what hit him.

All eyes turned to her, but Carol only saw one pair. Blue eyes, the color of the ocean on a sunny day, staring back at her. The eyes belonged to a Nordic God of a man. *Him. It's him.* His blond hair, trimmed neatly, stood out in stark relief to his chiseled, tanned face. Unlike most of the men in the room, he was not in a uniform, wearing navy pants that stretched tightly over his massive thighs. He was over six feet tall, muscular shoulders pulling at the material of his white dress shirt. Massive arms crossed over his chest, his feet standing apart, she could imagine him standing on the deck of a Viking ship. *He looks so much bigger than he did lying on the pavement.*

Carol's attention was slowly pulled away by the approach of a very pregnant woman, assisted by a policewoman. Focusing on the victim's wife in front of her, she gently took her by the arm and began to explain what the surgeon would be doing as she led her to the surgery waiting room. Turning, she glanced back one more time at the only man in the room she noticed. This time, she noticed one more thing about him. His smile. His face was illuminated by a beautiful smile. Straight white teeth. Full lips. Breathtaking. And it was directed at her.

Carol's shift was technically over, but she stayed with Sofia and Jon to make sure all the charts were completed. Looking at the clock, she decided to run back up to the surgery waiting room to check on the policeman's status and see his wife one more time before heading home.

"Guys, I'm going upstairs before I leave. I'll see y'all tomorrow, same time, same station," Carol joked.

Jon, raising one eyebrow, looked her up and down. "Uh hmm, are you sure you don't want to go check out mister tall, blond, and gorgeous?"

"Who?" Carol asked, feeling the blush creep back onto her face.

Sofia laughed, "Oh lordy girl. Don't think we didn't see that hunk of a detective staring you down in the waiting room earlier. He looked like you were the last popsicle on a hot summer day."

At that, Carol had to laugh in spite of her embarrassment at being caught ogling the Viking. "Guys, I swear, I'm going upstairs to check on Mrs. Whitten. I honestly never thought about that hunk being up there. He's probably long gone by now." Pushing her hair behind her ears again, she wistfully said, "And why on earth would he look at me? I don't think I would fit his image. He looks like the type that goes for all tits and ass."

Jon and Sofia exchanged looks.

"Hon, have you looked in the mirror recently?" Sofia asked. "You're drop dead gorgeous. Blonde, beautiful, sweet on top of all that, and hell, you make the rest of us look like chopped liver. What's not to love about you?"

Carol opened her mouth to speak but found Sofia's hand shoved up in her face before she could utter a word.

"And don't give me that crap about your parents. We all know your parents only love each other, their money, their big ass house, and their country club friends."

At that, Carol had to laugh again. "I know. Believe me, years of counseling taught me that no matter how much I tried, I just couldn't ever get them to see the real me." Pausing momentarily, she looked back over at her friends. "But it's all good, guys. I'm not looking for a gorgeous hunk to fight my dragons and carry me off. I'm fine with who I'm and what I'm doing now."

Waving to them, she walked over to the elevators. The fourth-floor surgery wing was packed with the crowd of policemen who were in the ER waiting room and had only moved upstairs. It looked as though Mrs. Whitten was well attended, so Carol turned to leave.

"Miss? Miss?" she heard a soft voice call. Turning, she saw Mrs. Whitten walking over. Moving toward her, she gave her a gentle hug.

"I just wanted to come up and check on you, see how you were doing and if there was anything I can do for you," Carol explained.

"Thank you for your kindness," Mrs. Whitten said.

"Please, call me Carol."

"I'm Jen," the woman answered, giving a tenuous smile. "The surgery nurse has been out several times and said that things were going well."

Reaching over to hug her once again, Carol said, "I'm so glad. I'll be back on shift tonight, so I'll come check on you again. Now make sure you get some rest. You and the little one," she said patting Jen's very pregnant belly.

Turning around, she ran face-first into a brick wall. A brick wall with arms that reached out to catch her before she fell. Looking up in shock, she saw what...or who she ran into. Her Viking.

Blushing a deep red, she stammered, "I'm so sorry, I wasn't watching where I was going." She tried to move away but found that his hands held her upper arms. His grasp was firm but not in any way painful and would not allow her to move.

"My apologies miss, I was in your way. Are you sure you're all right?"

Carol stood rooted to the floor staring up into a face so handsome it almost hurt to see all of that beauty. His blond hair, like hers, was yellow blond. Trimmed neatly, she wanted to see if it felt as good as it looked. His square jaw, slightly stubbled, led to a strong, thick neck. His wide shoulders tapered to trim waist, leading to thick thighs. His clothes were tailored to fit his muscular frame.

Her eyes made their way back up to his face where she found his twinkling blue eyes looking deeply into hers.

"Like what you see, miss?" he asked with a smirk.

Blushing even deeper, Carol jerked back from his hands as she saw the open elevator doors about to close. Jumping inside as the doors shut, she refused to look at the man left standing there. Grateful for the empty elevator, she leaned heavily on the back wall as it descended back to the first floor.

Tom, stunned that the beauty ran out on him, stared numbly toward the closed elevator door. Jake, walking over, clapped him on the back.

"Losin' your touch, man?" he asked Tom.

"Damned if I know. God, she was gorgeous, wasn't she?"

"So what're you doing still standing here, dumbass. Go find her."

Snapping out of his trance, he ran for the stairs next to the elevator. Racing down the four flights of stairs, he pounded out of the ER into the parking lot looking all around.

She was short, but her blonde hair made it easy to find her in the crowded parking lot. Seeing her weave through cars, he took off running again. "Miss, miss," he called.

She turned around as she reached her car, one hand already on the door handle. Emotions flitted across her face. Surprise, fear, irritation.

"Is there something I can do for you?" she asked, attempting to be polite.

He stopped several feet away, knowing that his size could be intimidating. "I'm sorry, miss. I think I offended you upstairs, and I never meant for that to happen. I wanted to offer my thanks for the way you spoke to James when he came in and for being so kind to his wife."

Visibly relaxing, she replied, "You don't have to thank me. I'm glad he's going to be all right. Were you friends?"

"Yeah, we were on a case together. It went wrong and well, you saw the aftermath."

"Did you get the person responsible?" she asked.

Surprised that she asked, he answered, "Yeah, Jake took him down." Seeing her questioning look, explained further, "He arrested him."

"Oh," was all she could think to say. Looking down, she could feel the blushing begin again.

"I hate to keep callin' you miss. What's your name?" he asked.

Looking up sharply, she asked, "Why do you want to know?"

"You want the truth, darlin'?"

She just nodded, keeping her gaze on him.

"Because I want to know the name of the woman I'm gonna take out to dinner."

Her eyes narrowed in suspicion. "You want to ask me to dinner? Why?"

Not used to this reaction, he faltered. Most women he approached were already flirting back or had already propositioned him.

"Well," he replied, running his hand through his hair in frustration, trying to figure out what to say next. He lifted his gaze back to her face. "You're the most beautiful woman I have ever seen. And I already know you're special." *Do I tell her I recognize her from the accident? Damn, then she will think this is a gratitude date.* "I wanna have a chance to get to know you." Looking down at her face, he cocked his head to the side, grinning. "Is that so bad? The idea of havin' dinner with me?"

Shyly looking down, she was quiet for a moment. Realizing he had never had to wait for a woman's answer, he began to get nervous. *Please say yes, angel. Don't shut me out.*

She raised her face to peer into his eyes. Blue eyes met blue eyes. His gaze never wavered. *He's telling the truth.* "I work the graveyard shift, so dinner is kind of out."

Noticing that she wasn't turning him down completely, he quickly pushed his advantage. "Well, how about a quick breakfast. At the diner just down the street. You'll feel better if you get some good food in you."

Sucking her lips in as she thought over his proposal, she looked back into his eyes. Nodding slowly, she agreed as she reached out her tiny hand toward him. "Okay. I can do breakfast. And my name is Carol."

Taking her small hand into his much larger one, he gently shook it. "Pleased to meet you, Carol. I'm Tom."

She turned to get into her car. Tom, still holding her hand, held her back. Raising her hand to his lips, he gently kissed her knuckles. Then he assisted her into the car, shutting the door.

Driving the short distance to the diner, she wondered what she was doing. *What does he want with me? I haven't been to the diner in a long time. What's on the menu? I don't even know him. This is a mistake.* She pulled into a parking space before the tangle of thoughts running through her mind had a chance to convince her to turn around and drive straight home.

Meeting a few minutes later at the diner, Tom held the door open for her. The waitress behind the counter waved them toward a booth, and they slid in facing each other. His long legs reached under the table, touching the side of her much smaller ones. Generally wanting to distance herself, she found that she liked the contact. Glancing up at his face, she caught his smile and found it was easy to return it.

Breakfast at the diner was a noisy affair, with townspeople coming in and out, greeting each other, catching up on each other's lives. Tom discovered it was hard to talk during breakfast in the busy diner and craved a chance to be with her alone. Looking over at Carol, he noticed her eating slowly and deliberately, as though afraid of eating too quickly. *Hmm, maybe she's trying to prolong this meal to spend time with me.*

After a few more minutes, Carol pushed her plate away, and as the waitress walked by, she called for their check.

Tom's eyes darted over to her face, confused by her hurry when half of her breakfast was still on her plate. *Damn, guess she's not trying to prolong the meal after all!*

"What's your hurry, Carol?" he asked, trying to keep the pout out of his voice.

She looked up in surprise, realizing that she had requested the check when he still had more to eat. Blushing, she rushed to explain. "I'm so sorry. I'm so used to eating by myself and grabbing the waitress whenever I can." Shyly she looked back down at the food left on her plate.

"Did you not like the food?" he asked gently, still looking for some clue to her behavior.

Shooting her eyes back to his, she admitted, "Oh, I love the food here! It was just a long shift and I really need to get to bed."

Feeling foolish for forgetting that she had just come off of a night shift, Tom grabbed the check that the waitress just laid down on the table. Pushing his plate away, he stood, reached for her hand and assisted her as she slid across the booth. He didn't let go of her hand as they wound their way through the crowded diner.

She couldn't remember the last time a man held her hand like that. Craving his touch, she kept her hand firmly in his, only letting go when he paid the cashier. Not sure what to do then, she let her hand hesitantly drop to her side.

Without skipping a beat, he clasped her hand in his again as they exited the diner. Walking to her car, she couldn't help but notice how right it felt to hold his hand. It was so much larger than hers. It had so much power in its grip. But that power felt...comforting, not overbearing. Concentrating on the feeling of their entwined fingers, she was surprised when he pulled her to a stop.

Looking up, she realized that they were already at her car. Blushing, she laughed nervously. "I guess I wasn't looking where I was going."

"You seemed lost in thought. I hated to interrupt," he admitted. "What were you thinking on so hard?" *Come on. This is where you tell me that you want to see me again. That you had a great time with me and you've changed your mind about dinner.*

Shaking her head gently, she just replied, "Oh, nothing of importance." Not knowing what else to say, she nervously said, "Thank you for breakfast. It was nice to eat before heading home."

A strange, warm feeling washed over Tom. *She's gonna make me work for this.* This thought was followed by the realization that he liked that.

"When can I see you again? I still want to take you to dinner."

She realized that she wanted that more than

she had wanted anything in a long time. *I want to see him. I want to talk to him. I want him to hold my hand again.* "Well, during the week, my life is basically sleeping during the day, take a run in the park in the afternoon, then work at night." Shrugging her shoulders, she admitted, "Not much of a life, but it's mine."

"What do you do when you're off work?" he asked, surprised at how curious and possessive he felt.

"Usually, I clean the apartment, read, run errands."

He looked down at the stunning beauty in front of him, honesty pouring off of her. *No bar hopping? No clubbing? No dancing till dawn?*

"When are you off next?"

Smiling that he still seemed interested, she replied, "I work three more night shifts and then I'm off Thursday and Friday."

"I'll pick you up on Thursday at six o'clock."

Sucking in her lips as she nodded her agreement, she said, "I live in the apartments near Cherry Grove Park. Number three-seventeen. I'll see you then."

Kissing her hand again as he assisted her into her car, he watched her as she pulled out of the parking space. *Oh, you'll see me before then, angel.*

Driving away Carol looked into her rear view mirror, seeing him standing in the parking lot staring at her. *Could he possibly be interested in me?* Smiling, she drove home, thinking of the Vikings in her romance novels. *Maybe, just maybe, there is a little truth to them after all.*

Tom stood in the parking lot, watching her drive away, still feeling the jolt from kissing her hand. *That girl is going to be mine.*

Chapter 5

That afternoon, Carol awoke refreshed from her long sleep. Stretching her body, working the kinks out from her long shift and then sleep, she felt the guilt of eating so much at breakfast. *A run. That will make me feel better and work some calories off. Not too many. Just a few.*

Minutes later she left her apartment, jogging toward the running path of the park next to her building. She began her stretching, sitting on the grass in the warm sun. Loving the feeling of the sun on her face, she leaned back, soaking it in. Her hair, pulled into a ponytail, hung down her back. Never worrying about her appearance when running, her baggy shorts and top were worn for comfort. Standing and finishing her stretching, she began down the trail.

Tom sat in his truck across the street, watching her disappear into the trees, knowing he would catch a glimpse of her again as she came out near the pond. *God, I feel like a stalker.* All he knew was that he just wanted to see her again.

Looking down at his own running apparel, he wondered what she would think when she saw him. *Excited to see him. Or scared of the creepy stalker.*

Never one to hold back, he jumped out of his truck and started jogging down the trail.

After a couple of minutes, she could hear the sounds of a runner behind her. Moving over to the right side of the path so that the next runner could pass easily, she was startled when they pulled up beside her keeping pace. Looking over quickly, she stumbled as she recognized Tom.

Reaching his arm out to steady her, he smiled down at her face hoping she was as glad to see him as he was to be back in her presence.

"Tom," she exclaimed, confusion evident on her face. "What are you doing here?"

They continued to jog as he pondered his answer for just a moment. Deciding that she wouldn't appreciate a pithy response, he stuck to honesty. "I just wanted to see you again as soon as possible. This just seemed like a good way to spend some time with you. Plus I need the exercise." He noticed the smile that barely turned up the corners of her mouth as she stared straight ahead while they ran.

After several laps around the pond and through the woods in the park he began to see that thankfully she was slowing. He knew he was in excellent shape, but the pace they were keeping was starting to wear on him. "You ready to rest a bit?" he asked hopefully, wanting to sit for a while and talk before she had to get ready for work.

A look of concern glimmered in her eyes as she looked at her watch. "I usually run a little more."

"Angel, you're in great shape and you don't wanna overdo it."

Glancing up at his face, searching for sincerity, she focused instead on the way his biceps were bulging under his t-shirt. And the t-shirt. The sweat had the thin cotton material plastered to his sculpted chest and abs. As her eyes slid downwards, she couldn't help but focus on his tree-trunk thighs as he pounded the jogging trail. Fighting the urge to reach out and touch all of that masculine perfection she just turned back to the trail, more determined than ever to keep running.

"Slow down," Tom pleaded, noticing the perspiration and redness on her face.

Shaking her head, she just mumbled, "Ate too much at breakfast. Don't want to get fat."

This is about breakfast? She thinks she needs to run off her breakfast? What the hell? This girl is gorgeous and has no clue.

Slowing down his pace, he gently pulled on her arm until she slowed her pace down as well. Afraid of making her skittish, he pretended to limp a little. "Sorry, my calf is sore."

Immediately contrite, she slowed to a stop. Her nurse's training had her leaning down to wrap her delicate hands around his lower leg. "I'm so sorry! You should have stopped a long time ago."

He loved the feel of her hands on his leg. He had only pretended to have a leg cramp to get her to slow down but quickly realized that the feel of her touch sent sparks through him just as it did when he had the accident. Looking down at the top of her halo of yellow hair, he hated to stop her ministrations but knew he had to discontinue the charade.

Gently taking her by the arms he pulled her to a standing position just in front of him. Bodies almost touching, she rested her hands on his waist while his fingers stroked her shoulders. Blue eyes gazing at blue eyes. He found himself drawn to her like a magnet, leaning down as she rose on her tiptoes, moving her lips closer to his.

"Whoa, move off the trail you two!" came a shout from two teenage boys rounding the path as they ran by.

Startled out of her trance Carol jumped back, embarrassment crossing her beautiful face.

Damn! What shitty up timing! Tom started to move forward, but she quickly stepped back again.

"I really need to get back. I have to get ready for work," she said, reluctance in her voice.

As they walked the short distance to her building, he asked, "So do you always run that far and that fast? Are you training for a marathon?" Taking her silence into consideration, he continued, "You said something about running off your breakfast. Was that what you were trying to do?"

Jerking her head toward him her blue eyes grew large as she sucked in her lips in contemplation. Shrugging her shoulders, she simply replied, "No. Not really. I just felt... full and thought a run would help."

Not trusting that she was telling the whole truth he decided not to pursue the point, which went against everything he was trained to do. As a detective, as soon as he found a discrepancy in a witness' statement he went in for the tough questioning. *Back off. Let this one slide. Wait until she trusts. And. She. Will. Trust.*

At the door of her apartment building, he

took her hand once again and raised it for a kiss. "I'm glad I came running with you. I didn't want you to think I was stalking, but I just really wanted to see you again."

Smiling up into his eyes, she was struck by how handsome he was. Even the sweat running down his body only made her want to pull him in for a kiss. "I had a good time too, Tom." Starting to pull her hand away as she turned toward the door, she felt herself gently tugged back. Looking up in question, she found herself staring into his lowered face as his eyes bore into hers. His lips touched hers in the softest kiss before he pulled away. So gentle. So kind. A whisper of a kiss that spoke volumes. The spark that she felt every time they touched made her lips tingle where his had been.

"See you soon, Angel," he said, smiling.

She watched him turn and move to his truck parked across the street. Walking up the stairs of her building, she realized she felt happy. Hopeful. Out of control. Pulling out her cell phone she called Ronda.

"You seem unusually stressed, Carol," Ronda commented.

"I was just feeling out of control and felt the

need to talk." Shaking her head, she looked down at her hands. "I haven't thought about my childhood in a long time and yet I found myself thinking about it more and more recently."

"Does this have anything to do with *the someone* that you met a while back?"

Carol blushed and nodded. "Yes, I suppose it does. We're not dating or anything like that. But he seems interested, although I have no idea what he sees in me. My God, he is gorgeous and could have any woman around."

"Does this make you feel out of control?" Ronda gently prodded.

"He took me to breakfast where I was so nervous I ordered too much food, ate too much food, then found myself running forever trying to get rid of the excess calories." Pausing to gather her thoughts, she continued. "I think he noticed. But I just covered it up. Nothing like scaring away a potential date by announcing 'Oh, by the way, I'm bulimic!' I think I handled it well, though."

"I'm sure you did, although you do realize that if you begin to see this man or any man for that matter, the subject will need to come up."

Nodding in resignation, Carol agreed. "Yeah, but it needs to be on my time. I'd rather he have a good image of me before the finds out that piece of information."

Moving on, Ronda pressed her about her childhood. "What specifically have you been thinking about?"

"It was after I was running. I remembered what it felt like to discover that I was chubby and how disappointing that was to my parents. I remember being summoned into their presence to discuss my weight."

"That must have been difficult. How old were you?"

Carol let her mind wander back to when she was twelve. She could see the events in her mind as clearly as if they were yesterday. Leaning her head back on the chair, she began to speak.

"I could hear the admonishment in my mother's voice even as she just said my name...

"Yes, ma'am?" I answered respectfully, as I walked into the dining room. My father sat at the head of the table with his coffee next to the morning newspaper. My mother, perfectly coiffed, sat next to him.

"Your father and I looked at your report card last evening. You have all A's in every subject except for gym. You received a B. What do you have to say for yourself?"

Before I could answer my father looked over at me, his eyes scanning me from head to toe. "You must have all A's to get into law school after getting into college. Receiving a B in gym class is unacceptable."

Looking down at my feet, I replied, "I have trouble running. I can't keep up."

"Look at me when addressing me, young lady."

Raising my gaze back up to my parents, I wished I wasn't such a disappointment. I tried, I really did. I made sure my hair was always fixed, and my clothes were always hung up. My grades were perfect, well except for the B in gym class. I was quiet, polite, and always respectful.

"Carol, your father and I just want the best for you, dear. You're a beautiful young woman, but you need to lose some weight. We think if you were thinner you would be able to maintain an A in all of your classes. We have hired a trainer to come after school and we are putting you on a strict diet."

My palms sweating, I ran my hands along my thighs, feeling the tightness of my jeans. I hate running. Sighing deeply, I simply smiled at my parents, nodding my head. "That would be nice mom. Thank you, dad."

Her father nodded his pleasure at his daughter's acquiescence. "We have to have you in top shape to run the law firm with your old man, right?"

Dismissed, I turned and walked through the dining room into the kitchen. Looking around to make sure no one was watching, I grabbed a few cookies as I headed up to my room. I'll run them off tomorrow.

As she finished her story, she looked into Ronda's understanding eyes. Sighing, she continued, "I have no idea why that incident popped into my head."

"You tell me that you have been running just for exercise and to get fresh air after being in the hospital for such long shifts. And yet, you have admitted to recently trying to run off the calories just like you did years ago. I don't think it is that unusual for your mind to travel back in time to when running was associated with weight loss."

"I hadn't thought of that," Carol admitted. "It was the combination of the invitation and wanting to make a good impression on Tom, but the idea of a relationship is scary."

"All relationships are scary because you bare yourself to the other person, not knowing if they will accept you or reject you." The comfortable silence flowed around the two women for a few minutes, allowing Carol to consider her words.

A small smile curved the edges of Carol's mouth. The tentative smile turned into a beautiful grin, as she looked over at Ronda. "I think I would like to try. I like the way he makes me feel," she acknowledged. "Safe, secure, and maybe even pretty. I like that."

"Well then my dear. I think you're still moving forward beautifully. You know that with bulimia you will have some setbacks. And that's fine. Life is all about moving forward, even if we occasionally move sideways or backward!"

Laughing, the two women rose from their chairs and embraced before parting.

Chapter 6

"Where you headin' off to?" Jake asked his partner, early the next day, having just come in from his run before work.

"Thought I would go to the hospital and see James."

"Uh huh. I think visitin' hours haven't started yet. You plannin' on checkin' out the ER while you're there?"

Tom grinned at Jake, "Well, I wouldn't be opposed to seeing who's there." Grabbing his jacket off the back of his chair he swung it around, dangling it from one finger across his shoulder.

"Well, take care of that angel. You don't want her wings getting clipped."

"No worries there, Jake. That woman's special," Tom replied, as he turned and walked out of the station.

Arriving at the hospital, he went up to James' room first to check on him. Jen was just coming and greeted him warmly.

"Hey, Jen," he said, looking down at her very pregnant stomach. "How's little Jimmy today?"

"Oh, he's ready to come out and meet his daddy, but I told him to wait a bit. Let me deal with getting James home before this one arrives."

Placing his arm around her, pulling her in for a hug, he replied, "You know you have all of us, right?"

She smiled up at him knowing the brotherhood of the police force would see her and James through and hugged him tighter.

Just then the elevator doors opened, and Carol walked through looking at Tom comforting Jen. Smiling as she walked over, she greeted them both, placing her tiny hand on Jen's arm, "How are you doing?"

Jen returned the smile, assuring Carol that she was fine. Carol's eyes raised to Tom's, once again stunned by the male glory in front of her. *He wants to take me to dinner?* She was just getting ready to greet him when her pager sounded calling her back to the ER.

"That's odd. My shift is over – they must be shorthanded right now." Hugging Jen goodbye, she turned to walk to the elevator.

"May I escort you to the ER?" he asked,

reaching beyond her to push the elevator buttons. "I'm heading out anyway."

Smiling her agreement they made their way to the ER, only to find it chaotic. A young man, wild-eyed and cursing, half-dressed with the hospital gown falling off was running down the hallway, pushing carts into the way of the pursuing security guard. Appearing to be intoxicated, he was swinging his arms around as though to hit something in his imagination. Before Tom could react, Carol ran toward the man, who knocked her down as he was stumbling forward. He fell to the floor as Tom and the security guard jumped on him, pulling out their handcuffs. The drunken man managed to kick out one last time, catching her on the shoulder knocking her into the wall.

"Goddamn it!" Tom roared. Fury overtook him as he hauled the man up, pulling back his arm to punch the drunken fool. The new security guard, not knowing what to do just stood back.

Scrambling off the floor, she launched herself between the drunk and Tom, barely missing his flying fist. "No," she screamed. "He's a patient!"

Tom, anger at an all-time high, grabbed Carol to pull her out of the way. Hauling her by her arms, he removed her to the side while shouting orders to the security guard, now accompanied by several other guards. "Get him handcuffed to a bed!" he growled.

Carol, shaken, realized that while Tom had her upper arms in a firm grasp, he was not hurting her in the least. It felt secure. It felt safe. It felt right. It felt—

"What the hell were you doing running toward his drunken ass?" Tom roared at her, shocking her out of her sense of calm.

Attempting without success to jerk away from him she looked up, eyes blazing, "I was doing my job. Trying to stop the patient from hurting himself or someone else in the process." She shook her finger at him, poking him in the chest, continuing her tirade. "I'm not some helpless female that's going to fall apart at the first sign of trouble." Poke, poke. "And furthermore, I'm not some female that's going to fall at your feet just because you decide to go all caveman on me!"

Blonde hair escaping her ponytail. Blue eyes snapping. Cheeks rosy from exertion. *She looks more beautiful as an avenging angel than ever.* Tom wanted to grab her and kiss her until she was silent. Then kiss her until she moaned. Then kiss her until she...*Damn!* Trying to discreetly adjust the tightness in his jeans, he looked down at her imagining all that energy pouring off of her aimed at him as he took her.

Whirling around, she walked down the hall, holding her head high. Her shoulder was in agony, but she was determined to not let him see her in pain.

Starting to follow her, he was called back.

"Hey, dickwad. Way to make a lady feel good!" Rob laughed.

Tom, glaring at his friend just growled, "What the hell are you doing here?"

Rob, still laughing, replied, "We're the ones who brought the drunk in." His eyes darted down the hall at Carol's retreating back and his laughter stilled. "Sorry about that man. I assumed the security guard would put him in a secure lockdown area while they were checkin' him out. She okay?"

"I don't know. That asshole kicked her pretty hard." Rubbing his hand over his face in frustration, he started walking in the direction where she was headed.

"Good luck," Rob called after him.

Tom just waved in return as he continued walking down the ER hallway toward the nursing station. Hearing familiar voices coming from one of the examining rooms, he started to interrupt until he heard a female's voice tell Carol to take off her scrub top. *Damn, what would I give to be in there right now?* Knowing he had no choice, he stopped outside.

"God Almighty, girl. You sure know how to pick a fight, don't you?"

"Sofia, I don't know what made me angrier. That drunk patient or caveman detective," Carol replied.

Tom, listening outside the room, was surprised when he was joined by a male nurse.

"Name's Jon. I'm a friend of Carol's. She getting patched up by Sofia?"

Tom nodded, eyeing Jon carefully.

Jon laughed. "Don't worry man. I'm just her friend. She's a great girl, but...well, I just don't swing that way."

Tom nodded once again, seeing an ally in Jon. Both men stayed outside the examining room, unashamedly listening to the conversation.

"Carol, honey, I've been married a long time. Nothin' wrong with a man going all caveman on you if his heart is in the right place. That's not the same as a dictator prick who just wants to control you."

Rob overheard a snort coming from the room.

Sofia continued. "Yeah, you know what I'm sayin'. You grew up with that kind of dictator. But honey, there can be the type of man who gives you everything he has to give and would give anything just to take care of you. That kind of man...well, you've never had that before. Might just be what your detective is and might just be what you need."

Just then a young, smiling, male doctor walked passed Tom and Jon straight into the examining room. "Miss Fletcher, I heard you were injured. I wanted to come down to make sure you were all right."

Jon moaned. "That prick, Dr. Driscoll, is always sniffing after Carol and she won't give him the time of day!"

Oh hell no, Tom thought. Pushing his way past Jon he walked into the room as well, with Jon close on his heels.

He stopped, glaring at the doctor who looked up in surprise. Glancing over Tom saw Carol, wide-eyed, holding her scrub top in front of her chest, with her shoulder in a sling.

Jon, quickly walking over to the examining table said, "Carol, I found your boyfriend waiting outside and knew you'd want him in here with you."

Her eyes snapped from Jon to Tom to Sofia

and then to Dr. Driscoll. Not knowing what to say, she blushed bright red.

Tom, furious with the doctor trying to use his interest in Carol to get into the examining room couldn't help but notice her gorgeous blush creeping from her barely covered chest to her hairline. Walking over, he wrapped his arm around her uninjured arm, kissing the top of her head. "I was worried, babe. Jon helped me find you."

Dr. Driscoll, scowling, turned and left the room muttering about unofficial people in the ER. Sofia and Jon burst into laughter at the retreating doctor's back.

Tom looked down as Carol looked up, not surprised to see her eyes flashing fury. Not letting go of her he leaned down, barely brushing his lips over hers.

"Angel, I can see you're all ready to pitch a fit, but let me lay this out for you. I was mad out there earlier 'cause I saw a woman, especially a woman I'm interested in, get kicked by an out of control drunk. That shit doesn't fly with me, Carol. Now I was waiting outside patiently with your friend Jon, when the next asshole comes walking in like he has a right to see your body just 'cause he works here. Jon didn't think it was cool, and I sure as hell didn't either. So we came in, made a play, not to embarrass you, but to make sure that asshole knows you're not on the market."

Carol, still grasping the scrub top to her chest, just blinked slowly. She heard Sofia say, "Damn girl. That is hot."

Blue eyes stared into blue eyes. Tom whispered, "You got me, Carol?"

"You're interested in me?" was all Carol could think to say.

Tom, leaning back in surprise, looked at her beautiful face. Shaking his head, he replied, "That's all you got from that? Yeah, I'm interested in you."

It did not escape Tom's notice that Sofia and Jon exchanged looks. Remembering what Sofia had said about Carol growing up with a dictator, he figured that might have something to do with her self-esteem. Vowing to himself to work on that later, he turned to Sofia.

"Is she ready to go home?"

Sofia nodded, "Yeah, her arm is just bruised, so we're putting it in a sling to limit the movement for a couple of days. The ER charge nurse told her to take three days off due to an injury at work."

Jon snorted at that. "They don't want her to file a complaint since the guard didn't do his job."

Tom noticed that Carol was still sitting perfectly still, with her pink scrub top clutched to her chest. Her back was perfectly shaped, her porcelain skin beckoned. He wanted to start at her ears and kiss his way down her neck to her shoulders, continue the path down toward her — . *Get your mind off her breasts and get her home.*

"I'll take her home," he announced to a grinning Sofia and Jon.

Carol, snapping out of her trance of the last several minutes, asked, "Just who do you think you're?"

"I'm the man who would give you everything... and give anything to take care of you," he announced, using Sofia's words from earlier. "Get dressed and I'll wait outside."

Dropping a kiss on the top of her head he sauntered outside, Jon following behind.

Sofia turned to her friend. "Girl, don't go getting mad. That gorgeous, protective man just made a play for you in a big way. He's not taking your freedom, Carol. He's just giving you all he has." Helping Carol get her top back on and then replacing the arm sling, she leaned into her friend's face. "Girl, you deserve someone who will take care of all that you're. You find that you can give yourself to a man like that, you will never be alone again. Think about it, Carol."

She just nodded, the dying adrenaline rush of the morning's activities coming on the heels of a graveyard shift, left her exhausted. Walking out of the exam room, she saw Tom leaning up against the wall, talking to Jon. He cut his eyes over to her and she felt their warmth flow deep inside of her. *What are you doing? You finally break away from your father and you fall into the arms of someone who wants control?* She stood there breathing deeply for a moment, pulling her lips in as she continued to worry. *But he makes me feel...safe.*

His mouth turned up in a grin as though he could read her thoughts, knowing that she was beginning to thaw towards him. "Come on. Let's go."

She walked over to him, uncertainty showing on her face. Looking from Tom to Jon, she saw her friend with a shit-eating grin on his face and she quirked her eyebrow at him in question.

"Take care, sweetie. Sofia and I'll hold down the fort until you get back." Leaning in to give her a hug, he whispered in her ear. "Carol, give this one a chance. He's great...and you deserve that."

Tom pulled her uninjured side in closely, tucking her tight into him as he propelled her out through the doors toward his truck. Clicking the locks he opened the door for her, but before she could step up into the cab, he lifted her up as though she weighed nothing and gently placed her on the seat. "I'll get you buckled up."

Letting him take charge was creating angst since she never let anyone take control of her. But it felt nice. Cared for. Loved. *Loved? Oh, my God…get a grip. Just a friend. Just a friend.*

Once buckled in, Tom leaned over barely touching his lips to hers. "You okay?"

Carol just stared, once again stunned into silence. She managed to nod, which Tom seemed satisfied with. Rounding the front, he hauled himself up into the driver's side.

Pulling out of the parking lot, Carol finally found her voice. "Do you remember where I live?"

"I remember. I had it checked out after our run the other day."

Shocked, she whirled her head around to look at the man in the driver's seat. The gorgeous man. The muscular man. The man who made her want to lock her lips with his. The infuriating, take charge, get-in-your-business man.

"You checked me out? You investigated me?" she asked, her voice beginning to rise with each question.

"Carol," Tom replied patiently, as though talking to someone who just wasn't getting it. "I wanted to make sure you were livin' somewhere safe. I checked to see if there were any registered sexual predators around. Gorgeous, single woman livin' alone. You're on my radar, and I plan on making sure you're safe."

"That doesn't strike you as stalkerish?" was the only response Carol could think of. *Is this his way of being in control? No, safe. It feels safe.*

"Plus you're kinda clueless," he continued.

Eyes wide in fury, Carol looked over at him again, all the warmth of the previous moment gone. "What did you call me? Clueless? Oh my God, what a jerk! I told you before I'm not some helpless female that's going to fall at your feet. You can just drop me off here – I'm walking the rest of the way!" she stated, putting her hand on the car door handle.

Tom looked over at her hand. "Babe, you try to get out of this moving truck and I swear to God, I'll paddle your ass right here."

Carol, so incensed, could tell tears were ready to fall, both from anger and fatigue, but fought them back with everything she had. *I will not cry in front of him.*

Parking at her apartment building, he turned

to face her. Seeing her distress, he knew she needed careful handling. "Angel, eyes on me." Waiting momentarily for her to pull herself together, he repeated gently. "Eyes."

Carol responding to the warmth in his tone, looked at him. Speaking in barely a whisper, she said, "Clueless. How could you call me clueless?"

Breathing in deeply, Tom reached over to cup her cheek. Relieved that she did not pull away, he explained. "Because you're gorgeous but seem to have no clue that you are. While that makes you nice to be around 'cause you're not always trying to shove your looks in everyone's face, you go around with no idea what men are thinking. And that could be dangerous. You've got a huge heart, wanting to take care of everyone, includin' some piece of shit drunk, but that could be dangerous too if you're not careful. The hospital's got guards. Hell, you had a trained detective right next to you and yet you tried to jump in."

Noticing that she was still staring at him but had leaned ever so slightly into his hand, he continued. "You're also a woman that doesn't play games, and that makes you priceless to me. I like what I see. I like what I know about you. I wanna get to know you better. I get that somewhere in your past you were controlled by someone that gets off on being in control. Angel, that isn't me. I wanna be in charge, but that's because it will always be all about you. Taking care of you. Getting to know you."

Carol let those words sink in, feeling the emotion in the truck cab soothe her pain. Cautiously, she said, "Tom, you may think I'm clueless and some of what you said was right. But I'm not dumb."

"Never said you were."

Sucking her lips in tightly for a moment, she plunged ahead. "I don't actually date…much. I can tell you're the kind of guy who has women falling all over you. I don't do well…with…feeling…I mean, I often feel…"

"Carol, you're no casual hook-up, if that's what you're worried about."

He hated seeing her wince at his words but knew that he needed to make sure she understood where he was coming from.

"I have been around. I'm not gonna pretend, but I've always been up front, never led anyone on, never cared about anyone. It was always just physical. Always been careful, and I'm clean." He watched Carol wince again. *Damn. I shoulda been more like Jake in the last couple of years and kept it in my pants more.* He hated the look on her face.

He wouldn't have been surprised to see the repulsion at his actions, but what he saw was worse. Self-doubt was written all over her face. Understanding now that she was struggling with herself, he brushed his thumb over her delicate face.

Leaning in closer, so that his lips were a breath away from hers, he continued. "Never been interested in a woman like I'm interested in you. I wanna take the time to explore what we've got. Wanna get the clueless out of your head and get you with me."

Seeing her close her eyes for a moment, he felt her lean into his hand even further. Smiling, he touched his lips to hers again. "You with me, angel?"

She barely nodded, and Tom needed no more encouragement. Taking her lips in a slow, gentle kiss, he ran his tongue over the seam, plunging in as she opened to him. The kiss turned harder, wetter, more emotion, more passion. More everything.

Carol, lost in the feelings, never wanted the kiss to end. *I have never been kissed like this. Never. God, he is going to ruin me for anyone else. And then where will I be? Alone.* Pulling back, she looked down, trying to still her racing heart.

"You were with me. You stopped doubting,

and you were with me. I don't know where you went, but the doubt came back."

Blue eyes stared into blue eyes. Smiling, Tom leaned back in for a quick kiss before getting out of his truck and rounding the front to open her door. Escorting her upstairs into her apartment, seeing her settled with some pain medicine and tucking her into bed before leaving, he smiled the whole time.

Chapter 7

"You seem nervous today, Carol. Is there something going on that you want to talk about?"

Carol looked across the coffee table at the soft spoken, caring counselor. Smiling, Carol spoke up, "Well, I do have a date tonight. I just don't know how I feel about it."

"Why do you have to feel anything about it, right now?"

"We're going to a restaurant that I'm not familiar with. It makes me feel…unsure."

Ronda gently prodded. "Unsure?"

Taking a deep, cleansing breath, Carol focused on her choices. Choices learned from many counseling sessions.

"Okay, I'm unsure because it's different. I still hate not knowing menus ahead of time and not knowing how the bathrooms are." Looking back up at Ronda, she continued. "I know that sounds silly. I haven't purged in years, but whenever I feel nervous, it's a hard habit to get out of."

"Well, let's look at the two separate issues. One, what are your choices when faced with something new. And two, let's examine why you're nervous. You pick which one you want to talk about first."

"Easiest first," Carol laughed. "My choices. When faced with a new situation involving food, I can go online and look at the menu ahead of time. I can always go for a salad if I feel too out of control." Looking at Ronda, she quickly added, "But being in a new restaurant does not mean I'm not in control. I can choose what I eat. I can choose to only eat the amount that fills me up. I can decide when to stop eating. I can choose to enjoy the food and not count the calories. And I'll continue to make the choice to not purge what I eat."

"How's that, doc?" she said smiling.

Ronda, laughing, answered, "If you were a new patient, I would accuse you of just saying what you think I want to hear. But I know you," she paused, looking fondly at Carol. "You have come a long way from that young woman determined to fight her way against her parent's image." Pausing again momentarily, she then asked, "So what makes you nervous about tonight's date?"

Carol, looked down at her hands in her lap for a moment, trying to find the words to express what she was feeling.

"I don't really know him at all. We met at the hospital when I was on duty, and he came in with other policemen. He's a detective. I looked at him, and it felt as though all of the air just got sucked out of the room." She spared a glance up to see if Ronda was laughing at her description, but Ronda was just nodding attentively.

"He chased me into the parking lot to ask me my name and to ask me to dinner," Carol smiled at the memory.

"I get the feeling there's something you're not telling me," Ronda queried.

"Well...okay, here's the crazy thing. The last time I was here, I told you that I met someone in passing. Well, it's him. But if he recognized me, he would have said something. So it must just be one of those crazy coincidences."

"Or fate, if you believe in that sort of thing," Ronda added, smiling.

Carol was quiet for a moment. "It's been a long time since I've been on a date. I mean a real date. I've gone out some with friends of friends, but I never felt anything for them. This guy, wow he makes me feel...desired."

"Is that a bad thing?" Ronda asked.

"No, not to most people, I guess. He is tall, well over six feet tall. Muscular, built like a huge football player." Laughing at the memory, she added, "In fact he was standing with two other men built just like him. It was like a wall of gorgeous testosterone!"

"That's a vivid description," Ronda admitted, raising her eyebrows.

Carol couldn't help but giggle. "Yeah, he's huge, muscular, very blond, handsome...and what on earth could he want with me?" she finished looking pensive. "I know what everyone says, Ronda. They say I'm pretty. I know I'm intelligent, and I think I'm nice, but pretty? I still struggle with that. And he looks like the kind of guy who could get a woman to drop her panties just by the crook of his finger. He is also very controlling, but it doesn't feel like my parent's control. It feels like I'm the most important thing to him." She looked down at her hands and blushed slightly.

Lifting her eyes back to Ronda's face, she added, "I don't have a lot of experience with men."

Ronda gently prodded, "You want to tell me about that?"

"Ronald became my escort to the family events by the time I had graduated from high school, but it never felt like we were dating. We went out, we went places, but I got the feeling that he did it more out of expectation. Our kisses were not very exciting and other than some heavy petting, we never had sex." Shrugging her delicate shoulders, she added, "I wasn't interested in having sex with Ronald and I think he was getting some on the side."

"How did that make you feel?" Ronda asked.

Looking out of the window for a moment in reflection, Carol then turned her gaze back to her counselor. "Honestly? I had no interest in having sex with Ronald but looking back, I'm sure that I felt unworthy since he was not as discreet as he could have been about other women."

"And later sexual experience?" Ronda probed.

Smiling, Carol shook her head at the memories. "Well, when I was finally out from under my parent's thumb, I dated a little. Not much, and certainly not lasting. I gave up my virginity in my third year of college willingly…mostly to see what all the fuss was about." Rolling her eyes, she added, "I didn't think much of it. Kind of hurt. Sort of messy. A lot of groping, grunting, and then it was over. And I thought this is what romance novels are all about? After that, I had a couple of more partners in the last five years, but nothing earth shattering." Shrugging her shoulders again, "Maybe I'm just frigid and can't get anything out of sex."

"I think with the right person, you'd find that you would relax and perhaps enjoy a sexual relationship. Maybe you just needed to focus on you becoming healthy first."

"You may be right. I definitely needed to focus on me. But now that this detective is interested in me, I wonder if I'll be enough for him?"

Ronda looked at Carol, knowing how far she had come in counseling, but knowing that there were some body issues still existing. "In our society, you're considered beautiful. But it is what you see when you look in the mirror that concerns me."

Carol smile reached her eyes as she replied, "Oh Ronda, don't worry. When I look in the mirror, I see healthy. Not too heavy, not too thin. But healthy."

"That is the best thing you could have told me today," Ronda exclaimed. "Well, that and then next time you'll have to tell me about the handsome detective!"

Chapter 8

That afternoon, Tom and Jake sat at their adjoining desks reviewing the case against the man who stabbed James.

"Looks airtight, Tom," Jake said. "Protocol was followed, he confessed, got the evidence, we should be good to go."

"I talked to Jen this morning. She said that James is doing great, and they may release him in a couple more days."

Jake, ever the detective, looked over at his partner. "And…?"

"What?" Tom asked, trying to look innocent.

"Don't think I don't know you asked Jen about that nurse you couldn't keep your eyes off of the other day. Don't you have a date with her soon?"

Tom, uncharacteristically quiet, replied, "Yeah, tonight actually." Looking up, seeing Jake's confused look, he continued. "I don't know, man. She's so Goddamn gorgeous and yet doesn't seem to know it. Most women I know flaunt everything they've got, and Carol just appears to feel very self-conscious."

Jake agreed, glad that his friend was truly interested in this woman and not just looking for a hookup. "She seems nice."

Tom nodded, "Hell yeah. Jen said she's come by every day to check to see how James is doing but that she always wants to know how Jen is doing as well. And she does that on her own time when her shift is up."

"So what're you thinking? You plannin' on just having a new friend with *your kind of benefits?*"

Shaking his head, Tom stared straight into Jake's gaze. "Hell no. Carol's a keeper. I know it. But she's a mystery I hope to start unraveling tonight. I just don't want to scare her off."

"Scare her off?" Jake asked in confusion.

"Look, I'm not like Rob, tapping everything that offers, and you taught me the good rule of finding my hook-ups out of town so I wasn't running into them with every case we investigated. But Carol's classy. She also seems skittish, like she could take off if scared."

"Then just be a gentleman and not some dick that wants to take her to dinner just to bang her...you'll be fine."

Shifting in his seat nervously, Tom admitted, "Plus I like to be in control and she's gotten burned in the past by someone who wanted to control her. Not like me. Not like I wanna take care of her."

"I don't know what to tell you, man. Haven't met *the one* yet. But I guess you're gonna have to show her that our kind of control is about her, not the man."

Standing up, Jake slapped Tom on the back. "Good luck, bro," he said as he headed down the hall with their report for the chief.

Tom arrived at her apartment early, not wanting Carol to have to wait. He could not help but stare as she opened the door. Her halo of blonde hair was pulled back into a low ponytail, with waves down her back. Her modest emerald green dress showed off her athletic figure to perfection, and her heels gave her toned legs the impression of being long even though she was a full foot shorter than he was. The silky dress hung perfectly on her figure, allowing Tom to see her curves that the hospital scrubs hid.

The drive to the restaurant was pleasant, and he found it was easy to converse with her. Small talk always irritated him, never really caring much about the woman he was with. But Carol? She was different. He glanced sideways, glimpsing at her profile. A glow seemed to emanate from her, a sense of peace surrounding her. Not flashy. Not in-your-face. A parade of past faces flashed through his mind, and he realized that he usually tuned out the women as they talked about fashion, movies, music, their friends, the bars they wanted to try. Carol? She was quiet, cautious. He realized that he had no idea what she was thinking.

He had chosen a restaurant on the outskirts of town, knowing that they not only offered excellent food, but also a quiet atmosphere so that they could get to know each other uninterrupted. *I hope she likes it. Why am I nervous?* It had been a while since he took a woman to dinner who actually interested him.

As she turned to walk in front of him toward the restaurant, Tom stared at the back of the dress, where it dipped below her shoulder blades. Fighting the desire to lick from her neck down her back, he placed his hand on the small of her back to lead her inside.

Walking in, the hostess looked up with a huge smile on her face. "Why Tom, it's been forever since you've been in to see me…us." Her tight dress showed her ample cleavage, and she worked it to her advantage as her eyes cut over to Carol.

Damn. I forgot Anita worked here. Glancing down at Carol, he saw no change in her demeanor at all. But with his hand on her back, he could feel the slight tenseness. If his hand had not been on her, he would have never noticed her tension. *How does she do that? How does she completely mask what she's thinking? No glaring, no frowning. Nothing.*

The hostess stuck her hand out toward Carol, saying with a smile, "Hi. I'm Anita. I'm an old friend of Tom's."

Carol robotically reached for Anita's handshake, feeling like there was more than just friendship between the two. *It doesn't matter. It doesn't matter.*

"He's great isn't he?" Anita continued to gush. "All us girls used to want to tie him to us, but you know Tom – always keeping one foot out of the bed and heading for the door!"

At that, Carol jerked her hand back, suddenly feeling as though she had been dropped into a situation in which she had no control once again.

Embarrassed, Tom slid his hand from Carol's back around to her tense shoulders and gently pulled her to his side. He could feel the tension radiating from her body while the smile plastered on her face did not reach her eyes. *Dammit.*

"Yes, well as you can see, I have a beautiful date and we have a reservation. You may show us to our table." Nervous, he hoped he was handling the situation correctly. The last thing he wanted was a former hook-up to ruin his evening with Carol.

"Sure thing, honey. But listen, the next time you're over this way, look me up. I'm always up for a night with you sugar, and I know you're always *up!*" Turning to Carol with a smile, she continued, "Normally I wouldn't be so forward, but we all know Tom. He's great with the benefits, but sticking around just isn't his thing, is it? Oh well, enjoy him while you have him."

By this time, Carol body was humming with anxiety. *A player?* Her palms were sweating, and a sick feeling crept into her stomach. *What am I doing here? This is so not me. He's not even interested in me.*

Tom growled, "Anita, show us to our table. Now."

Eyes narrowing in confusion, the hostess turned and sashayed over to a corner table next to a window with a view of the mountains in the background.

Assisting Carol with her seat, Tom took the seat next to her instead of across from her. She still had no appearance of anxiety over meeting Anita, but he noticed that her hands shook ever so slightly as she picked up her menu. *Whatever is in her past, she has learned to hide her emotions.* He desired to take her in his arms and not only protect her from anything now but also to wipe away whatever stole her joy in her past.

Looking over their menus, he noticed her subtle scent drifting his way. Ever so slight, with just a hint of floral. Noticing everything about her, he tried not to stare. Her hair that beckoned his fingers to sift through the strands. Her china doll face with delicate features. Slim hands, belying their strength. She took the napkin and gently unfolded it as she placed it in her lap before perusing the menu. *Most women are already draping themselves over me, and she seems completely unaffected.* Confused as to how to read her, he began looking over the menu as well.

As Carol's eyes expertly scanned the menu, she mentally calculated the lowest calorie meal without seeming obvious. She stilled her nerves, trying not to look at him, having already memorized his every feature. Navy slacks, cut to fit his muscular thighs. Light blue dress shirt, with the cuffs, rolled at the wrists. *Tall. Blond. Built. Strong jaw, ocean blue eyes that twinkle, and kissable lips. Kissable lips? Oh Jesus, read the menu. Read the menu. Remember, this is just dinner. Nothing more. If he wants a new fuck-buddy, he can look elsewhere!*

His leg brushed against hers sending a tingle all the way from her knee to her core. She clenched her thighs to ease the pressure. *Read the menu,* she chanted like a mantra.

Tom smiled, noticing the slight movement as she pressed her legs together. *So she's not as unaffected by me as I thought.*

The waiter came over and took their orders.

"I'll have the baked chicken with steamed vegetables," she stated as she eyed the rolls the waiter had put on the table. Melted butter slid off of their sides, pooling in the plate under them. *Chicken — 140 calories. Steamed veggies — 60 calories. I could have one roll. 120 calories without the butter. I could run more tomorrow.*

"I'm glad you ordered food and not just a salad," he commented, unknowingly interrupting her calorie counting.

She smiled, but once again it did not reach her eyes. Shrugging softly, she admitted, "I like to eat."

Tom, his eyebrow lifted in question, stated, "Well, I don't know where it goes, 'cause you're a tiny thing."

The smile left her face as she turned to look at the majestic view outside the window. He felt the loss of her smile immediately, wanting to do nothing more than have it back on her beautiful face again and directed at him.

"Tell me about being a nurse," he asked, hoping to pull her out of her silence.

Whipping her head around to look at him, the change in Carol's demeanor was instantaneous. "I love it!" she said, her smile returning in its full glory. "I have been a nurse for about four years and it's everything I ever wanted it to be."

Tom, thrilled to have found the topic that sparked her apparent joy, prodded more. "What about the ER? Is that where you want to work or did you just get stuck there?"

"Oh no," she replied, placing her hand on his arm. "I think the ER is the most fascinating place to work. Every day is different. Every hour is different." Feeling the strength of his arm muscles under her hand sent a spark through her, reminding her of their first meeting when he was injured. Jerking her hand back, she glanced into his eyes.

He felt the spark as well, also remembering her touch when he was almost unconscious. He felt the loss of her hand and reached out to grasp her hand in his much larger one.

"You were telling me about the ER?" he asked, his fingers tracing gentle circles on her hand.

"I love never knowing what will walk through the door. It really keeps me on my toes. And sometimes there's such a connection with a patient." Looking deeply into his eyes, she said, "Like your friend's wife, Jen."

"Do you often make a connection?" he asked, thinking about his accident. *Does she recognize me? Does she realize it was my hand she was holding?*

"Well...there was one person, when I held their hand after they were injured, I felt a connection," she spoke quietly, lowering her eyes, afraid to see what his memories were.

"I was injured recently, and I swear to God, an angel held my hand," he spoke, leaning so that his voice was just a whisper in her ear.

Immediately raising her eyes to his, she barely spoke. "You remember?"

Leaning further so that his lips were touching her ear, "I remember everything about you."

Sucking her breath in sharply, she turned her face so that her lips were next to his. "You thought I was an angel."

"No babe. I knew you were." And with that, he completed the distance so that his lips touched her with the barest hint of a kiss.

Eyes wide, she was stunned, then confused. "So is that what this is? Tonight, I mean? You wanting to thank me?"

Placing his hand gently on her cheek, turning her face back to his, he replied, "I looked for you for weeks. I couldn't get you out of my mind. And when I finally saw you in the ER, that was it for me. I was gonna move heaven and earth to make you mine."

She found that the warmth of his words wrapped around her like a blanket. Smiling, she allowed him to pull her in for another whisper kiss.

The waiter arrived with their food and Carol found herself glad for the distraction. Focusing on the food, she was a master at eating small portions while making it look as though she was just taking time with her food. She forced herself to focus on Tom and their conversation, not mentally calculating the calories. *Why am I doing this now? I have been so healthy! It's that damn invitation from my parents, being here with Tom, and Anita.*

Their conversation flowed as they swapped stories of her adventures in the ER and his adventures as a detective.

"So tell me about your two friends that were

in the ER with you?" she asked.

"You saw me there and didn't come in and say something? Hell Carol, you could've saved me weeks of looking for you," he admonished.

"How was I to know you were interested?" she shot back.

Tom just shook his head in frustration. "Clueless."

"Would you stop saying that?"

Holding her eyes with his, "Anyone who looks like you ought to know, any man would be interested."

"Carol? Carol Fletcher?" a male voice came from behind them.

Tom turned, scowling at the interruption, his irritation focused on a man, dressed in an expensive suit, walking over toward them. Tall, slender, with his dark brown hair styled as though he spent a great deal of time in a salon. The man never looked over at Tom but kept his eyes on Carol as he approached.

Confusion, replaced by recognition showed on Carol's face. "Ronald?"

Ronald Harriston, the son of one of her father's associates and a man her father had deemed worthy to be husband material, kept walking until he was right next to Carol, on the opposite side of Tom. Leaning down he kissed her cheek, causing Carol to jerk back uncomfortably. Tom, already irritated at the interruption, was willing to make a concession to a friend of hers, but seeing her reaction he stood up quickly, moving forward forcing Ronald to step back.

Carol attempted an introduction to intervene. "Ronald, it's been a long time. Tom, this is Ronald Harriston, a friend of my father. Ronald, this is Tom, my da—"

"Her boyfriend," Tom finished. Taking control of the situation, he placed his left hand possessively on the back of Carol's neck, extending his right hand toward Ronald.

Ronald looked surprised but shook Tom's hand nonetheless. "Your father hadn't mentioned that you were seeing someone." Sizing Tom up, he continued, "I'm more than just a family friend, I'm an old *friend* of Carol's."

Bristling, Carol stated, "I don't report everything to my father, Ronald. I haven't for a long time, as I'm sure you know." Outwardly calm, she could feel the panic building. *The invitation. I have got to deal with that soon.*

"Your parents miss you, Carol. They say you don't come around very often to see them."

"I see them occasionally." Anger mixed with the panic made Carol feel lightheaded. *You can do this. You can do this.* "You know as well as anyone that they don't approve of my career."

"So you're still playing nurse at the hospital."

"Playing?" Carol sputtered.

Tom moved so that his body was between Carol and Ronald, forcing Ronald's eyes up to his. "I think it's time you moved on."

The feeling of being out of control overtook Carol. She looked down at the food still left on her plate, the smell of it turning her stomach. "If you gentlemen will excuse me, I'll be right back," she said as she moved past Tom, walking toward the restrooms.

Ronald watched her momentarily before turning back to Tom, realizing his mistake upon seeing the fury on his face.

Tom growled, "As an old friend, you get one pass, man and that was it. I catch you starin' at my woman's ass again you'll be eatin' through a straw. You got me?"

Ronald smirked, "I apologize. Good evening." He turned and moved away, leaving the restaurant.

Damn. A perfect dinner ruined by that asshole. And Anita. Could it get any worse? Getting angrier by the moment, he forced himself to calm down. Glancing toward the ladies' room, he noticed an older woman approaching him.

Looking at her questioningly, he asked, "May I help you, ma'am?"

"I'm sorry," she spoke softly. "I was just in the ladies' room and I think your date is ill."

Quickly thanking her, Tom strode over to the door of the restroom. Hesitating, he knocked before opening the door. Scanning the room to make sure it was clear of others, he only saw Carol's shoes under one of the stalls. The sound of retching came from the stall, followed by a sob.

Heading over to the sink, he took one of the clean wash clothes, soaking it in cold water.

Walking to the door, he knocked. "Carol. Let me in."

"Tom! What are you doing here?" she said, panicked.

"Babe, let me in." He pushed gently on the door. Pulling her out of the stall, he wrapped his arm around her, supporting her, holding the wet washcloth to her face.

"What happened? Are you sick?"

"I had to get rid of it. I had to get rid of dinner," she spoke in a whisper, her body shaking.

Tossing the cloth into the trash can, he wrapped her in both of his arms, pulling her body into his tight embrace. Rubbing her back with his hand, he willed her body to calm.

"What happened, babe?"

Shaking her head from side to side, she pressed her face into his chest.

"Eyes on me," he ordered gently.

She lifted her face, leaning way back to peer into his eyes. Pulling her lips in tightly again, she breathed through her nose, trying not to cry.

"What happened?" he softly asked again.

"I'm sorry."

"I don't want you to be sorry. I want you to tell me what is going on."

Looking back down, she spoke in a whisper. "I...sometimes...purge when I'm stressed. I...I... haven't done it in a long time. Just..." She shook her head, not wanting to see the repulsion she knew would be on his face. *No one knows this. Why did I tell him?*

Tom brought one hand around to cup her face, gently pulling her face up to his. "Eyes, sweetheart."

Pulling her lips in again, she brought her eyes up to his. Blue eyes met blue eyes. No repulsion. No anger. No aversion. No distaste. Just warmth. Comfort. Care.

"Are you seeing someone to help you?"

She nodded. "I have been seeing a counselor since I was twenty years old. First at the University, then I found someone here in town. She retired, and I have a new one, but I hardly have to see her now. Just when I feel like I need it."

"You know what makes it worse?"

She nodded again. "Stress, new situations, feeling out of control...pretty much everything that has been happening in the last few days." She paused for a moment, seeming to work something out in her mind. Raising her eyes back to his, "Anything to do with my parents."

Tom nodded, not wanting to keep asking questions at this time, especially standing in the middle of the ladies' room. "Let's go, Angel." He kept her tucked tightly as they walked back out of the restaurant. Not looking at the questioning glance of the hostess, he walked her out to his truck helping her up into the cab.

The ride home was silent. Carol was mortified that she had confessed to him her illness. *Well, it was nice while it lasted. Mental note to self— never confess to a hot guy that you throw up sometimes on purpose. A total mood killer.*

Arriving at her apartment, Carol's hand on the car handle, she quickly said goodnight as she began to open the door.

Tom's voice rumbled through the truck. "I once told you what I'd do if you open that door before I was ready."

Her head snapped around, a questioning look on her face. *I have already laid myself bare, might as well make it final.* "Tom, you don't have to play nice right now. I know what I have. I know how to help myself, but sometimes, when life is stressful, I have to remind myself to make healthier choices. I didn't do that tonight, and you have no idea how sorry I'm about that. But the fact of the matter is that I shared something with you that I haven't told anyone. I don't even know why I did it, but I can't take the words back. But you don't have to pretend that this doesn't repulse you. Let me just preserve as much dignity as I can out of this evening, and say goodnight."

Not saying a word, he jumped out of the truck, stalking around to her side. Opening her door, he reached in and plucked her out of the seat. Squealing, she wrapped her arms around his neck to keep from falling.

Carrying her upstairs to her door, he slowly slid her body down his as he set her on the ground. Not letting go, he held her tightly from chest to knees. "Keys."

Confused, she reached into her purse, handing him her keys. Opening the door, he ushered her in. Looking around, he saw a perfectly ordered apartment.

The living room walls were painted a pale color and held a large burgundy sofa and chairs. The walls of the dining room were a darker color and surrounded a table with four chairs. The apartment had wooden floors, and a rug was in the middle of the living room. She also had a large screen television on the wall opposite of the sofa. A huge window took up most of the wall at the end and overlooked the park next door. He could see a hall dividing the apartment and assumed the bedrooms were down there.

Pushing her gently toward the back hall, he ordered, "Babe, go put something comfortable on. I'm waiting here. We're talking about some of this shit that's got you so clueless and we're talking tonight. So go change clothes."

Cool blue eyes narrowing, she hissed, "Stop ordering me around. I'm not a child, and I do not need a caveman telling me what to do!"

Sighing as he realized that he wasn't making a very good impression, he closed his eyes for a moment. Opening them again, seeing her staring at him, doubt and questions in her gaze, he began.

"Carol, I'm a man who wants to take care of you. I'm not trying to order you around just for the hell of it, and I'm not trying to take anything away from you." Stepping close, encouraged that she remained still, he continued as he placed his hands gently on her shoulders. "I want to talk to you and I want you comfortable while we do it."

Taking a deep breath, Carol nodded. Walking into her bedroom, she knew why she agreed. *He's too nice to just dump me at the door, so he wants to explain why we can't see each other anymore. Well fine. I'll give him that.* Taking off the dress and heels, she pulled on yoga pants and a soft t-shirt. Tossing her hair into a messy bun on top of her head, she quickly brushed her teeth to get rid of the acid taste.

Looking into the mirror, she shook her head. *Why did you do that? You haven't purged in a couple of years. You gave in when you saw Ronald and the mention of dad, along with that damn invitation, and that 'old friend' Anita. You scared off Mr. Hot detective out there, all by giving in to the temptation. You're a fool, and you deserve this guy running for the hills away from you.*

Taking a deep breath, steeling herself for what was to come, she walked back into the living room. She noticed him giving her a head-to-toe scan. Seeing him sitting comfortably in the middle of her sofa left her wondering where she should sit. *Where does one sit when getting dumped? Jesus, Carol...get a grip.*

Before she could decide what her next play should be, Tom raised one arm. "Come here." Seeing her hesitation, he said it again, this time, the warmth of his words beckoned her. "Come on, babe."

Walking toward him he reached out, snagged her hand, and gently pulled her down on his lap.

Confusion must have shown on her face because he questioned, "What's wrong?"

"Is this the usual breaking up position?"

"Clueless."

"Will you stop calling me that?"

"When you stop acting it, I will."

Huffing, she decided to let him have his way. The sooner he said what he needed to say the better. Then she could go back to her lonely existence.

Tom hauled her around so that she was straddling his lap, facing him. Holding onto her hip with one hand, the other hand curled around the back of her neck.

"Carol, weeks ago, I got a gift. Got visited by an angel and swear to God, I knew I needed that person in my life. I spent a couple of weeks scourin' the city lookin' for you. When I laid eyes on you in the ER, I knew...*knew* I wanted you. Not one thing has changed. Nothin'."

He paused a second to make sure she was following him. Her eyes, glued to his, kept him going. "Found out you got shit for parents. I don't know the story, but hope you trust me soon to let me in. Found out you've got an eating disorder. That only makes me want to take care of you more, but it sure as hell doesn't make me want to leave. I hate that I have got a past reputation with some women, and I can't stand the thought that brings you pain."

She started to lower her head, but his hand on her neck gently kept her face on his.

"But Carol, this is you and me together. We get all this shit out in the open and we deal. We talk it out. We work it out. Hell, sometimes we even fight it out. But babe, if you want this as much as I do, then you and me are happening."

His words flowed over her, seeping into all the hidden crevices of doubt and pain. Her eyes went warm, and tears pooled in them threatening to spill over. *Care. Comfort. He's not rebuffing me. He wants me. Me.*

A tear escaped down her cheek, and he wiped it with his thumb.

"You want to work things out with me?" she asked, still looking unsure.

"That's that clueless shit I was talking about.

You're gorgeous. You don't seem to know it, but we're gonna work through that 'cause someone has taken that from you. You're smart with a good job, a caring job, an important job. I have got a feeling your folks don't see it that way, and that matters to you, but we're gonna work through that too. I'm feeling goddamn lucky that a woman like you is givin' me a chance. You don't seem to realize that either. But getting my drift, sweetheart? We're gonna work through that too."

She thought back to Sofia's words again. *But honey, there can be the kind of man who gives you everything he has to give... and would give anything just to take care of you. You've never had that before...might be just what you need.*

Her hands shot up from his shoulders to the sides of his face, and she pulled him in for a kiss. Her lips moved over his, feeling, memorizing. He let her take control for a moment before deepening the kiss. He angled his head, pulled her in and took over.

Carol, lost in the kiss, could no longer tell where she ended and he began. His tongue explored every crevice of her mouth tangling with her tongue thrust for thrust. Sucking her tongue into his mouth before slowly letting it slide back, he heard her moan appreciatively.

Nipping at her lips, he then smoothed over the sting with his tongue.

She lost all sense of time as the kiss continued. Long. Hard. Wet. Feeling as though she needed him for her very breath, she sucked him in.

He found himself just as lost in the kiss. Never had he kissed a woman for so long, usually turning kisses into just the preamble for sex. Kisses were only the way for a man to get a woman turned on, wet, ready. But this. This was something even he had no experience with. Sliding his hands down to her ass, he kneaded the globes. She was tiny, but her ass filled his hands perfectly.

Grinding herself on his jean covered dick, she felt the need to create the much-needed friction.

Tom, wanting to take care of her, moved quickly, rolling back onto the couch with her tucked into his side. Sliding his hand down the front of her yoga pants, he found her folds slick and ready. Gently pushing a finger into her slick channel, he began thrusting first one finger and then adding a second. *Jesus, she is tight. How will I ever fit without hurting her?* His dick ached as it pressed against his jeans, but he wanted this to be all about her. Continuing the kiss while fingering her, he could feel her inner muscles clenching.

Panting, she could feel her orgasm building as she kept riding his fingers. *I have never felt this before. Maybe I'm not frigid.* "Tom, Tom," she moaned.

"Eyes, Angel. I wanna see you when you come."

Blue eyes gazed at blue eyes, as she plummeted over the edge. Her inner walls clenching around his fingers, she rode out the waves of pleasure.

Finally coming back down, she relaxed as he slid his fingers out of her pants and into his waiting mouth. Watching him suck her juices off of his fingers, she leaned back up to kiss him, tasting herself on his tongue.

Lying together on the couch for a few minutes in blissful silence, he then rose and pulled her up with him. Walking down the hall toward her bedroom he paused at the door.

"Can I stay, babe?"

Smiling a dreamy smile, she answered, "I think I would lock you in if you tried to leave."

Laughing, he walked into the bedroom, pulling her along with him. She went into the bathroom first, changing out of her yoga pants, pulling off her bra, but leaving on her t-shirt and panties. Returning to the bedroom, she saw him lounging against the headboard. *I have never had a man look at me the way he does.* Nervously, she licked her lips as she hesitated.

Tom noticed her nipples pebbling through her t-shirt. *God, she is beautiful.* Willing his dick to behave, he held out his hand to her.

She slid in beside him and he pulled her in tight.

"Just lettin' you know, we're not doing anything tonight."

Carol, twisting around to peer into his face, was ready to question when he continued.

"Babe, you've had a rough night. I want you to rest, and I want to be here with you to make sure you do. I also don't want to leave now and have you go back to being clueless by talking shit inside your head. So I'm here. We're sleepin' together and then we're gonna start working on what we talked about earlier."

Leaning in to kiss her gently, he raised back up. "Got me?"

Relaxing with a smile on her face, she reached up to caress his cheek.

"Yeah, Tom. I got you."

Tom, breathing easy for the first time all evening, just replied, "Thank goodness."

Smiling, she snuggled in as he pulled her tightly against his strong body. She slept all night. No fears. No dreams. Just peaceful sleep.

Chapter 9

T om woke the next morning, staring at the beautiful woman lying in bed with him. He never stayed with a one-night stand and the few fuck-buddies that he had over the years meant nothing to him other than a chance to have a steady partner for a couple of months. He never felt anything for them, other than physical for the one-nighters, and some friendship for the buddies.

Grimacing, he thought about those buddies. After a while, the women wanted more commitment from him that he did not feel, so the relationships ended...if he was honest, they usually ended badly. That was why he stuck to one-nighters. They were physical, no promises of tomorrow, and no hurt feelings.

Looking back down at her, he knew this was different. Curled up on her side, with her hand tucked under her pillow. Tousled, yellow blond hair framing her face like a halo. Rosy lips, slightly open as she slept. She was such a puzzle.

Strong, yet fragile. Thinking back to their conversation of the previous evening, he knew she shared more with him that she had her friends. *Something's there between us. I know it. I know she knows it. I just have to make sure she keeps knowing it.*

Her eyes opened sleepily, and she gazed at the handsome visage in front of her. Hard, defined muscles covered his chest and abs, tapering down to a trim waist. Raising her eyes, she focused on his strong jaw, covered in beard stubble that made her wet thinking about it between her thighs. Continuing her perusal, she looked farther up into his blue eyes that were staring back at her. She blushed, realizing that she had been caught ogling the man in her bed and tried to roll away.

"Oh no," he said as he rolled on top of her to keep her from leaving. "I have been starin' at all this beauty for a while. Don't want it hidden." Leaning down, he touched his lips to hers in a gentle kiss, which quickly became a hard, wet, tongues clashing, sucking, nipping good morning kiss.

She felt the fires building in her core, began to grind her hips, feeling his swollen dick pressing between her legs. Running her hands along his back, she marveled at the feel of the muscles there as well. *Jesus, he is built.* Feeling the power of his muscles as he began to move against her, she desperately hoped he was ready to take this to the next level. *Please, no more talking right now. Just take me. Take all of me. Mark me. Make me yours.*

He felt her body responding and knew she was ready for him. Sliding his hand to the bottom of her t-shirt, he slowly peeled it upwards, lifting it over her breasts as he then pulled it off her and tossed it to the side. He palmed her breasts as they filled his hands. He loved the feel of them; full, but not heavy. Looking down at their perfection, rosy-tipped, aching for his mouth, he leaned over taking one in his mouth. Pulling it deeply in, he rolled his tongue around the hard pebble. Sucking, nipping, he worshiped one breast while his hand rolled the other nipple between his thumb and forefinger.

She grabbed his head, holding him to her breasts as the electricity fired down to her sex. Sliding her hands down his neck toward his back, she felt his muscles cord underneath her touch. Hips undulating against his straining cock, she threw her head back and moaned.

He raised up, hearing her mewl at the loss of contact. Grabbing her panties with one hand, he pulled them down and off, then slid his finger into her folds. Crooking his finger deep inside, he began the movement that quickly had her purring as he watched her face in fascination. *Never watched a woman's face like this before. Never cared before.*

She felt the pressure inside build as his fingers continued their dance inside of her wet sex while his other hand fondled her breasts. Almost panting, she couldn't seem to make the last climb up toward...what, she didn't know. She just knew she had to get there.

Crooking his fingers, he hit the spot that took her over the edge. Screaming out his name, she closed her eyes in ecstasy, as the orgasm pulled her into oblivion.

He felt her muscles contract around his fingers as he watched her face when she came. Leaning down he pulled his fingers out, licking them before taking her mouth in a hard, wet kiss.

Tasting herself on his kiss, she wanted more. More kiss. More Tom. More everything. Opening her eyes, she saw him gazing down at her. Smiling, she reached down grasping his cock through his boxers. "One of us is overdressed," she said, raising her eyebrow.

He laughed as he pulled back up off the bed. Hooking his thumbs in the waistband of his tented boxers, he halted for a moment looking down at her beauty. Petite, slender, perfectly shaped. His eyes lifted to hers staring back at him. Blue eyes gazing at blue eyes.

"Carol? You ready for this?" he asked. "Cause we do this, you're mine. And I'm yours. No turnin' back." Looking down, holding her gaze, he held his breath. She began to smile, tentative at first, then her smile filled her face. Letting out his breath, he grinned back. "Gotta hear it. You with me?"

"Yeah, Tom. I'm with you," she replied, raising her arms to the top of his boxers, covering his hands with her own.

Pulling them off he lay down beside her, stroking her, memorizing her, finding what brought out the moans. "Love this body, Angel. You're so beautiful. Inside as well as out. Just fuckin' beautiful."

At that moment, she knew what it felt like to be beautiful. She felt it. Experienced it. Understood it. At that moment, she didn't care what image she saw in the mirror. She just reveled in the knowledge that to Tom, she was beautiful. Smiling, she pulled him to her, locking her mouth with his.

Rolling over, bracing up on his elbows, he towered over her, taking over the kiss. Slow at first, it quickly intensified. Tongues tangling, exploring, sucking, nipping then soothing with soft licks.

She once again pushed her hips up toward his, desperately seeking the friction needed.

Tom slid his hand under his pillow, coming out with a packet. Looking at her surprised expression, he chuckled. "Put that there last night, babe. Wasn't sure, but was hopeful."

He quickly rolled it on, then placed his swollen cock at her entrance. "Eyes on me. I wanna see those gorgeous eyes when I'm inside of you."

Sliding his cock into her wet folds, he slowly pushed to the hilt. *Jesus, she's tight. Does this hurt her?* The realization that he never cared before washed over him. "I'm not hurting you am I?"

Answering by grabbing his ass, looking into his eyes, she said, "Go for it, baby."

"Hell yeah," he growled as he began to pump in and out of her dripping sex. Harder and harder, keeping his eyes on her face, watching her bite her lip as her head was thrown back. He'd wanted to take it slow and easy, but he felt out of control with this woman. He wanted to own her, mark her, make her his. Pounding, the friction building, he kept his eyes on her.

"Eyes," he called out when he first felt her inner walls contract around his cock. Her eyes jerked open and she screamed his name again as a second orgasm exploded inside. Tom continued pounding for a few more thrusts before he made one last thrust, neck straining, emptying himself.

He rolled to the side as he crashed down, pulling her along with him to keep from crushing her. Holding tightly to each other, heavy breathing synchronized, they lay for a long time. Not speaking. Just hands slowly caressing. Pulling her body in closer so that he felt every inch, he knew this was it. What he had been looking for. The missing piece of his life. This was forever for him. *Is it forever for her too?*

"You're so quiet," she murmured, staring at his chest, afraid to look up and see what might be in his eyes. *He's so much more experienced than I'm. Maybe that sucked for him. Maybe my body didn't satisfy him like he hoped it would. Maybe…*

He placed his hand under her chin, raising her face to his. Quickly assessing her, he shook his head. "Don't get clueless on me, Carol. Never had anything like that before. Never had sex with anyone I cared about." He sighed when he saw a flash of pain in her eyes. "Stay with me, Angel. Don't go back inside yourself where you can't know what we've got here. I told you last night, I hate like hell I have gotta past that causes you pain. But we're laying it to rest right here and right now."

Carol, wide-eyed, looked at Tom, doubt showing across her face. "How?" she asked.

"By getting it out in the open. Didn't want to do it now, laying in bed after we just made love for the first time, but it seems those ghosts are in your head, so we're gonna get rid of them now, so they don't ever come back up."

Raising up, he leaned his back against the headboard, then pulled her up so that she was resting against him.

"Babe, I'm thirty years old. Not any surprise I have been with women. Jake, Rob, and me played football in college, and we acted like we were the big dogs on campus. Had women, not one of them meant anything and honest to God, I couldn't tell you the name of any of them. I worked as a policemen in Richland for a few years before coming back here. Again, I was young and had a lot of one-night stands. Always purely physical. Never meant anything. Wasn't looking for anything so that fit what I needed."

Carol was quiet, listening, surprised that his words did not hurt. It seemed as though they were talking about someone else. A Tom of long ago. Not her Tom. Not the Tom she had now.

He leaned over, staring into her eyes for a moment, then satisfied with what he saw, he continued. "Moved back to Fairfield to become a detective to be where Jake and Rob were. We were best friends, brothers almost since we were little and I found that by my mid-twenties, I wanted that back in my life.

"Hooked up some once I was back in town. Mostly one-nighters, but had a few friends with benefits. Found that those always ended badly 'cause I never wanted anything more, and they usually thought that it was gonna lead somewhere."

Carol shifted in his arms so that she was straddling him, wanting to see in his eyes. Placing her small hands on his muscular shoulders, she nodded. "Keep going."

Liking the feel of her naked sitting on his lap, encouraged by the change in her demeanor, he continued.

"Jake taught me a valuable lesson. He found that being a detective it was a damn nuisance to be investigating a crime and run into a town hookup. He tended to go out of town for his needs, saying it just worked better for him. Made a lot of sense to me, so I haven't had any women in this town in years. And when I did go out, it still meant nothing to me but a physical release. Won't deny I had a couple of friendly hookups more than once with a woman I liked, but that was all it was. And when it was over, it was over. Rob, well he can't keep it in his pants, and that will come back to bite him in the ass one day when he finally meets someone that he feels about like I feel about you."

Seeing that Carol was still listening, still gazing into his eyes, he was encouraged that maybe one of her dragons could be slain today. "So, this is how we lay this shit to rest. You with me, so far?"

Carol nodded, still satisfied with his recapping of his sexual past.

Tom gently cupped her angelic face with his hands. "Listen carefully. I have never loved any woman. Sex was physical or at the most a little pleasurable fun. That was then. This is now. Now is you. You're not a one-nighter. You're not a fuck-buddy. You're not a friend-with-benefits. You and me are gonna keep seeing each other. We're gonna move forward. You're mine, and I don't share, so you also don't have to worry about sharing me. So get the clueless about us out of your head. There is no comparison of you to any other woman. You're it for me. You still with me?"

Carol leaned in just until their mouths barely

touched. She breathed him in. Closing her eyes for a second, she touched her lips to his.

Tom was quiet, not sure where her head was at. Encouraged by her gentle kiss, he still felt a trickle of fear, wondering what she was thinking.

Leaning back, she smiled up at him. "I'm with you, Tom." Taking a deep breath, she sucked her lips tightly for a moment. Relaxing, she smiled again. "Okay."

Eyebrow cocked in question, he asked, "Okay? Okay what?"

"I choose you. I know you have a past, and you've laid it out. No more surprises. No more wondering if your past relationships are going to come around like Anita in the restaurant. If they do, I know you're with me. And you've never really *been* with them. Not emotionally. So yeah, I'm with you."

"Thank goodness," he growled crashing his lips down on hers. This kiss built in intensity until they were one person. One being. Needing each other to breathe, to live.

Feeling the blood rushing back to his dick, Tom lifted her, and she slid down onto his waiting cock. Then she rode him until she shattered into a million pieces. And then he lifted her, continuing to thrust up into her until he found his release. Then they collapsed once again, this time, his past not between them.

As Tom got ready for work, Carol fixed breakfast. Her eyes feasted on him as he walked in from the bedroom. Dark jeans, tight across his thighs, light blue button up shirt paired with a navy tie, and a khaki sports jacket carried across his arm. As her eyes traveled back up to his face, she blushed as she once again was caught ogling him.

"Angel, you keep lookin' at me like that and I'll never make it to work."

Ducking her head, she turned back to the stove to plate the eggs. Massive arms encircled her from behind, pulling her back to his front. "Oh no, don't get shy on me now. You wanna look, babe, you go right ahead and look."

Tilting her head back, she took his lips in a soft kiss but pulled away before he could deepen it. "You've got to get to work, remember?" she replied in a sing-song voice.

Taking the plate in one hand, he smacked her ass with the other as he walked over to lean against the counter. "When do you go back to work, Carol?"

Picking up her plate and walking to the bar, she replied, "This is my last day off because of my shoulder. I go back on the graveyard shift tonight."

"I'm not a fan of the graveyard shift. A lot of crazy shit goes down in the ER at night, and there's no denyin' I'd like you in my bed."

"I have never had a reason not to work that shift before," she replied honestly. "I haven't dated in a long time, the only real friends I have work the various shifts…and the money is really good."

"You hurting for money?"

"No…" Carol's eyes darted to the side, breaking eye contact with him.

Setting his empty plate in the sink, he turned to face her directly. "No what?"

"I just pay my own way for everything and well…my student loans were large. I didn't get any help from my family," her eyes shot up to his, "but that's okay. I mean lots of people don't have any support from family."

"Come here, babe," he ordered gently, holding his hand out.

She walked around the bar and into his arms. Holding her tucked tight against his chest, he rested his chin on her head. She could hear his heartbeat pressed against her cheek.

"Carol, we made real strides earlier. Got rid of some of that doubt you had going on. I know somethings up with your parents, and we gotta deal with that later when you're ready. Right now, I gotta get to work. When will I see you again?"

"I'm not sure. I won't know my schedule until I get there."

"Okay, babe. You can text it to me once you know." Tom pulled her in closer, kissing the top of her head.

She pressed her cheek closer to his chest, feeling the comfort of hearing his heartbeat. With his arms completely enveloping her, she felt warm, safe, comforted. Not controlled. But protected.

"I hear your heartbeat," she whispered.

"It beats for you, Angel," Tom replied as he leaned down to capture her lips in a kiss, before leaving for work.

Closing the door, Carol leaned against it for a moment, thinking about the past twenty-four hours. Knowing she needed to call Ronda, she wasn't dreading it. *Yeah, I have got to tell her about my setback last night. But I have also got good news. He likes me. He really likes me.*

Chapter 10

Walking into the ER nurse's break room several days later, Carol saw Jon at the candy machines. "Hey stranger," she called out. "We haven't worked the same shifts recently."

Jon smiled, hugged her, then pulled her down into one of the chairs at the table. "Oohh, I have got news."

Laughing, she said, "What's going on?"

"Well, I have been trying to work more day shifts since...I met someone."

Grabbing her friend in another hug, she begged, "Tell me about him."

"A couple of weeks ago I went clubbing in Richland." Seeing her raised eyebrow, he quickly explained. "Girl, it was not a bad club. Just a friendly bar that plays jazzy music. Was with some friends, and they introduced us. He's nice. Don't know if anything lasting will happen, but for now, it's all good. So what about you and Mr. Hottie Detective?"

The door opened as Sofia walked in. "Oohh,

are we talking about Carol's Mr. Gorgeous Ass Detective?"

Blushing, Carol couldn't help but smile.

"Oh lordy, my girl is finally getting some!" Sofia shouted, high-fiving Jon.

"Guys, hush! Not everyone around here needs to know about my sex life," Carol admonished.

Sofia and Jon looked at each other, grinning ear to ear. "Well, at least, you now got a sex life to talk about," Jon retorted.

Before the conversation could go any further, their pagers sounded. Heading back into the hall, they were alerted that the police were bringing in a prisoner injured in a fight.

The man was coming in on a stretcher, his clothes ripped and bloody. Rob was with the paramedics transporting the prisoner with three policemen in attendance. Taking him back to one of the ER exam rooms, Carol began to remove his clothes to ascertain his injuries.

Rob stayed for a couple of minutes watching Carol as she leaned over talking softly to the patient. Smiling at what he saw, he was beginning to understand why Tom was so enamored. She seemed real. Genuine. Thinking that he'd like to settle down with one woman himself but not sure where he was going to find the right one, he was happy for Tom. Catching her eye as he walked out of the room, he smiled and gave a head nod.

Carol continued to work on the patient as Dr. Driscoll came into the room. Smiling, he leaned over closely to her as she was cleaning the wounds. "Dr. Driscoll, you need to step back; you're in my light."

"Carol, you know you can call me Charles." He continued to smile at her as she continued to ignore him. After a few minutes of watching her work, he wrote in his notes that the wounds were severe enough that the patient would need to stay overnight for observation. He left and Jon popped into the room to see if she needed assistance.

"I have got it," she assured him. "Your shift is over. Go on home."

As Jon left the room, another man was escorted in with one of the policemen. Explaining that he was the wounded man's brother, he wanted to be close by. The two officers conferred, at first denying the brother the chance to sit in the room.

"I don't see how it could hurt," Carol spoke up. "He isn't going anywhere right now."

"Ma'am, all due respect, the prisoner is a major drug dealer from the Richland area, and he was in our area scoring. He got into a knife fight with another dealer. We got the tip and we got the man. We're not about to take a chance that he will escape or that his brother won't assist in some way."

Tight-lipped, Carol continued to work on him. The brother sat quietly in the corner chair watching.

Speaking softly to the patient, she cautioned when he would feel the pinch from the needle, and she administered pain meds in his IV as directed by the physician. "You're going to look like you were in a cat fight for a couple of weeks, but I promise I'm excellent with stitches. You take care of these, and people will hardly notice the scars."

He kept his eyes on hers, distrust showing on his face as well as pain.

After several minutes, the brother spoke. "I know my brother's been in some bad trouble miss, but I sure do appreciate you being so nice to him."

Carol looked over, smiling, and replied, "He's not a prisoner to me. Nor a drug dealer. He's just another patient."

The man smiled and raised his eyes to her, staring intently as he continued to make conversation.

"Brother's name is Calvin. Mine's Bert. My parents gave up on Cal years ago when he got into drugs and gangs. He went from bad to worse, so they washed their hands of him. But me, I just couldn't let him go entirely. We don't hardly see each other, but we'll text occasionally."

Carol continued working with Calvin, understanding the policemen's attitude but feeling sorry for Bert as well. As she finished the stitches, she began to clean the blood off his body as much as she could. Sofia came by to see if she needed help, but Carol waved her off.

The attending physician completed the admission orders and taking over for Carol since some of the wounds were at risk for infection. As the hospital attendants were rolling Cal's bed out of the ER room to move to a hospital bed upstairs, the policemen followed along.

Bert stood, then hesitated as he looked over at Carol. "Miss, I do thank you for your kindness. I know my parents aren't here, but if they were, they'd appreciate it too." Looking at her name tag, he commented, "Carol. That's a real pretty name for a real pretty lady."

Starting to feel uncomfortable under the constant gaze of Bert, Carol quickly washed her hands and moved toward the door. "You really should head on up in the elevator with your brother so you'll know which room they put him in."

Bert nodded and followed her closely out into the hall. "Carol," he said, putting his hand on her arm, "I hope to see you around again sometime."

Carol just smiled politely, turned, and walked back over to the nurses' station. Standing there facing Sofia, she said softly, "Casually look behind me and see if that man has left."

Sofia quickly glanced over Carol's shoulder, seeing Bert staring at Carol before walking over to the elevator. "He's gone now, hun. You okay?"

Sighing, Carol nodded. "Yeah, it was probably nothing. You know how some people are just overly grateful for what we do, but he just kind of gave me the creeps."

Leaning over the counter, Sofia patted her hand, then looked at the clock. "Well, it's your lucky time, Carol. Your shift is almost over, I have got a break coming up, and I want to hear about Mr. Sex on a Stick Detective boyfriend!"

After questioning more of the witnesses of the earlier fight, Tom and Jake walked back into the station. Settling their large, muscular frames into their seats, they pulled out the files and reports that needed to be completed. The Chief came over to receive his update and the three men discussed the case against Calvin.

"He's in the hospital overnight, instead of his ass being in jail?" Jake asked, irritation showing on his face.

Tom swiveled around in his chair, looking at the chief as well. "You've gotta be shittin' me."

The chief looked over his shoulder, calling for the two patrolmen who had been in the hospital with Calvin to come over. Both men walked over immediately, answering the questions that were being fired at them from all three.

After reporting the trip to the hospital, assuring the chief that there were two guards at his hospital door, they mentioned the brother. "Seemed harmless, but we left orders that he could never be alone with our prisoner."

Tom surmised, "Don't know if he'll keep showing up with a shit-head brother like that."

The two officers glanced at each other smiling.

Noticing, Jake barked, "What?"

"Well, gotta tell you the sweet nurse attending Calvin had his brother drooling all over himself trying to get her attention."

The room filled with dead silence. Tom, standing to his six foot, four inch height, followed by Jake standing right beside him, both looked down at the officers.

With deadly calm, Tom asked, "What nurse? What did she look like?"

Now nervous, one officer replied, "A real cute, blonde nurse. She was real sweet, talked to Calvin the whole time, not that the fucker was thinking about anything except how much pain he was in. She was tiny, looked like some kind of fairy."

At that, Tom leaned down into the officer's face, "What about the brother?"

Just then, realization dawned on the other officer. "Shit, I heard you were datin' a nurse."

Tom cut his eyes to the last one who spoke, before stealing his stare back to the first reporting officer.

"Tom," Jake said in warning, placing his hand on his friend.

"What did you say about the brother?" Tom repeated.

Licking his lips, the first officer reassured him, "We were there the whole time. Nothin' happened, I swear." Hearing a growl from Tom, he continued. "It's just that the brother is kind of weasely. The kind who seems harmless, but is creepy at the same time. He was staring at her the whole time she was working on Calvin. Tried to make conversation with her. Noticed her name badge. Even heard him say he would like to see her again."

The other officer was quick to add, "But she just smiled pleasantly and walked away. I could tell he made her uncomfortable, and she sent him on up with us to Cal's room."

Tom leaned down and snagged his jacket, throwing it over his shoulder as he stormed out of the door.

Jake sat down at his computer immediately searching for information on the brother. The chief dismissed the other officers, then turned back to Jake.

"He gonna be okay?"

"Yeah," Jake replied tight-lipped. "But he's gonna' go check on Carol."

"Never thought I'd see the day," the chief said, shaking his head. "Thought Tom would never find someone he cared about." Walking away, Jake could hear the chief muttering to himself, "Good man. Good man."

Jake, concerned about Carol, couldn't help but smile. *Yeah, looks like Tom has finally found his match.*

The knocking on the door seeped into Carol's consciousness. Slowly waking up, realizing the pounding wasn't going away, she raised up to look at the clock. It was eleven a.m., and she had only been asleep for three hours. Dragging herself out of bed, she stumbled into the living room to peek through her door's keyhole. *Tom. What is Tom doing here?*

Opening the door, she looked up into his blue eyes. Eyes that she couldn't read right now. "Hey, what's up?" she asked stepping back so that he could enter.

Tom walked passed her then turned around, looking at her sleep-rumpled hair, squinting eyes, and then his eyes traveled down. *Damn, she's gorgeous just out of bed and totally clueless about it.* Her sleep shorts barely covered her luscious ass, and the camisole top did nothing to hide her breasts or her nipples poking through the material.

Adjusting himself, he reminded his dick that he wasn't here for a booty call. "I came to check on you."

Staring up at him in confusion, she replied, "I was sleeping."

"I know that, babe. What I don't know is

why you didn't call about last night."

Still confused, she rubbed her sleepy eyes with her fingers trying to focus on the hotness in front of her that seemed to be irritated.

"Honey, I don't know what you're talking about. Can't it wait until later? I have only been asleep a couple of hours."

Sighing, he walked over wrapping his arms around her, enveloping her in his embrace.

"Ummm. That feels nice. I could go back to sleep right here in your arms. Although the bed would be nice too," she said looking up at him.

"Angel, I'm waiting for an answer."

Pulling back from his embrace so that she could focus on his face again, she replied, "Tom, I don't know what you're talking about. What about last night?"

"You had a patient. His brother made you uncomfortable? You didn't think I'd wanna know?"

Pushing her way out of his embrace her sleep fogged mind cleared. "Patient? Who told you? It couldn't have been Sofia or Jon because, like me, we can't talk about patients." Her voice rose as the anger slowly poured over her. "The cops were there. They told you." Then as understanding dawned on her, she looked up glaring. "Oh my God. They told you about his brother hitting on me? And you come over here to be the big, bad boyfriend? Oh no, Tom. No way."

By now, her chest was heaving with anger as she stalked toward the living room before turning around to face him again.

Tom, stance wide with his hands on his hips, glared back. "Not asking you to break rules. Not asking you to tell me shit about your job I don't need to know. But some man makes you feel so uneasy that others around notice it, I wanna know."

"So what, Tom? So you can show up at his door and pound the little man down? News flash, Tom, I'm a big girl. I have been on my own a long time taking care of myself. I don't need you to fight my battles."

"Like throwin' up the other night because things got rough?"

She jerked back as his words slapped her. "Oh no, you did not just throw that in my face."

Tom rubbed his hand over his face and looked down. Taking a deep breath, he lifted his eyes to hers, seeing in her anger.

"Angel, I'm sorry. I don't ever want to say something that hurts you and honest to God, that's not how I meant it." He walked over to her shaking form, wanting nothing more than to wrap his arms back around her, but knowing she needed a little space.

Carol, wary, looked up at him, judging his honesty. "Apology accepted." Sighing, she looked down at her feet momentarily, then speared him with her gaze. "What do you want me to say, Tom? I'm not going to run to you every time a man looks my way."

"Babe, I get that. What I want you to get is that you do your job. You do your job well. People are gonna be grateful and tell you that. But what I wanna know is if or when someone gets in your space or in your mind and makes you uncomfortable. That shit doesn't fly with me. I don't wanna hear from someone else that my woman was uneasy. That comes from you."

Carol looked back down, seemingly in thought. Tom walked the few steps needed to re-wrap his powerful arms around her.

"I'm not trying to take anything away from you. I'm not trying to control you. I just want you safe."

Nodding against his muscular chest, she felt her anger ebb.

"Gotta confess, babe. I'm a man who likes to be in charge. I like to take care of what's mine. But I'm new to relationships, so I'm gonna go overboard sometimes."

Leaning her head way back, she looked into his eyes. "I guess we both have to get used to this."

"Carol, I meant what I said earlier. I'm never gonna throw anything in your face. I never meant it that way. I know you've struggled with makin' right choices when it comes to stress. I just wanna take some of that burden off of you."

Sighing, she tucked herself back against his chest. "Tom, I have come a long way since my teenage and college years of eating and throwing up or running it all off as a way of dealing with stress. Most things in my daily life don't affect me at all that way. I handle it and move on. I just still struggle with dealing with my parents. Or reminders of them. That is where my biggest struggle comes from. Not my job. Not you getting mad. All this, I can handle honey."

He rested his chin on her head, loving the feel of her in his arms. "I guess we'll figure this out as we go."

Giggling, she agreed. "Yeah, Tom. That's usually what relationships do."

Squeezing her tighter, he kissed the top of her head.

Carol smiled, listening to his heartbeat against her ear. "I hear your heartbeat," she whispered.

"It beats for you, Angel," he replied.

Chapter 11

F or the next several days, Carol noticed Bert coming by the ER security desk but he was turned away each time. Finally on the third day, she walked over to one of the security guards. "Marcus, that man who keeps coming in. What does he want?"

"Carol, I was just going to come look for you. I wanted to let you know that as of right now, I'm making a formal report on him and banning him from this area."

Marcus, known for taking his guard duties seriously but also for having a jovial humor, surprised her. Shocked, she asked, "Why? What did he do?"

"He doesn't need to be down here. Says he's visiting his brother, and since his brother came in through the ER, he claims that this is the only way he knows how to get to his brother's room. He's been denied for the past two days and shown the front entrance. Now he comes in today, asking about you."

Eyes wide, she felt a trickle of fear move down her spine. "Me?" she said in a whisper.

"Yep. Said you'd been real helpful, and he wanted to know when you got off shift today so he could thank you."

"You didn't tell him, did you?"

Marcus replied, looking hurt. "What kind of idiot do you think I'm, girl? Hell no, I didn't tell him. He gave me the creeps, and I told him to leave and not come back. And, I'm filing a formal report banning him from this ER."

She placed her hand on his arm. "I'm sorry Marcus. I know you wouldn't tell him. He does seem creepy, but maybe he truly is just lost and then wanted to say thank you."

"Now who's being idiotic, girl? You keep away from him; you see him, you turn and run. In fact, isn't your shift about over? You let me know, and I'll walk you to your car."

Thanking him, she headed to the break room. Seeing Sofia, she told her what was going on.

"You going to call Mr. Hot Stuff?" Sofia asked.

"Can't you just call him Tom?" Carol asked laughing.

"Why? When my names are so much fun and so much more appropriate."

"Anyway, to answer your question, I guess I had better. He wasn't too happy with me when I didn't let him know. It was weird, Sofia. He was demanding, but not like my parents. He's caring, but in an entirely different way than Ronald ever was. I just don't know what to think, but I'll assure him that Marcus is walking me out."

Giving her a quick hug, Sofia walked out calling, "Honey, that's what I was talking about. There can be a man that likes his control – in the bedroom and out of it. That doesn't make him an asshole if it is all about you. And from what you're telling me, Mr. Tight Pants is all about you! And you can tell him that I said hello!"

Her mood lighter, Carol grabbed her cell phone as she put on her coat. Tom answered on the first ring.

"Hey, sweetheart. What's up?"

"I'm just letting you know that Marcus is walking me to my car. It seems that Bert has been showing up asking about me, so Marcus is filing a report and ..."

"Carol, you stay right where you're. Don't step outside that hospital. I'm coming."

She huffed, "Tom, this is ridiculous. Marcus is big, protective, and he's armed."

"I'm telling you this is non-negotiable. Do.

Not. Leave. The. Building. Without. Me."

"You don't think this falls into the category of you going overboard."

"Nope. Not until I have had a chance to ascertain the situation myself. Jake and I are on our way."

Carol was standing at the security desk, looking at a grinning Marcus.

"So your Mr. Hot Detective is coming to get you?"

"You've been talking to Sofia," she accused.

He just laughed before his attention was then taken away by an ambulance entering the area. Turning back to her, he warned, "Don't go out by yourself."

"I promise," she replied. "I'm just standing right outside the door so I can see Tom when he comes. See you tomorrow."

She moved to stand outside the ER doors, walking slightly to the side so that she would be able to see the road leading to the hospital. Suddenly, a movement in her peripheral vision startled her. Whirling around, she saw Bert walking up to her from the side.

Glancing back toward the ER entrance, she saw Marcus with his back to her. Backing away from Bert, she moved closer to the doors, next to the unloading ambulance. Feeling protected there, she looked at Bert but did not smile.

"Carol, I have been looking for you. I missed you the past couple of days."

Determined to shut him down, she spoke sharply. "Bert, this is my place of work and you cannot come here looking for me. You have already expressed your gratitude for helping your brother, so there is no other reason for us to talk."

A kicked puppy dog look flashed across his face. "But I just wanted to see you again. You're so nice and awfully pretty."

Raising her hand, she replied, "Bert, the security guard has informed me that you're going to be banned from here. Do not contact me again."

Heavy, hard, fast footsteps were heard coming from behind her. *I know those footsteps. Oh lordy, this could get ugly.*

Whirling around, she plastered a huge smile on her face while striding to him.

"Tom, I wondered when you'd get here honey."

Tom, sizing up the situation, wrapped her in a big hug and smiled down into her face. "Hey, babe. You ready to leave?" Jake stalked up beside Tom, creating a wall of protection. Tom eyed Bert over Carol's head, staring straight into his eyes.

Bert looked nervous and turned his gaze to the sidewalk.

"Well, I guess I'll be going Carol," he said. "It was nice seeing you again."

Tom pulled Carol back so that he could see her expression. "Tell me now, what is going on. I wanna know what's happening so I know how to respond."

Just then Marcus walked out of the door. "I see she found you. Good."

Marcus, Jake, and Tom watched as Bert walked through the parking lot. Marcus cursed, "I told him to stay away." Looking at Tom, he said, "I have put in a request to ban him."

Rounding on her, Tom looked down in anger. "Carol, what the hell were you doing out here by yourself? I told you to wait inside."

Embarrassed to be chastised in front of Marcus and Jake, she retorted, "I was just standing by the door, Tom. Marcus was right inside. I was not out in the parking lot; I just wanted to be able to see you when you drove up."

Tom, his arm still wrapped protectively around her shoulders, looked at Marcus. "What's up?"

As Marcus explained the situation with Bert, she could feel Tom's body getting more solid.

Still. Every muscle tight. *Oh, Lordy.*

Stealing a glance up at his face, then over to Jake's face, she dropped her eyes quickly. *Breathe. Just breathe.*

Tom could feel when the change in Carol's demeanor appeared. He could feel the slightest trembling in her shoulders and noticed her staring at her tightly clasped hands. *Comfort. She needs comfort.* He slowly rubbed her shoulder and back, rubbing his hand gently up and down.

Jake took notes on Marcus' reports, noting Tom was holding on to his anger by a thread while trying to comfort Carol.

Jake commented, "We're gonna check him out more thoroughly. So far, he's checked out fine. Lives with mom. Dad died a few years back. Has nothing to do with his brother's drug business. Something's not right, though."

Marcus nodded and assured them he would walk Carol to her car at the end of her shift, and when he wasn't on duty, another security guard would take care of her.

"Angel, you on board with this?" Tom asked, giving her shoulder a slight squeeze.

Grateful that he was finally asking and not just telling, something she was sure he was not accustomed to doing, she looked at all three men, replying, "Yeah. I think that's a good idea.

I'm not afraid of Bert, but I admit he gives me the creeps even if he's just being nice."

"Nothin' nice about making someone uncomfortable, Carol," Jake spoke. What and who was important to Tom was important to him.

She just nodded, feeling safe once again. Noting that Jake and Marcus had been doing the talking, she glanced up at Tom. His expression was hard, but his eyes were warm as they looked back down at her. Smiling a small smile, she felt her body being pulled in tighter to his.

"Taking you home, babe. Where are you parked?"

Carol pointed in the direction of her car, as Tom and she walked away from the others after having said their goodbyes.

After buckling in, she looked over at Tom, noting the expression on his face. "Are you still mad?" she asked softly.

Sitting in the driver's seat with his hands on the steering wheel, he sat quietly for a moment. Just as she thought that he wasn't going to answer, he looked over at her, his eyes doing a sweep of her face before settling on her eyes.

"Angel," he said shaking his head, "I'm pissed as hell, but not at you. Pissed at Bert. Jake and I'll be paying him a visit."

"Oh Tom, don't hurt him!"

"While I may want to pound the shit out of him for makin' you uncomfortable, I'm a cop. And Jake'll be with me to make sure." He held her eyes, his face no longer as tight. "Carol, letting you know now that I want you filing a restraining order on him." Holding his hand to her lips as she began to argue, "Nope. Not relenting. If I could be around you twenty-four-seven, I would. But since I can't, I'll do anything to keep you safe."

Leaning toward her, stopping only when his lips were barely touching hers, he continued. "Gotta say, while I love being able to sleep with you whenever we want to at your place, I don't like you living alone."

Breathing him in, she leaned back slightly. "I haven't told you yet, but I'm getting a room-mate." Moving forward to kiss him, she felt the loss as he reared back.

"A roommate? Who'd you get? Have you checked them out? Do you know them?"

Rolling her eyes, she sat back on the seat. "Geez, Tom. I can handle getting a roommate, you know. I have been living on my own before, and I have had roommates for a number of years. Anyway, I found her on Craig's List."

Carol stared in fascination at the instant change in Tom's face. *Purple. He's actually purple! Oh shit.*

"Are you fuckin' kidding me? Craig's List?" he roared. Taking in her honest response, he mentally counted to ten. "Angel, I'm trying here. Honest to God trying. You see right in the world and try not to see shit around you. A man like me, in the job I have, I see shit every day. Your goodness touches me, babe, but I want to make sure the shit doesn't touch you."

Rubbing his hand over his face breathing deeply, he continued, "I want her name and address. Gonna check her out for you. Please."

Carol nodded her agreement. After the incident with Bert, maybe being extra cautious wasn't such a bad thing.

Exhaling her agreement, he leaned back over, sealing his lips onto hers. Licking her seam, he slid his tongue into her mouth, slowly exploring as his tongue danced with hers. The kiss went on for several minutes, growing in intensity as he felt his dick swell uncomfortably in his pants.

"Damn. I gotta have you drop me back off at the station, and I don't wanna go in with a hard on." Hearing her giggle made him smile. *I like that. Like hearing my girl happy. Wanna keep that happy in her as much as I can.*

"When is your next day off?"

"I work two more nights, and then I have three days off," she replied.

"You gotta do what you gotta do, but I'm not crazy about you working the graveyard shift all the time."

She looked into the handsome face of the man she had come to care for. Smiling shyly, she said, "I have been thinking about that, honey."

❧

On Carol's next day off, Tom came by to pick her up for dinner at Smokey's. He stood at her breakfast bar while she was still in the bedroom getting ready. He noticed that all of her mail was neatly stacked on the counter except for a large cream colored invitation lying to the side. His eyes caught the wording for the Fletcher and Harriston Annual Charity Cotillion. She walked in, seeing the letter in his hand.

"This a stressor?" he asked.

She looked down at the invitation. "Yes and no." Eyes back to his, she wasn't surprised to see the questioning look in his face. "Yes, it is a stressor. Anything to do with my parents is a stressor. But no, because I'm refusing to let it affect me. I'm refusing to give in to urges."

Opening his arms, he beckoned, "Come here, Angel."

She ran into his arms, feeling the blanketing warmth as she was surrounded by all that is Tom.

Satisfied that she was not beginning to panic, he kissed the top of her head. "Proud of you, babe. You seem to be losing some of that cluelessness."

Carol, leaning back in his arms, looked straight up into his face and glared. "What a backward compliment!"

Laughing, he patted her ass saying, "Let's go eat."

"Tom," she said softly. "Tonight, after dinner, can we talk?"

"Carol, you don't have to ask that. You wanna talk, we talk."

Nodding, she smiled. "Okay then. Tonight, we're going to deal with the stressor called my parents."

"It's 'bout time. I didn't want to rush you, but glad you're ready to lay that shit out so we can deal."

That night at Smokey's, Carol had the opportunity to spend more time with Tom's best friends. Funny, charming, handsome. The trio of gorgeous men caused quite a stir among the women hanging in the bar. The barflies began to circle, but Jake and Tom quickly shut it down. Tom did not want anyone to make Carol uncomfortable and Jake never hooked up in town, and certainly not with a mostly drunk, half-dressed woman hanging out in a bar. Rob had more difficulty keeping the women at bay. His reputation of often going home with someone made the women hover, but he was determined to show Carol a classier side than his reputation.

Sharing a booth that was frequented by Wendy and Bill, the bar owners, the foursome laughed and talked into the evening. Jake and Rob understood what Tom had found in Carol. Drop dead gorgeous, but never flaunting it, as though she had no idea how beautiful she was. Funny, smart. And totally into Tom. Both men had seen women out with one of them, trying to catch the attention of one of the other. But not Carol.

She laughed her way through dinner listening to the stories of the three friends growing up on the same street. Looking at Tom, she remarked, "I can see why you wanted to come back here to live. You three just seem like you're triplets, having shared experiences for so long."

Tom nodded. "Yeah, my parents moved when I was in college to be closer to my grandparents, but Fairfield was always home."

As the men continued to reminisce, Carol perused Jake and Rob. Jake was quieter, more thoughtful. *He needs a good woman. Someone kind. Soft. Caring. Someone who will take care of him while letting him take care of her.*

Rob was a different matter. Louder, more boisterous, definitely with a reputation as a player. He seemed to revel in his freedom, but with the right woman, she could see him settling down, ready to take charge and take care of his woman.

"Where'd you go?" Tom asked, leaning over to brush his lips to her ear.

Ducking her head in embarrassment, she admitted, "I was thinking of Jake and Rob." Seeing the expression on his face, she giggled. "No, no, not like that. I was thinking about how they needed good women to be with."

Tom still stared at her, with one eyebrow cocked in question.

"I mean, they could have what we have."

He pulled her in tightly to his side with his heavy arm around her shoulders protectively. Kissing the top of her head, he smiled over her head to his friends. *They think I'm pussy-whipped. Yeah, well, maybe they are right. Wouldn't change a thing...not a Goddamn thing.*

Chapter 12

That night, back in her apartment, Tom and Carol settled onto the couch. She attempted to sit on one side, but he was not having it.

"Sweetheart, when we lay shit out to deal with it, I want you on my lap."

Smiling, she sat on his lap, head draped on his shoulder. Sitting quietly for a few minutes, she wondered how to start.

"My parents aren't bad people, Tom. I wasn't abused. I had a huge house, a nanny, all the comforts."

"People don't have to physically abuse you to be abusive."

Nodding, she agreed. "I know Tom. Believe me, years of counseling has taught me that. Growing up, my parents were just very distant. For my dad, it was all about the job. The law firm. The perception that his family was the epitome of wealth and class. For my mother, it was all about my dad. His money, the trips, the country club, the wealthy and influential friends.

I was just an accessory, part of the perfect picture that they wanted to present."

Squirming to get more comfortable, she continued. "Of course, I didn't realize it at the time, but food simply became a stress reliever for me. If I ate everything on my plate, my parents wouldn't fuss at me about something. I loved sweets, and I would hang out in the kitchen with the cook who constantly fed me treats."

Looking into his eyes, she added, "Tom, I know you can't possibly understand this, but food became my friend…my comfort. But then came the weight. By the time I was in middle school, I was chubby."

She looked over his shoulder at a distant spot on the wall, her mind going back about twelve years. Tom, realizing that she had disappeared into her past, gently put his hand up cupping her face. Her eyes cut back to his.

Smiling, she continued. "Middle school is hell for everyone, but when you're rich, chubby, and socially awkward, it is even worse. Suddenly after about thirteen years of never noticing me, my parents sat up and realized they weren't happy with the way I looked. I always made good grades, but I had to be the best in the class. They hired a personal trainer to run me daily to get the extra weight off, but nothing ever seemed to make them really notice *me*. I was just an image that they had in their minds. Their image."

Sighing, Carol was silent for a moment.

"When did you first began purging?" Tom asked softly, his hand still cupping her expressive face.

"I was fourteen. The trainer had me out running earlier in the day. I came in and heard my parents arguing. My mother wanted to provide me with an escort to their annual charity event, someone that was the son of a wealthy politician. My father was insistent that Ronald was going to be my escort. In my mom's eyes, Ronald wasn't high enough on the social ladder. To my father, he wanted Ronald and me to become lawyers, get married and continue the family law business, serving the wealthy.

"Listening to my parents plan out my future made me head into the kitchen. I ate everything I could get my hands on. Chips, cookies, soda, some fried chicken that was in the fridge." Shaking her head, "I couldn't believe that I ate so much. But then it hit me. I was going to have to fit into a party dress. So I ran to the bathroom and stuck my finger down my throat. It was gross and disgusting, but it all came up. Everything."

"Was that the beginning?"

"Yeah. After that, I realized that I could eat whatever I wanted when stressed out and then just get rid of it. I also continued the running, mile after mile, burning every calorie I could possibly get rid of.

"Tom, you have to understand that this became my way of life. My way of handling my parents. My life. Or rather their life. They liked the slimmer me. It made them proud. So I would eat to my heart's content, then just purge and stay slim."

His face was tight. Solid. Angry. Shaking his head, he wanted to hit something. Or more to the point, someone. But he knew she did not need his anger right now. She needed his understanding. Taking a deep breath, he tried to remove the frustration out of his head. "So what changed? What made you seek help?"

"I was finishing my first year of college. Dating Ronald and hating it." At this, she felt his body tense. Capturing his gaze, she kissed his lips softly. "I never loved him, honey. He never meant anything to me. He was simply my father's choice. He fit the image of me that my father wanted to project."

Feeling his body relax and his blue eyes warm, she continued. "I ended up in the ER with food poisoning and that night changed my life." Smiling at the memory, she continued. "The hustle, the bustle, the nurses were so kind and efficient. I was struck by the realization that this was the world I wanted to be in. I'm not a lawyer. I don't want to work with or for my father. And I sure as hell did not want to be with Ronald Harriston. The image that my parents had for me had drilled into me, just wasn't the image I had for my life.

"So I changed my major, broke up with Ronald, and started living on my own. Well...eventually."

"Eventually?" Tom asked, not understanding.

"Well, it's not like I suddenly grew a pair of balls."

She felt Tom's chuckle rumble through his chest before he threw his head back and laughed. "Thank God you didn't grow balls, girl!"

As their laughter subsided, she sighed loudly.

"Was it bad? With your parents?"

"Yeah. I managed to keep it a secret for a while. I still saw Ronald on the weekends for a while before breaking up. I didn't tell my parents about my major change. I kept wanting to, but every time I thought about it I would begin purging more. It was actually in an Intro to Psych class that I realized that I had an eating disorder and sought counseling. I thought it would be hard to say all the things that I had held inside for years, but once I started talking, it all came out."

"Kinda like now?" he asked. He brushed her hair away from her face, staring into the beautiful eyes that he could lose himself in.

Smiling her agreement, she leaned her head back down on his shoulder, resting her body as the weight of her secret floated away. *He accepts me. He doesn't see me as a freak. He's still here.*

"And the rest of the story?" he prompted.

"That's all there is, honey." She lifted her head off of his shoulder. "I graduated on my own, working my way through college with the help of some student loans. I came to Fairfield when the ER job opened up. I found a counselor here, and I still see one occasionally when needed."

Shifting her body around as though she weighed nothing, Tom had her straddling his lap. "That's not all. What about the confrontation with your parents? What about your relationship with them for the past several years? What about the invitation to the charity event? What about you purging the night you saw Ronald?"

Huffing, she looked away with a slight pout on her face. "I have gone through so much tonight. More than I have ever told anyone other than my counselors. Can't that be enough tonight?"

"Angel, eyes on me," he gently ordered. She lifted her gaze to his. "I know this isn't easy for you. You gotta know babe, that you sharing means the world to me. But I take care of what's mine. And I can't take care of mine if I don't know what all I'm up against. That was why I got bent out of shape with the Bert situation. Same goes with your parents."

He let that sink in for just a moment, then continued. "I want to know how all this went down with your parents. From then to now."

Taking a deep breath, she pulled her thoughts together. "Ronald was suspicious that something was going on. He was in his last year of college, already having been accepted to law school. He came to visit me unexpectedly, and I had nursing textbooks all over the room." Chuckling, "I swear, I think he would have been less upset if he walked in finding me sleeping with another man!

"Anyway, Tom I don't want to drag this out anymore, so I'm going to give you the quick and dirty. He went straight to my parents. I was summoned to their house. Dad held the checkbook, so I went. It was ugly. My father threatened to disown me; my mother complained that I had been a disappointment to them and becoming a nurse was just one more thing that did not fit their image. I held firm. Broke up with Ronald, who has never forgiven me. Walked out of my parent's house and headed back to school. I spent the night throwing up. They tried to change my mind with forceful tactics. Dad canceled my bank cards that night. My apartment roommate, another nursing major, was kind enough to not make me pay rent for a while. I went to a different bank, got student loans, got a job and continued my studies."

"What about now?"

"I see my parents just a couple of times a year. It's never pleasant. They always manage to have Ronald there. He is now a junior partner, and they are still hoping that he and I'll get together. We have evolved to where we send Christmas cards and the occasional phone call on birthdays."

She paused momentarily. "Honey, I don't worry about their image of me anymore." Taking his face in her hands, she pulled him in carefully. "Tom, the only image I care about is the image I have of myself. Carol's image. That's what counts. That's the image I'm working on."

Allowing her to pull his face toward hers, he whispered, "And what is that image?"

Smiling against his lips, she breathed him in. "I'm a nurse. I'm your woman. And I'm just me." Touching her lips to his, she kissed him with all the emotions she had bottled up inside. Sliding her tongue into his waiting mouth, she explored, allowing her tongue to tangle with his.

He allowed her to take charge of the kiss, knowing she needed to exert some control. Soon he was lost in the feeling of her tongue stroking his, her sucking it into her mouth, nipping at his lips. The blood rushed to his dick, but he willed it to behave. This was still about Carol, her pace, her control. The kiss seemed to continue forever until they were both breathless and panting.

Leaning away from him, her lust filled eyes searched his. She still saw questions there, pulling her back into their reality. "You want more, don't you? You want to know about the invitation?"

Tom held her tightly, willing to give his strength to her. "I just want to know how things are now."

"Each year my parents host a huge charity

event but don't let the words 'charity' fool you. It's an expensive dinner; people are desperate to get the invitations. It's the place to see and be seen. I started going when I was about sixteen. Hated them. I was the pudgy kid that just happened to be the daughter of the man hosting. Dad even had to pay someone to dance with me or escort me. I hated it. I haven't gone since I changed majors and left my parent's support. This year, I received an invitation. I have no idea why. I have no desire to go. I haven't responded. But getting it in the mail, well…I admit, it sort of made me go back into some of my more unpleasant memories. Then I was just started to go out with you and that was stressful. Ronald was a total unpleasant blast from the past. It was just all too much that day and I gave into the weakness."

"Carol, you're not weak. You're one of the strongest women I have ever met." Blue eyes held blue eyes. "Proud to be yours and proud to call you mine."

The smile on her face radiated straight to his heart. Blonde hair framing her beautiful face, blue eyes shining, and that smile. *God, I'd give anything to have that smile turned toward me every day for the rest of my life.*

She giggled and looked down.

"What's going on in that pretty head of yours, Angel?"

"Oh, it's silly. It's just that I actually toyed with the idea of going this year and taking you. Just to really show them that I have moved on. But that is silly."

"You want to go, we're going. We're officially dating. No reason we shouldn't go."

"It could be brutal, you know," she said hesitantly.

Placing his hands on either side of her face, he leaned forward till his lips rested on her forehead. "Babe, I'd walk through fire for you. Believe me, your parents don't scare me at all."

Pulling her face up, he placed his lips on hers. Gently. Softly. With just the slightest pressure.

Grabbing his face in her hands, she took the kiss deeper. Their talk now over, she wanted him and was determined to let him know.

He pulled back just far enough to separate their lips. Carol, missing the contact made a mewling sound. He waited until he had her eyes.

"We good?"

Her brow crinkled as her lust filled mind tried to understand what he was saying.

Tom chuckled. "Stay with me, babe. This is important. Told you we were going to take care of you being clueless. Laid out my past reputation, so that shit was dealt with. Now you shared about your parents and about your eatin' disorder. And now you know I'm not going anywhere. You don't face this alone. You don't face them alone. You've got me and I have got your back. We're in this together."

He held her face as he watched her beautiful blue eyes fill with tears. Trying unsuccessfully to blink them back, they slid down her cheeks.

"I have never had anyone have my back before," she whispered.

Wiping the tears with his thumbs, he replied, "Well you've got it now. So are we good?"

"Yeah. We're good," she said, smiling through her tears.

"Thank God," he growled as he took her mouth, this time hard, wet, possessive. Full of power, full of lust, full of love. Standing with her in his arms as though she weighed nothing, he stalked into her bedroom.

She was light in his arms, but he felt every curve as she slowly slid down his front. His hand held fast to her ass, keeping her feet dangling above the floor, pressing her into his aching dick. Capturing her moan in his mouth, he continued to pour his soul into her as their lips stayed sealed in a kiss.

With her arms wrapped around his neck, he could feel her hands gripping his back. Feeling moisture against his face, he reluctantly released the kiss and leaned back to peer down into her tear-filled eyes.

"What's wrong?" his voice gravely with both need and worry.

Shaking her head, she gave a slight smile. "I just love you so much. It's okay if you don't love me back, but I can't seem to stop what I feel. I really love you, Tom Rivers."

He walked over to the bed and gently laid her down with his body covering hers. Still dressed, they lay pressed from chest to feet. Keeping his face as close to hers as he could while still being able to focus on her luminous blue eyes, his voice shook with emotion.

"Carol, you're it for me. I felt something the moment I first saw your beautiful face. Something changed deep inside of me. Touched me. Stayed with me. I wanted to know you and since that time, everything I have learned about you just makes me want to stay with you forever. I love you too, Carol. If you know anything about me, you know I'm loyal. I'll love you till the day I die."

Wiping her tears with the rough pads of his thumbs, he moved back in to capture her lips.

Pouring everything he had into the kiss, he willed her to take from him everything she needed. *Strength. Courage. Hope. Comfort. Protection. Love.*

Carol felt him capture her soul in that kiss. For the first time in her life, she didn't feel alone. He was slaying her dragons. And it felt right. It felt good. Allowing him to have some control didn't make her out of control. With that realization, she answered his kiss back, sucking on his tongue until she could hear his moans deep inside of her.

He lifted himself up onto his knees, pulling her up with him. Quickly he pulled her shirt over her head and divested her of her bra. Palming her breasts with his hands, he lowered his head to suck a nipple deeply into his mouth.

Leaning her head back, her hands in his hair, she felt her world tilt with the sensations tugging from her breasts to her core. Sliding her hands down, she captured the bottom of his tight navy t-shirt and pulled it over his head, his lips only leaving her breast for the second that it took the material to pass.

Moving from breast to breast, he gave equal attention to the luscious rosy-tipped globes. *How could I have ever thought that fake tits were attractive?* he thought. Her natural breasts and ethereal beauty captured him. Enthralled him. Owned him.

Her hands found their way to the top of his jeans as she undid the button and slid the zipper over his enormous cock. Sliding her hand down the front of his boxers, she wrapped her fingers around his silky manhood, moving her hand up and down its length.

Moaning, he pulled away from her nipples, looked deep into her eyes and asked, "You got a problem with me being in control? I swear it will always be about you."

Blue eyes gazed at blue eyes.

"I trust you. With all my heart," was her reply.

Smiling a slow smile that reached the twinkle in his eyes, he just nodded. "All right, Angel. Lay back down and keep your hands on the bed. Keep them there until I tell you to move them."

Smiling back, she slid back down to the mattress, lying perfectly still, wondering what he was going to do.

Tom unzipped her jeans and pulled them off her body slowly, kissing her skin as it was exposed. As the jeans landed on the floor, he kissed his way back up to her satin panties. He slid them off as well, then moved his hands to her knees where he gently pulled her legs apart, totally exposing her delicate sex to his view.

Carol lay there, mesmerized by the sight of this handsome man, staring at her. She watched as he lowered his head between her legs and began to lick her wet folds. The sensations threatened to overtake her, and she threw her head back on the pillow. Her hand automatically sought his head, but he quickly withdrew.

"Hands on the bed. You don't move till I tell you."

She stilled her hands, but her fingers clutched the sheet underneath her, holding on like a drowning person grasps a life preserver. *That's what he is...my life preserver.*

Tom licked her moist folds then pushed his tongue up into her as far as it would go, loving the taste of her as much as he loved hearing her scream his name when the orgasm hit her.

He stood up, licking his lips as she watched in fascination. Ridding himself of his jeans and boxers, he faced her in all his glory.

Her eyes lit up at the sight of the Viking standing in front of her. *No romance novel hero ever looked like that.* Her reality was so much more than anything she had ever read. Or could have ever been prepared for.

"On your knees. Place the pillows under your hips and grab hold of the headboard. Smiling as he watched her acquiesce, he patted her ass in a gentle stroke.

"You ready?"

Carol nodded her answer, but a smack on her ass was his reply.

"I ask, you answer. I wanna hear you say it."

"I'm ready, Tom."

Slamming his desperate cock into her waiting sex, he groaned at the tightness. *Damn, she feels incredible.* Careful not to hurt her, he pounded away, reaching one hand around to fondle her breasts, tweaking her nipple in the process.

Carol couldn't remember ever being more turned on, the feel of his cock sinking deeper and deeper into her. The friction was creating an electrical current that started deep in her core and vibrated out in all directions. She could feel herself racing to the end, desperate for the release of crossing the finish line. She felt his hand slide from her nipple to her clit, fingering the swollen nub. That was all it took for her to reach the goal, the electrical current exploding in fireworks that shook her whole body as she screamed his name once again.

"Hang on, angel," came Tom's voice, rough with need. He continued to pound in and out several more strokes until, neck straining, veins standing out, he grimaced and yelled out as he found his release deep inside her warm core. Continuing to thrust a few more times until he was drained, he collapsed onto the mattress, pulling her against him.

Sweating, panting, gasping for breath. Smiling. After a few minutes, they looked at each other. Blue eyes gazed at blue eyes.

He pulled her in, one hand protectively wrapped around her and the other hand cradling her head to his massive chest. Lying still for a few minutes, they just reveled in each other and the love they had declared.

Pulling the cover over them, they settled in for sleep.

"I hear your heartbeat," came her soft voice.

"It beats for you," came the gentle reply.

Chapter 13

After Tom had left for work the next morning, Carol stood at her breakfast bar, staring at the invitation. *I can do this. I can pick up the phone and do this. It's a simple call. Actually, mom won't even answer – the maid will answer. So I can just leave a message. Okay. I can do this. Here I go. Oh Jesus, Carol, just do it!!*

Grabbing her cell phone in her hands before she chickened out, she dialed her parent's home number. One ring. Two rings. *Good, let the answering machine pick up.*

"Hello."

"Mom? I wasn't sure you'd be home."

"I'm always at home on Thursday mornings Carol, getting ready for the Ladies' Auxiliary Book Club. But then you would know that if you stayed in touch."

Sighing, Carol pressed her fingers into her temple as though to relieve the ache that was sure to follow. "Sorry, mom. But that goes both ways, you know. You and dad don't call any more often than I call you."

Silence greeted her.

"I wanted to call to let you know that I received the Charity Dinner invitation, and I have decided to come this year."

"You're serious?" her mother asked. "Well, that is certainly a change. Decided that you have stayed away too long? Well, I'll arrange a date for you. In fact, I'm sure that Ronald will be more than thrilled to escort you this year."

"Mom, you don't understand. I'll be bringing my own date."

"Who?" her mother asked sharply.

"You don't know him. He is the man I have been dating for a little while and he will be escorting me to the dinner and to meet you and dad." *There, I got it out. Breathe in. Breathe out. You got this girl.*

Silence. Nothing. No sound. No huffing on the other end of the phone. Just silence.

Hanging her head, Carol suddenly felt drained. "Mom. Are you still there? Am I welcome or not?"

"Well, you certainly have to admit that your news is most surprising. Who is this person you're seeing?"

"His name is not important, mom. He isn't going to show up on any of your social registers.

What is important is that he is the person I'm with, and he will be escorting me to the dinner. So just put me down as attending with one guest."

"All right, Carol. We will play this your way, as always."

Shaking her head now, as it still hung down, Carol could feel the familiar feeling of bile rising. Willing herself to keep her breakfast down, she needed to finish the call. "I have to go, mom. I have to be at work in a few minutes," she lied.

"Still playing nurse?"

"Yes, mom. I'm still playing nurse."

"Wait. Before you go, let's set up a time to get together."

"Who?" Carol asked incredulously.

"Just you and I, dear. We haven't had lunch in forever, and maybe it would be good to meet before the dinner."

Just say no. Just say no. "Sure mom. When and where?" *God, I'm such an idiot.*

"How about Sunday for brunch. We could meet at the little Bistro in Jefferstown; that's halfway between Richland and Fairfield."

Carol surprised that her mother would agree to drive any distance to see her, then realized that her mother would have a driver. "Sure mom. I'll see you there about eleven. Gotta go to work now. Bye."

Hanging up before she could throw up, she sat on the stool trying to regulate her breathing. *Choices. It's all about choices. I can meet with her. I'm strong. I'm in control. I can do this.* Continuing to self-talk until the desire to throw up passed, Carol stood up, feeling stronger than she had in a long time.

Putting in a phone call to Ronda to update her on her events and progress, she spent the rest of her day off house cleaning and running errands.

❧

"Nervous, babe?" Tom asked as Carol spent an inordinate amount of time getting ready for the brunch with her mom.

Pulling her blonde hair into a soft twist at the back of her head and securing it with an elegant clip, she looked at him in the mirror. *God, he's gorgeous.* Peering at the tall, muscular, blond Nordic God lounging back on her bed made her pulse beat faster. *What I could do with him if I wasn't heading out to meet my mother.*

"You keep looking at me like that, girl, and you'll be late for your brunch if you even make it at all."

Blushing at having been caught ogling him, she reached into her jewelry box to put in simple earrings.

"You avoiding the question?" he asked softly.

"No, just trying to figure out how to answer," she said as she raised her eyes back to his in the mirror. "I'm nervous. I always feel as though I have to be perfect around her."

"Look in the mirror." Seeing her questioning gaze from her mirrored reflection, he explained. "No, look at you in the mirror." He watched her eyes move from his back to her face. "Now tell me what you see? What image is looking back at you?"

Carol looked at the image in the mirror. Clear skin. Bright eyes. A smile played at the corners of her mouth, softening her appearance. "I see me. I like what I see," she added.

Tom stood moving directly behind her until her wrapped his muscular arms around her from behind, totally encasing her in his embrace. *Comfort. Acceptance.*

～

Carol drove into the crowded parking lot of the Bistro, looking for a parking space. Not wanting to be late, she found a spot and quickly checked her makeup in the mirror. Looking at her reflection, she reminded herself that her mother would never be satisfied, so she just needed to be happy on her own. Taking a fortifying breath, she walked briskly into the restaurant. Moving through the crowd waiting for a table, she walked to the hostess station.

"I'm here to meet Mrs. Estelle Fletcher. I'm Carol Fletcher."

The young woman checked her list, looked up with a smile and said, "Of course, Ms. Fletcher. Your party is this way."

Carol followed the hostess toward the back of the restaurant, looking around at the décor. As the hostess stopped, Carol looked sharply at the table. Coming to a standing position to greet her....Ronald. *What the hell?*

"Where's mother?" Carol asked, feeling anger beginning to boil.

"Come now, is that any way to greet an old friend?" Ronald said while taking her by the elbow to escort her to her seat.

"Ronald, this is not funny. I came to have brunch with mother, and I find you here instead. What the hell is going on?"

Ronald, looking around admonished, "Carol, lower your voice. You're making a scene. Sit down, and I'll explain."

Carol wanted to scream, cuss, and then stomp out of the restaurant but instead, years of breeding pounded into her, had her sitting down, quietly steaming.

Ronald deftly waved the waitress over to the table. "We're ready to order now. I'll have the ham and spinach omelet and the lady will have the eggs benedict with fruit. We will both have mimosas and coffee."

Carol stared at Ronald as though he had two heads. "You ordered for me? You have no idea what I wanted to eat."

"Carol, we were friends from the time we were born and we dated for years. I think I still remember what you like to eat."

"Liked to eat, Ronald. Liked. Past tense. As in you no longer know me. We haven't been together for over five years, so I hardly think that qualifies you as knowing what I want."

"Calm down, Carol. If it is that important, I'll call the waitress back over."

"Never mind. Let's just get this over with. And you never told me where mother went to."

"Your mother really wanted to meet with you. She feels bad that it has been so long since you have spent time together. She called me this morning to say that she was feeling ill, but did not want you to waste a trip out here and so she asked if I would step in and have brunch with you instead."

"She could have called me and canceled the brunch, Ronald. I do have a phone, you know."

"She was afraid she would miss you, and she also just thought it would be nice if we had a chance to chat like old friends once again."

Carol sat quietly for a moment, stewing over her mother's actions. The mimosas were served, and she found herself reaching for hers immediately, needing the fortification.

Lifting her eyes to Ronald, she took him in. Tall, but not as tall as Tom. Well-dressed, dapper, but not like her Viking. Handsome, but not gorgeous. Smooth, manipulating. Not like Tom, who as he says, let's get it all out so we can deal with the shit. Smiling, she couldn't help but think of how much Tom had come to mean to her.

Ronald saw her smile and relaxed. "I knew once you had a chance to think about it, you would realize this was a good idea."

Glaring at him over her mimosa glass, she almost choked as the liquid went down the wrong way. "A good idea?" she sputtered. She continued to cough for a minute, trying to get the liquid to go down the right direction.

Ronald glanced around with an uncomfortable look on his face. "Can't you cough quieter?"

"Are you kidding me?" she asked. "You're more concerned about other people looking than me choking?"

Ronald reaching across the table to take her hand said, "Of course not, that came out wrong. Please forgive me."

Pulling her hand back from his, she suddenly felt very weary. "I think I need to leave. This was a bad idea, Ronald. I feel tricked by my mother, and we just don't have anything to talk about."

"No, no wait. Our food will be arriving in just a moment, and I promise, I'm just here out of a favor to your mother. She did mention that you were coming to the Charity dinner?"

"Yes, I'm. Did she also mention that I was bringing a date?"

The waitress brought their food over, and Carol had to admit to herself that it smelled heavenly. Looking at the eggs benedict, she couldn't help but quickly add up the calories in her head. *Stop. This is fine. Just eat a little, eat healthy, and you'll be fine.*

Nodding, Ronald replied, "Yes she did. Is it that man that I saw you with several weeks ago?"

"His name is Tom Rivers and yes, that is

who you saw me with."

"What does he do for a living?"

"Ronald, I'm not going to sit here and be questioned about my choice of boyfriend." Fighting the desire to shovel the food in, she forced herself to pace. Slowly cutting bites of food, assisted her in not eating too much too quickly. Angry that she had to use these tips again, she knew that stress was always going to manifest itself in overeating.

"Well, I thought he seemed very nice the evening I met him. I was pleased to see you with someone so caring."

Narrowing her eyes, Carol assessed the man sitting across from her. Something's not right. Ronald and her parents had never given up on her becoming his wife so that the law firm could stay in the family.

Plastering a smile on her face, she agreed. "You're right. He is a very nice man." Looking down at her half-eaten brunch, she knew she couldn't eat another bite. "Well, Ronald, this has been nice, but I really must be going. I have to work tonight and want to get home in time to get some errands run first."

Not hiding his surprise, Ronald stared at her. "You work at night?"

Laughing, she replied. "Yes, Ronald. Nurses

have to pull all sorts of shifts. I usually work the graveyard shift in the ER."

Visibly paling, he retorted, "I can't imagine what kind of man lets his girlfriend work at a hospital in the middle of the night!"

The smile leaving her face instantly, Carol stared at Ronald with thinly veiled indignation. "He is the type of man who sees me for exactly who I'm. Loves me for exactly who I'm. And does not try to make me into anyone else." Rising, she tossed her napkin on the table. "Good day, Ronald. I suppose we will see each other at the dinner, but I think that will be the last time we associate." Turning, she walked steadily toward the door. Striding through the awaiting crowd, she headed to her car.

"Carol wait," a deep voice called out from the entrance. Not recognizing the voice, she whirled around. Jake was jogging over, concern etched on his face. Dropping her gaze to her feet, she felt her heart drop. *Oh great. How do I explain this?*

"Carol," he spoke gently. "Are you all right?"

Raising her head to look directly into his eyes, she smiled. "Jake, what are you doing here?"

Blushing slightly, Jake seemed to debate

what to say for a moment. "I was…having brunch with…a friend."

Remembering what Tom had told her about Jake only seeing women outside of Fairfield, she realized that he must be out on a date. Blushing herself, she looked back down, not knowing what to say.

"Are you all right?" he prodded. "You looked angry back there."

"I'm fine, Jake. Thank you." She reached out, placing her small hand on his arm. "Really, thank you. That was," she pointed toward the restaurant, "supposed to be brunch with my mother. She pulled out and sent an old family friend instead. We don't see eye to eye on most things, so it was not a pleasant meal. But I'm fine."

"All right. I just wanted to check on you after I saw you leave so abruptly. Are you okay to drive back?"

"Absolutely. I'm all right, so please…go back and enjoy your brunch."

He nodded as he assisted her into her car and watched her pull away. She watched him in her rear view mirror. *Good friends. That's what Tom has. Good friends. And good to me too.*

The drive to Fairfield was going to take about an hour and a half, and she felt anxious as she started the drive. There was a rest stop about thirty minutes down the road and without thinking, she pulled in. Walking into the empty ladies room, she could feel the unexpected, but familiar, feeling of wanting to purge. *Damn. Why now?*

Standing over the toilet, she leaned against the stall wall. The idea of the eggs benedict swirled in her mind, along with thoughts of her mother's and Ronald's manipulations. Reaching her fingers to her lips, she forced herself to bite them instead of sticking them down her throat. *Ronda says to talk to someone supportive when the urge comes. But I never had anyone who knew my secret. My shame. Until now. What if he rejects me?* Shaking her head to clear her thoughts. *He won't.*

Pulling her phone out of her purse, she dialed his number. Picking up on the first ring, she heard his familiar voice.

"Hey, angel."

Silence. For a moment, she couldn't think of anything to say.

"What's wrong? Where are you?" She recognized the concern in his voice.

"I'm on my way home, honey," she said weakly. "I just…needed to hear you…your voice."

"Carol, tell me right now what is going on.

You're scarin' me. Where are you?"

"I'm at the rest stop halfway home. I just felt like I needed to... um... you know. And I thought of...calling you. If...I talked to you, then...um...I wouldn't do anything."

"Let me come to you. You stay there, and I'll come right to you."

"No, no. I don't need you to do that. I just needed ...to hear your voice. I just needed...to know you're there."

"Sweetheart, I'm here. I'm right here for you. You don't need to do this. You're strong. You're beautiful. You're a survivor. And babe, I love you so much it hurts sometimes."

Smiling, Carol held the phone tighter as silent tears slid down her face. "I know. I just needed to hear it right now." Taking a deep breath, she wiped her tears. "I'm good. I'm going to get back in my car and head home."

"Come straight to my place. My house is closer than your apartment. I'm gonna be right there waiting and I want you here with me. Drive safe, and I'll see you, okay."

"Yeah, Tom. I'll come straight there." Hanging up, she used the restroom and went over to the sink to wash her hands. Looking into the mirror, she stared. Her hair was still pulled up into the sleek bun from earlier. Taking her clip out, she let the blonde tresses fall messily around her face. Using a paper towel, she wiped some of the makeup off then looked back into the mirror. Looking back was Carol. The Carol she knew. The Carol she liked. The Carol that smiled back at her in the reflection.

She knew where Tom lived, but had never been to his house. He usually picked her up from her apartment, and she got the feeling that his house was…sacred. Something not to be shared with just anyone. He had told her that he lived in the house he grew up in, on the street where he became best friends with Jake and Rob. When his parents moved away, they deeded the house to him.

Driving into Tom's driveway, she grinned as she saw him lounging outside on the porch waiting for her. Her car had barely stopped when he threw open her door, pulling her out and into his embrace. Not willing to let her go, he kicked her door closed, saying, "Lock 'em." She held on to his neck while clicking her car remote in her hand. Tom carried her up the porch stairs and into his house, still not willing to let her go. Sitting down on the couch, with her straddling him, he cupped her face, his eyes searching hers. Satisfied with what he saw there, he pulled her back into his chest.

"I been waiting for you, getting more pissed by the minute," he said, stroking his hands up and down her back. "Shoulda never let you go by yourself."

Carol was silent, trying to find a way to tell him that brunch was a setup. Breathing deeply through her nose, she let out a huge sigh.

Tom, misinterpreting her sigh, assumed that she was upset with him. "I'm so sorry, Carol. I shoulda protected you from your mom."

Leaning away from his chest, she raised up to look at him but found that she could only stare at this chest. Not willing to look him in the eyes, she hesitated.

He ducked his head down to try to meet her gaze but finally placed his fingers under her chin, lifting her face. "Do you forgive me?" he asked.

"Oh Tom, there's nothing to forgive," she quickly assured him, making eye contact. "I just have to tell you something and you're not going to be happy. And I just don't know how to tell you. And I..."

He placed the fingers that were on her chin onto her lips, effectively shushing her. "Just say it. If you purged, we'll deal. If we need to call your counselor, we'll do it right now. Whatever you need, I'm right here with you, every step."

Acceptance. Love. Comfort. Care.

Filled with courage, she leaned back so that she could see his face as she began to talk. Taking a deep breath, she began. "Tom, what I'm going to tell you is going to make you mad. But you have to promise me that you'll stay calm. I handled it, and it's over."

His face, no longer as soft and gentle as it was a moment ago, was holding fast to her eyes. "Angel…," he warned.

Plunging ahead, "Tom, the brunch was a setup. My mother did not come; instead, she sent Ronald."

He plucked her from his lap, setting her gently back on the sofa before he walked across the room, cursing. "Are you shittin' me?"

Hopping up from the sofa, she walked over with her hands raised to calm him. "Tom, I'm all right."

"Fine? Fine? You called me, crying in a bathroom, trying not to give in to the urge."

"I know. I know," she said with resignation.

Tom, fury pouring off of him, paced the room in frustration. She stood silently, knowing he needed a few minutes to calm. He stopped by the window, standing still, looking at the view outside. Finally taking a deep breath, he turned back around, walking over to her, wrapping her in his embrace. "Sorry, sweetheart. I'm just trying to get hold of my anger."

Hugging him tightly, "I know, honey. I'm so sorry."

Pushing her away gently so that he could look down in her face, he admonished, "You've got nothing to be sorry for. But you need to tell me everything," he said looking sternly. "I mean everything."

"Honey, there's not much to tell. I got to the restaurant and was shown to the table. There sat Ronald. I was going to leave but wanted to know why he was there instead of my mother. He told me that mother called this morning because she was ill and asked if he would meet me instead."

"Do you believe that?" Tom asked, doubt showing on his face.

"No." She sighed sadly, and Tom pulled her back into his chest, holding her tightly. "I think my mother wanted to send him, constantly hoping that I'll fall at his feet, I suppose. He started asking about you, so I knew mom sent him to find out about you."

"How did it end?"

"I got angry and left. I ate a little but was so

irritated that I felt ill while eating, so I did not overeat."

Looking up into his face, she continued, "I saw Jake. He came to check on me when I got to my car. I think I interrupted his date."

"You must have been visibly upset for Jake to come check on you."

"I guess he saw me having lunch with a man, and I did leave rather abruptly."

He pushed her hair back away from her face, peering deeply into her eyes. "No secret, I'm pissed as hell right now." Leaning his head back, staring at the ceiling momentarily, he then looked back down. "But proud of you. You were strong. You were tough. You felt the urge and called me." Bending over to kiss her lips softly, he then pulled her back into his embrace.

"Babe, you gotta know, I plan on taking care of this."

Carol jerked back in his arms. "How? What are you talking about? You can't do anything, Tom. There is nothing to do. It was a situation, and I handled it."

"You think I'm gonna sit back and let someone fuck with my girl. Even if that person is her mother and some old friend? Not happening."

"Tom, you can't fight all of my battles for

me. Some things I have to handle on my own."

Tom said nothing, neither agreeing nor disagreeing. *This isn't over, Angel. No one messes with what's mine to care for.*

Pulling him in, she leaned up on her tiptoes to nuzzle his neck, loving the rough stubble and imagining it between her legs. She pressed her legs together to ease the building pressure. As he chuckled, she felt the rumbling deep within his chest as she tried to pull him closer.

"Impatient?"

"I just really need you, Tom. All I could think about for the last part of the drive was getting here and jumping you!"

Growling, he lifted her in his arms, and she wrapped her legs around his waist. Walking the few steps until her back was pressed against the wall, he claimed her mouth, plunging his tongue deep inside.

She met him stroke for stroke, her tongue dancing with his, as the kiss deepened. Pressing his swollen dick against her, he rubbed his tight jeans against her core, providing the friction she craved. Pulling her top down below her breasts, he jerked her bra cups down exposing the creamy curves and rosy nipples that he had been imagining. Sucking a nipple deeply into his mouth, he pulled and tugged as he laved the swollen bud.

Her head banged against the wall behind her as the sensations overwhelmed her. Sliding her fingers through his blond hair, she pulled him in closer as he worshiped her breasts. First one and then the other, giving equal attention to her needs. The more he sucked on her nipples, the more she rubbed her clit against his rough jeans.

He held her up with one hand on her ass, as the other hand slid into her silky panties, thrusting up inside of her wet folds. *Wet. Ready.* Another finger joined the first and began their movement inside of her, eliciting more moans that he captured with his mouth. Just then, he felt her walls convulse around his fingers as she dug her fingers into his shoulders, crying out his name. He looked into her face, eyes closed, lashes resting on her flushed cheeks. A smile playing at the corners of her lips. *I gave that to her. Me. No one else.*

Slowly letting her legs slide down to the floor, he held her tightly. His blue eyes captured hers in a gaze that continued for several peaceful moments.

Finally breaking the silence, she asked softly, "What are you thinking?"

Leaning his head down so that his forehead touched hers he breathed her in. "Thinking about us. Thinking about you being here." He paused for just a moment. "Never had a woman here. Ever. You're the first."

You're the first. Carol heard those words, allowing them to wash over her, filling the cold, lonely places deep inside. *I'm the first he ever let in. Into his home. Into his heart. Me. Just me.*

"I love you, Tom Rivers," she whispered.

Smiling, Tom turned as he took her hand and led her upstairs to the bedroom. Glancing around, she saw the master bedroom decorated in masculine colors of dark blue and gray. A comforter covered the king-sized bed and matching curtains that were pulled back to allow the sun to warm the room, framing the windows. Before she could peruse the room anymore, she was pulled back around to face Tom.

"You can check out the house later. Right now, I want my woman in my bed. Naked."

"How caveman!" she laughed.

"You feeling good from what we were doing out there?" Seeing her nod, he continued, "You excited about what's gonna happen in here?"

Grinning, she just nodded again, sliding up closer to him moving her hands on his impressive chest as his massive arms encircled her.

"It'll always be about you."

Rising on her tiptoes, she darted her tongue out and licked his mouth. "Well, then, let's get to it," she dared.

With a growl, he picked her up and gently tossed her down onto the bed. Pulling his t-shirt up over his head, he threw it on the floor. Unzipping his jeans, he pulled them down, kicking them off.

Carol leaned up on her elbows, watching the strip show in front of her. His body was sculpted from years of football and now his regular workouts. The muscles in his biceps bulged as he maneuvered his clothes off. Twisting back around to face her, she could see the broad lines of his abs as they tapered down to his waist. His tight black boxers were tented in the front with his impressive erection. His trunk-sized thighs flexed as he leaned forward, grabbing a condom from the nightstand.

"Tom?"

His eyes darted over to hers in question.

"I'm...um...on the pill. My periods were messed up from...my eating..."

"Carol, I'm clean. Swear to God, I have never gone without a condom, and we get tested at work. I'd never put you at risk."

"I know," she said with a sweet smile.

His eyes captured hers once again. Blue eyes

gazing at blue eyes. "What do you want?" he asked, his voice tight with need.

"You," was all she said, in a whisper.

Tom scooped her up in his arms as he rolled over, placing her on top. His mouth claimed hers, nipping, sucking, thrusting his tongue deeply inside. The kiss took on a life-force of its own, pulling them both in. Unzipping her dress in the back, he slid it the rest of the way down to her waist. Palming her breasts, he was once again struck by their perfection. Her breasts were full, rosy-tipped, but not heavy. *Perfection.*

Not able to wait any longer, he lifted her and settle her wet entrance onto his straining cock. "Ready, babe?" he growled.

Seeing her nod, he pushed his dick up, watching as she threw her head back and felt her dig her fingers into his pecs. With his hands on her waist, he assisted as she rode him, watching to see her face when she came.

Carol could feel the different sensations from this position, and the depth of his cock inside of her created a friction that was unlike anything she had felt before. Closer, closer. She could feel the energy from her nipples to her core. Just when she thought she couldn't take the need anymore, she screamed his name and felt her orgasm wash over her in waves of pleasure.

Feeling her inner walls clench around his straining dick, he let her orgasm milk him before he rolled them over so that he was back on top. Looking down into her face, gentle with the expression of satisfaction, he asked, "Can you take it?" Seeing her smile and nod, he wanted to make sure she understood. "Can you take it hard?"

Her eyes opened up, focusing on his, her gentle expression curving into a brilliant smile. "Oh yeah."

With that, Tom slammed into her, driving deeply into her welcoming sex. Her orgasm had softened her walls and the slickness allowed him to pound into her without fear of pain. The feeling of her surrounding his dick without a barrier almost had him exploding before he was ready. Buried deep in her, all thought left him as he could feel himself close to coming and wanted her to come again first. Continuing his strong pace, he reached between them and fingered her swollen clit. Tugging on it gently, he could hear the change in her breathing.

Climbing higher, she was sure that she had to reach the end soon. Crying out his name once again, she felt herself fly over the edge as the sensations washed over her, pulling her along.

Tom continued thrusting for a few more strokes until his head reared back, and his neck muscles strained as he poured himself into her. She milked him until he didn't think there could possibly be anything left. Crashing down onto the bed, he rolled so that he didn't crush her, pulling her tightly into his arms.

Sweat mingling, panting together, they lay, each lost in their own thoughts.

Tom pulled her in tighter, as though he could slay all of her dragons with just his embrace. *Love. I love this woman. I need her.* Sliding one hand upward to cup the back of her head, he pulled her in even closer to his chest.

Carol could feel his heartbeat slowing down from its frantic pace. *Safe. Secure. Cared for. Comforted. Accepted. Loved. He loves me.* Smiling, she listened to his heart beating next to her cheek.

Raising her eyes up to his, blue eyes gazed at blue eyes.

"I hear your heart beat," she whispered.

"It beats for you, Angel," he whispered back.

Chapter 14

C arol had one more week of graveyard shifts before she began working the day shift. Pushing open the door to the break room, she was pleased to see Sofia and Jon putting their belongings in the lockers.

"Hey guys, I didn't think that I would see you tonight," she greeted.

"Yeah well, I gotta pull some extra nights to cover some bills. Ross' truck quit on him, the downstairs toilet is leaking, and the baby has an ear infection. I swear, we just get caught up when life knocks us back down again," she moaned as she hugged Carol. "By the way, you've got to get over to the security station. Mr. Hunka Hunka Burnin' Love sent you some bodacious flowers."

Curious, Carol headed toward Marcus' station, seeing the huge bouquet from down the hall. Not able to contain her grin, she bounded up to him.

Cocking his eyebrow, "You think there's

something here for you, little girl?" Marcus joked.

"Hmmm, do those gorgeous flowers happen to have my name on them?"

Taking his time, pretending to look carefully for the card, Carol impatiently grabbed the card from amongst the blooms. Opening the envelope marked '*Carol Fletcher*', she looked at the card inside.

You're my life. You're my love. You will be mine. I want us to be together always.

Sofia and Jon, each peering over a shoulder, chimed in, "Awwwwww."

Carol, staring at the card with a confused look on her face, caught the attention of the other three. Realizing they were expecting a reaction from her, she looked guilty.

"Damn, I hope when I send flowers to a girl they have a better reaction than you, girl," Marcus exclaimed.

Blushing, Carol explained, "Oh they're gorgeous. It just...seems...well, it just doesn't sound like Tom."

"Oh honey, you know how florists are," Jon stated. "They just get the order and then they embellish the notes with their own words."

"Oh," Carol said, sounding slightly disappointed. Shaking her head, "I'm sorry guys. I'll call him once my shift is almost over." Picking up the vase, she headed back to the break room. Placing the flowers in the center of the table, she opened her locker to pull her cell phone out of her purse. Knowing he wouldn't get the message until he woke the next morning, she texted her thanks.

Tks for the flowers. They r beautiful. Luv u 2!

The ER was busy that night, but Carol was grateful since the shift seemed to fly by. She only had another hour to work when she decided to check her phone to see if Tom had received her text. Meeting Sofia outside the break room door, they entered together. She was surprised to see Marcus, Jon, and Tom standing by the table with the flowers.

"Tom," she greeted with a smile on her face, starting to walk toward him. He turned around, and the look on his face melted her smile instantly. Halting in mid-step, she looked between the three men. "Honey, what's wrong?"

Tom's long stride made it to her in two

steps, and he wrapped his arms around her tightly.

Protected. I feel protected. But protected from what? Carol leaned her head back to look into Tom's face. "Tom?"

"Sweetheart, I didn't send those flowers. What I want to know is who the hell did?"

Twisting her head to look at Marcus still standing by the flowers, she saw him shaking his head. "Tom, man. I'm sorry. I don't know. They were on the guard station desk when I clocked in at eleven."

"Call the person on the shift ahead of you. I wanna know who accepted the flowers and which florist delivered them. There's no God-damn florist name on this envelope. I also wanna see the security tapes. If I have to get a subpoena, I will." Tom barked out orders, and Marcus jumped to obey. He headed out to talk to the security guard who had the shift ahead of him.

Carol, wide-eyed, saying nothing, looked up at him. "Tom?"

He heard the fear in her voice and tightened his arms. "Don't worry. I'll take care of it."

"Tom, I don't understand. Who would send me those flowers?"

"Don't know, babe." He wrapped his strong

hands gently around her upper arms, pushing her away from him so that he could lean down to peer into her eyes. "But from this moment on, you do not leave this hospital alone. Either I, Jake, or a security guard walks you to your car. Angel…Do. You. Get. Me?"

Visibly paling, Carol nodded slowly. Lowering her eyes, her thoughts flying fast and furious. *Bert? Could it be Bert? I wonder if Tom has thought of him?*

With one arm still holding Carol tightly at his side, he pulled his cell phone out of his pocket and dialed. "Jake? Gotta problem. Someone sent Carol flowers with a suspicious note. I wanna know where Bert Penski is, right fuckin' now. Yeah. Yeah. Later."

Slipping his phone back into his pocket, he pulled Carol to his front again. One arm wrapped around her shoulders and one hand holding the back of her head, pressing her tightly against his chest. "I want you clocking out now and I'm taking you home. Got shit to do today, checkin' things out, but I want you to stay home, locked in. I'll come back this evening and we'll eat before I bring you back to work tonight."

Not feeling any movement from Carol, he used his hand on her head to tilt her head back gently, taking in her eyes. "Angel? You're gonna be fine. Promise."

Giving him a small smile, she nodded then laid her head back on his chest. *This is where I belong. Right here, my head resting on his chest.*

༄

Tom and Jake pulled into Bert's neighborhood within the hour. The old neighborhood had seen better days, but most of the tiny row houses were fairly neat. The identical houses were all built in the late 1940's, after World War II when the soldiers were coming home. A few of the homes had been renovated, but many were the same original size. In front of some were junk cars, overgrown weeds, and some sketchy characters. Others were well kept with trimmed lawns and flower beds.

"This the neighborhood Bert and Cal grew up in?" Tom asked.

Jake nodded but kept his eyes peeled as he drove down the road. "What did the security tapes show?"

Tom cursed, "Nothin', man. The asshole didn't come in a florist truck. Came walking from outside the camera range, beyond the hospital parking lot, with the flowers. Jeans and a jacket. Had a ball cap; kept it pulled down.

Mid height, mid weight. Nothing distinguishing. Waited outside the ER door until an ambulance came up. Slipped in with the group, set the flowers down on the security desk, then walked back out the way he came."

"Sounds more professional than Bert," Jake surmised.

"Don't assume that weasel couldn't figure out how to do that. He knows he's been banned, so he's got to find a way to get to her."

Stopping outside Bert's house, they perused it carefully. Quiet in the early morning, it looked completely unassuming. Not one of the newly renovated homes, but not junked either.

Tom put his hand on the truck handle, but before he could open the door, Jake quietly asked, "You cool?"

Tom cut his eyes quickly over to his best friend and partner. "You think I'm gonna go off, half-cocked, and get myself arrested?"

Unwavering, Jake looked Tom in the eyes. "Didn't say that, man. Just want you to hold your shit together."

"Got it," was the only reply.

The men knocked on the front door, waiting for just a moment before it opened by a small woman, suspicion in her eyes. "You sellin', I ain't buyin'," she said as she tried to shut the door.

Jake and Tom flashed their badges, halting the closing of the door. Looking up at their faces, she scowled. "I don't know nothin' about Cal. He ain't been here in a long time. He was trouble as a kid and trouble followed him. He ain't here and I ain't seen him."

Tom growled, but Jake spoke over him quickly. "We're not here for Cal. He's in custody. We're here to talk to Bert."

The woman's eyes opened wide, then narrowed in anger. "My Bert's not done nothin' wrong. You ain't got no call harrassin' him. He don't know nothin' about his brother."

Tom cut her off. "We need to talk to Bert. Is he here?"

"Ma, who's at the door?" said a voice from inside the house. Bert appeared at his mother's side. His eyes looked at Jake in confusion, then over to Tom, recognition settling in.

"Yeah, you remember, don't you, Bert? You remember seeing me at the hospital with my girlfriend."

Bert, drawing himself up to his unsubstantial height, looked up at Tom nervously. "Ma, you go on back and start breakfast. I'm just going to talk to these gentlemen for a moment."

Mrs. Penski scowled again as she turned and

walked back into the house. Bert stepped outside, looking up at the impressive men standing in front of him, sweat beginning to pour off of him.

"Nervous, Bert?" Tom asked. "You got something you're nervous about?"

"I don't know what you mean. Why did you come here looking for me?" he asked, licking his lips.

"We need to know where you were last night between nine and ten o'clock."

Bert's face showed confusion. "Last night? I...I was here. At home. With Ma."

"Anybody else around? Anyone who can support that claim?" Tom bit out.

Bert's eyes shifted to the side. "Well, Ma can. We were watching that new lawyer show on the TV and it didn't start until nine o'clock and went off at ten o'clock." Bert looked back up at them hopefully.

Tom growled, shifting his stance in anger. Jake took over, placing a hand on Tom's shoulder. "Anyone besides your mom who can verify you were here?"

"No. It was just us. My pop's been dead for a couple of years, so it was just me and Ma. What's this about?"

"Nothin' you need to be concerned about.

We're just investigating a situation at the hospital. You were banned and we're wantin' to make sure you're not violating that ban."

"Miss Carol? Did something happen to Miss Carol?"

Tom jerked away from Jake, putting his palm on Bert's chest pushing him backward till he was pressed up against the front door. "You don't say her name. You got me. You don't see her. You don't talk to her. And you sure as hell don't try to contact her."

Jake pulled Tom back, barking, "Tom."

Bert looked up in fright, his Adam's apple bobbing.

Tom turned and walked back to the truck as Jake finished up with Bert. *Damn.*

Jake joined him, and they drove out of the neighborhood, not saying anything for a few minutes. "You believe him?" Jake finally asked.

"Hell if I know. The video was unclear, but it coulda been him. Convenient that his ma is his alibi."

"We'll keep working it, man. Just make sure Carol stays sharp and aware of what is going on around her," Jake warned.

"Oh, I plan on staying right with her. Plus she's got a new roommate moving into the apartment with her in a couple of days."

Jake looked over, with a smirk on his face. "You already checked her out?"

"Hell yeah. Girl checks out. No police record. Credit check is good. Worked for the same employer for a while. Gonna be an elementary teacher here in town."

"Sounds perfect for Carol," Jake added.

"Gotta tell you, it's been nice for us to be able to have privacy at either place, but when I'm working, I'd rather her have a roommate." Tom looked over at his partner, raising his eyebrow. "Who knows, Jake? She just might be interested in you."

"Hell, a young teacher is not what I'm lookin' for. But you can always try to hook her up with Rob. He needs someone to tame his ass."

Laughter filled the truck, breaking the tension.

"I heard you on the phone yesterday, ordering a tux. What's up?"

"Carol's parents have an annual big-shit dinner and she hasn't been in years. She and her parents are...estranged. But they asked her to go this year, and she wants me to escort her. Seems like her parents weren't too happy about her becoming a nurse, so I sure as shit don't expect them to be too happy with her dating a cop."

Jake turned to look at his longtime friend, knowing the look he saw on Tom's face. "You don't seem like someone who's nervous to meet the parents. You look more like someone who wants to stir the shit to see if it smells."

Tom, smiling, said nothing.

Chapter 15

Tom walked to Carol's door, dressed in his tuxedo, tugging at the neck. *Why don't they make these big enough to move around in? Hell, I would even take being able to breathe in this suit right now!*

Still distracted as the door opened, he was unprepared for what greeted him. Not often speechless, he found himself simply staring at the vision presenting itself in front of him.

Her dress was the exact color of her eyes – summer sky blue. The beaded halter bodice and fitted waist hugged her curves to perfection. The silky layers floating from her tiny waist to the floor swirled around her feet. Her blonde tresses were pulled up into a soft twist at the back of her head, tendrils hanging down, accentuating the elegant style.

As his eyes were busy devouring her appearance, she was perusing him as well. His muscular build filled out the jacket of the tailored tuxedo as it narrowed to his waist. The tailored pants could do nothing to hide the build of his thighs, nor the bulge she noticed. Her breath caught in her throat as her eyes traveled back up to the face of the handsome man standing in front of her. His eyes had made their way back to her angelic face at the same time.

That was when he noticed the twinkle in her eyes as she smiled up at him. Stepping into the apartment, he pulled her gently over to the mirror in the entranceway. Turning her so that she faced the mirror, he stood behind her with his hands on her shoulders.

"What do you see? Tell me everything you see."

Eyes meeting in the mirror, blue eyes gazing at blue eyes. She looked at the image in the mirror.

"I see an incredibly handsome man, who makes my heart beat faster just by having him near."

"What else?"

"I see us — we look good together. We look…right." Her eyes sought his once again, as though to see if she was answering his question correctly.

He nodded. "What else do you see?"

Looking back at herself, she smiled. "I see a very healthy me. I see a nice looking woman, who is strong and competent." Her eyes, still twinkling, sought his again. Smiling, she added, "I like what I see. I like the image looking back at me."

He wrapped his arms around her gently. "Damn straight, Angel. Damn straight. We're working that shit out. Bit by bit." He moved his hand around to the front, placing his fingers under her chin to lift her face to his. "But this image of you has nothing to do with your dress, your hair, your makeup. You're just as gorgeous first thing in the morning!"

She rose on her tiptoes to plant a soft kiss on his lips. "I love you, Tom Rivers."

"I love you too, babe."

Draping her light shawl over her shoulders, they headed out into the night. Neither knowing what to expect from the evening. Both knowing they could face anything with each other.

The venue had valet parking, and when they arrived at the ballroom in Jefferstown, a young man opened Carol's door to assist her down from Tom's truck. A growl from the driver's seat had him snatching his hand back as his eyes cut over to the impressive tuxedoed man sitting behind the wheel.

"You may take the keys – I'll assist the lady."

She couldn't contain her giggle as the young man sprinted over to Tom's side of the truck to retrieve the keys. Tom rounded the front, striding to her door. Peering at the beautiful woman inside, he shook his head for a moment before lifting her out. Keeping his large hands around her waist, he waited until she was steady on her feet.

Curious, she asked, "Why are you shaking your head?"

Chuckling, he kissed her forehead. "Just can't figure out how I got so lucky. You're so Goddamn beautiful. Takes my breath away."

Smiling, she stuck her arm out for him to take. "Gonna buy a lady a drink, sailor?" she joked.

"Yes, ma'am," he replied before leaning over to whisper in her ear. "And when we are done with this shindig, I'm gonna do a lot more to you than buy you a drink."

"Promise?" Carol asked, eyes large with hope.

"Guarantee," Tom stated, willing the blood to stop rushing to his dick, just thinking about peeling off the silky creation she was wearing. "Damn, let's go before I throw you back into the truck."

Taking a deep breath, she allowed him to

take her by the elbow and lead her inside. *Please let my parents act normal tonight.*

Entering the ballroom, Carol was taken back to many years ago when she last attended. How different everything seems now. Then, she was an awkward teenager with a paid escort desperately bouncing between wanting to fit in and wanting to hide. Now, she was walking in on the arm of the most handsome man there. She immediately saw the heads of women turning to see who had entered and their eyes lingering on Tom as they walked by.

While she was noticing the women blatantly staring at Tom, he was scowling at the obvious lust in the eyes of the men leering at Carol. He initially had his hand on her back as they were entering the room, but quickly moved his hand around to settle on her waist, pulling her in gently to his side.

She noticed that the venue seemed much the same as years before. The circular tables, covered with white and silver cloths, were laden with food. Women of all ages were elegantly dressed; their evening gowns rivaled the colors of the floral arrangements covering the tables.

Before she could begin her search for their

table assignment, she was greeted by a familiar voice. Turning, she saw her father, distinguished as always in his dinner tuxedo, walking toward them. Her mother, perfectly coiffed in a gold evening gown, next to him.

"Carol," her father spoke in his smooth voice. "I see you have decided to finally come to our annual gathering." Reaching her, he leaned down to kiss her cheek, then pulled back with a scowl when Tom did not remove his arm from around Carol's waist.

"Father. Mother," Carol greeted. "It's nice to see you again." Turning to smile up at Tom, she could feel his hand give her waist a gentle squeeze, giving her courage. "I'd like to present my boyfriend, Tom Rivers. Tom, these are my parents, Harold and Estelle Fletcher."

The men shook hands, both measuring each other with their eyes. Turning to Carol's mother, he kissed her proffered hand.

Carol's mother eyed her dress carefully before giving her approval. "I see that my taste in clothing finally rubbed off on you, my dear. Your dress is beautiful. We will show you to our table. You, of course, will be sitting with us." Before she could even think of a reply, her mother turned, taking her father by the arm and leading them to their table.

Tom heard Carol sigh and as he looked down, he noticed her smile seemed less bright. "Let's go, Angel. These men around here have stared at my woman long enough. Maybe if I get you seated, they will keep their tongues in their mouths."

Her smile returned as she leaned into his towering frame as they made their way through the tables following her parents. The head table was already partially filled, leaving five empty chairs. As they approached their seats, the men at the table rose to greet the ladies. Her smile faded as she felt Tom's hand tighten around her waist. Sitting at the table was Ronald, with his parents joining them.

Tight-lipped, she greeted the Harriston's politely. "Ronald. Mr. and Mrs. Harriston, how nice to see you. May I introduce Tom Rivers."

The men shook hands, although Tom couldn't resist holding the handshake a moment longer with Ronald in a silent warning. Once they were all seated, she noticed the chair on the other side of Tom's was empty. "Will someone else be joining us?" she asked her mother.

"Yes, my dear. A new friend of Ronald's will be joining us. I believe she is running a few minutes late."

She. Thank God. At least Ronald will have his

own escort so he won't be bothering me.

Even Tom relaxed at that news. *Thank God I won't have to peel that prick off of Carol tonight.*

Carol began to relax as the dinner was served. People tended to talk less as they were eating, and if her parents were occupied, then they always ignored her.

"So Thomas, I understand you're a policeman."

The table was quiet as all eyes turned toward Tom. Carol's spoon halted halfway to her mouth as she stared at her father.

"Yes, sir. I'm a detective with the Fairfield Police Force." He held the eyes of Mr. Fletcher, refusing to look away or back down from what he knew was a challenge. *Intimidation doesn't work on me, jackass. Go for it!*

"Well, that must be fascinating work," Mrs. Fletcher said, with a false smile. She opened her mouth to say more, but Ronald's friend arrived at the table.

"Sydney, how nice to see you again," Ronald greeted.

Carol, having set her spoon down, grateful for the reprieve, looked up to see a gorgeous brunette wearing a skintight dress that showed bounteous cleavage move to the table.

Ronald began to make the introductions

when Sydney exclaimed loudly, "Tommy, how good to see you again!"

Tom's head swung around as his stomach dropped at the sound of his name. *Damn! How the hell did she get here as Ronald's friend?*

Ronald, seemingly surprised, asked, "Oh do you know Mr. Rivers?"

Leaning over, cleavage threatening to spill out of her dress, she kissed Tom's cheek. "Oh yes, we are old, *close, intimate friends.*" Looking over at Carol, Sydney smiled and asked, "And who are you?"

Carol couldn't find her voice. *Close. Intimate. Friends. More like fuck-buddies!*

Tom discreetly removed Sydney's hand from his shoulder, introducing her to Carol. "This is my girlfriend, Carol Fletcher."

Giggling, Sydney pressed her hand to her enormous breasts, drawing as much attention to them as she could. "Oh, Tommy. A girlfriend? When you and I were well acquainted, I never thought that just one woman would be enough for you!" Taking the seat next to Tom, she was sitting between him and Ronald, but her attention was definitely on Tom.

Horrified at the turn of events, Carol shot a glance at her parents, expecting indignation. Her father sat stone-faced, but her mother looked…smug. Glancing at the other members of the table, she realized that no one seemed shocked other than her and Tom. Ronald and his parents had smiles on their faces.

The room felt small, tight. There was no air to breathe. Carol could feel her vision blurring. *Set up. We've been set up.*

She couldn't look at Tom, afraid of what she would see. Interest in Sydney? Perusing her gorgeous body. Remembering times gone by. Comparing her to….*don't go there. Breathe. Breathe.*

She felt Tom shift in his chair, placing his arm around her shoulders, pulling her in for a gentle hug.

"Angel?" Tom whispered.

She stared at her plate.

"Carol. Look at me," he quietly ordered and she slowly raised her eyes to him.

"Let's leave. This is fucked, and you know it. I wanna get you out of here."

Barely shaking her head, she said, "No. It's fine. I just… I…um…let's just eat."

The meal ruined for her, she attempted to take a few more bites, but the food tasted like cardboard.

Mrs. Fletcher began her sly assault again. "Tom, we were talking about you being a policeman. I was just wondering if that career pays very much."

Carol gasped, but Tom squeezed her knee.

"It pays the bills and then some," he answered deftly. "But more importantly, I go to work every day lovin' what I do and knowing that I do something worthwhile."

Carol's father looked at him speculatively, but her mother just had a sour look on her face. Turning to Sydney, Mrs. Fletcher asked, "How did you meet Tom?"

"Oh, when Tommy and I were close, he headed out of town every chance he got to have a good time. We met at a bar in town here, and he was always *up* for some fun if you know what I mean," she laughed, placing her hand back on Tom's shoulder.

Tom growled, furious. Furious at Sydney. Furious at Ronald and the Fletchers, who he felt sure had set this up to discredit him. *I can see them fuckin' with me, but how the hell can they mess with their own daughter this way?* He could see Carol struggling, but had no idea how to make the situation better without causing a scene.

Carol was trying to eat, but her hands were beginning to shake. *Full. I feel full. I need to get rid of it. I just need to get rid of the food, and this will feel better.* Carol felt Tom's hand on her knee again, this time rubbing softly, pulling her back from what seemed like an abyss. *Breathe in. Breathe out. I can do this. I'm healthy. I'm with Tom. I'm capable of making the right choices.*

Tom felt the change in Carol's breathing as she seemed to gain control over her emotions again. Realizing that no one at the table had a clue what Carol was going through made him angry for her that she always had to battle this alone. Not her parents. Not Ronald. No one. *Well, not anymore. She is not alone.*

As Carol's head cleared, she heard her mother speaking again. "Well, I guess I shouldn't be surprised that she chose a common policeman to date since she is still playing at nurse herself."

Tom had had enough but before he could speak Carol stood up, placing her hand on his arm. "You say what you want about me, mother. You sit here, all sanctimoniously, but you haven't worked a day in your life so don't speak to me about a career. You want to talk about me, go ahead. But don't you dare, DARE speak to Tom that way. He's the best thing that ever happened to me, and I thank God every day that he came into my life."

Turning to Ronald, she continued. "And you. I used to think that you were my friend, but you're just as bad as them," she said pointing to her parents. "Don't believe for one minute that I don't know you set her up to be at this table. I don't know how you investigated Tom to dig up something, but if this is the best you can come up with, that's pathetic."

She then turned her ire toward Sydney. "And you. What did you hope to accomplish? To reconnect? Well, get this straight – you may have been his fuck-buddy, but I'm the one he holds all night!"

Beginning to shake, Carol turned and ran to the ladies' room before Tom could stop her.

Tom stood up, tossing his napkin on the table like a gauntlet. Leaning over, he put his fists on the table and he stated in a cold, deadly voice. "You wanna fuck with me, bring it on. But never fuck with Carol, ever again. You got me?"

Turning, he stalked toward the hall near the entranceway where the restrooms were located, leaving a stunned table behind.

Mr. Fletcher said nothing, just staring thoughtfully at the back of Tom as he walked away. Mrs. Fletcher barely glanced at Sydney as she waved her hand in her direction. "You may leave. Your part is over."

Shrugging, Sydney left the table, disappointment written on her face.

Tom made it to the ladies' room but hesitated outside the door. Just when he was ready to barge in to check on her, she came out.

Carol looked up with a look of surprise on her face that quickly melted into tears. "Oh Tom, I'm so sorry," she sobbed.

He crossed the space to her in two steps, grabbing her tightly and held her against his chest. Pressing his hand against the back of her head, he rocked her gently. "It's okay. I'm here now. It's okay. I got you." Over and over, he chanted the soft words as her sobs subsided.

When she finally was able to catch her breath, he continued. "Don't worry about it. We'll call the counselor first thing tomorrow and I swear, I'll never let you around those people again. You're not gonna purge because of them."

She leaned her head way back so that she could look into his eyes. Concerned blue eyes met teary blue eyes. "Tom," she said softly. "I didn't purge. I wasn't in there purging."

Still holding her head in his powerful grip, he looked down in confusion. "Then what are you sorry about?"

"For them," she exclaimed, sweeping her hand out toward the ballroom. "For my parents, that have never paid attention to me until I finally made a decision that went against their image of what I should be. For Ronald, a man who escorted me around like I was a prize he won, but who never cared for me. For all of it. I'm so sorry that you were insulted by them."

He chuckled as he pressed Carol's head back into his chest. She could feel the rumble from deep inside of him and couldn't help but smile as her head shook with his mirth.

"Angel, you got nothing to be sorry for. The way you stood up to them…sexy as hell, girl. Babe, I couldn't be prouder of you and proud of being with you than I'm right now. In fact, how about you and me ditchin' this joint and heading home. I have been thinking about peelin' this dress off of you since I first saw you in it!"

Smiling up at him as he twisted her body so that she was firmly planted into his side instead of his front, they walked down the hall. They had only taken two steps when they were halted by a sound behind them.

"Tommy?"

Tom hung his head. *Damn. Does this nightmare just keep going on and on?* He could feel Carol turning around, but he immediately wanted to protect her, so he kept her pulled in tightly to him as they both turned together to face Sydney. *Shuttin' this shit down right now.*

"I just wanted to apologize to both of you," Sydney said, looking embarrassed as she forced herself to make eye contact. "That was horrible, and I had no idea...well, I just wanted to apologize." She turned to walk away when Carol stopped her.

"Sydney, this was a set-up wasn't it?" Carol asked, almost fearful of the answer.

Sydney, gorgeous in her own way, looked back at the angelic creature standing pressed into Tom's side. *He loves her. I can tell.* "Yes, it was."

"But why? How?" Carol's words seemed to stutter.

Sydney, looking up at Tom's granite face, knowing he barely contained his fury, answered, "A man came into the bar I work at asking if anyone knew Tom Rivers. We got into a conversation, and I let him know that Tom and I had...um...been... um...friends." Her eye cut back to Carol's in a silent apology. "He told me that he would like me to come to a formal event, sit with Tom and that things would work in my favor."

Carol's brow furrowed in question.

"He said that Tom would have a date that he was interested in and that if I showed up looking sexy, Tom would want me and he would get

Tom's date. It sounded simple and I honestly didn't see anything wrong with it." Sparing a glance at Tom, she could tell that he had gone from furious to almost explosive. "But once I got here and saw the way you two were, I knew she was no casual fu—um…date. I'm really sorry."

Sydney turned to walk away, then stopped again. Looking at both of them, she said, "You two are the real thing. I can tell and anyone who can't is a fool." She then turned, walking down the hall once again.

Tom, having wanted to avoid the conversation, looked down at Carol's angelic face. Her beauty went so far beyond the average woman. It was haunting. It stayed with him. It pulled him in and wrapped itself around him.

"Babe, I'm sorry about her. I never imagined that we would run into anyone from my past. I just—"

Carol pressed her fingers to his lips. "I know. None of this is your fault. It's strange to run into one of your old girlfriends."

"She was never a girlfriend. It was never more than physical," he quickly interjected. Carol winced slightly and Jake cursed silently. *Damn, how do I make this right?*

"Well, one of your…um… former friends

with benefits." Taking a deep breath, she continued. "But what's important is that we're still together in spite of my family's machinations, and I didn't purge."

Pulling her back into his chest, he held her as close as he physically could. Pressed together from chest to knees, arms wrapped around each other, they presented a beautiful couple to anyone passing by.

"I can hear your heartbeat," she whispered.

"It beats for you, Angel," was the reply.

Neither saw her father standing around the corner, taking them in.

Chapter 16

L aughing with Marcus and Jon, Carol walked out of the hospital with them toward her car. As they approached, Marcus grabbed her arm, holding her back. "Stay with Jon," he bit out.

Jon moved protectively in, wrapping his arm around her shoulders as they both looked at Marcus staring at a note taped to her window. He leaned in to investigate the note without touching it.

"What is it?" she asked, hoping it was just an advertisement. That hope died as her eyes scanned the parking lot, seeing no other notes on anyone else's cars.

Marcus' only answer was to pull his cell phone from his pocket and hit a few keys. She looked up at Jon, who shrugged as he kept his eyes on Marcus as well.

"Tom? Marcus. Gotta note taped to her car. No, man. I didn't touch it. Yeah. Parking lot C."

"You have Tom on speed dial?" she asked.

Marcus and Jon both looked at her, incredulously. "Girl, you gotta note taped to your windshield and you're worried about who's on my speed dial?"

"But Marcus, you just called Tom, and maybe it's nothing. Maybe it's an ad for pizza."

This time, Jon squeezed her shoulders until she looked up at him. "Sweetums, no one else has a note on their car and Marcus has looked at it close enough to decide it's suspicious. Don't you think Tom wants to know?"

"I just don't want to be such a bother to everyone. Like I'm the fragile little female that everyone needs to protect."

Marcus walked over, stopping in front of her. "Girl, you're sweet as can be and everyone likes you. No one thinks you can't handle things, but if that note is what I think it is, then we need the police here to collect it as evidence."

Visibly paling, she stared at Marcus. "What do you think it is?"

Marcus and Jon shared a quick glance, but Carol caught it. "What? What are you not saying?"

"Don't know, honey, but it could be threatening, so we want the police to gather it and don't want our fingerprints all over it," Marcus explained.

By this time, the sound of a large pickup truck gunning through the parking lot could be heard.

"Oh lordy," Jon exclaimed, giving her shoulder another squeeze. "The Hunk Calvary is here."

Jake's truck had barely come to a stop when Tom came barreling out of the passenger door. Stalking over to her car, his eyes found hers first and she watched as he did a head to toe scan of her body.

"I'm okay, Tom," she said softly, wanting to assure him.

Tom gave Jon a head nod, before turning to Marcus, who had walked back over to her car. Jake joined them, pulling on his gloves. Tom allowed Jake to remove the paper from her window and stood over his shoulder as it was opened. Carol waited, not breathing, to see what was in the note.

"Damn!" Tom cursed, as he turned and walked a few feet away. Jakes's eyes looked at his partner before glancing back over to Carol, who was pale, not breathing, just staring at Tom's back.

"Tom," Jake warned quietly.

Understanding his partner's plea, he turned

and went to her as she willingly left Jon's protective embrace to plant herself full body into his. He wrapped an arm around her middle, and the other hand cupped the back of her head, cradling it to his chest.

"What did it say?" she asked. "Please tell me."

Jake walked over with the note as she turned in Tom's embrace so that she could see what was in his hand. Marcus and Jon leaned over as well, curious as to the contents.

To the beautiful Carol. I hope that one day you realize how special you're. And that day you will be mine. Not his.

The air that she had been holding rushed out of her body. Glad for the support of Tom's arms, she twisted her head around to look up at Tom, needing to know what he was thinking. His handsome face was tight with anger, but his eyes softened when they went down to look at her.

"Tom, it's not too bad," she said tentatively. "I mean, it's not threatening."

Tightening his hold on her body, he growled, "Don't go there, babe."

"Go where?"

Jake looked at his partner, knowing he was holding on by a thread. "Carol." He waited until she looked up at him. "This is harassment. Someone's stalking you, harassing you, frightening you. A threat is implied. It does not have to state explicitly that you're in danger." He paused, letting his words sink in, continuing to hold her eyes as she was still wrapped protectively in Tom's arms. "Do you understand, honey?"

She nodded silently, not knowing what she thought or how she felt. Twisting back around again to look at Tom, she whispered, "I want to go home."

"Don't want you there by yourself."

Jon spoke up quickly. "I'm off now. I'll go home with her and will hang there until you get off work."

Tom cut his eyes over to Jon and nodded. "Appreciate it, man."

Carol huffed. "I don't need a babysitter."

All four men spoke at once, and she quickly threw her hands in the air in defeat. "Okay, okay. But we're taking my car, Jon. Yours is totally unreliable."

Jake nodded at her, then walked back to his truck with the note bagged in plastic. Jon grabbed her keys from her outstretched hand

and hopped in the driver's seat.

Tom turned her around, still wrapped up in his embrace. First kissing the top of her head, he then leaned down to make sure she was connecting. "I want you in your apartment. I want Jon with you the whole time. I want you to stay there till I get off duty. I want you safe, sweetheart."

Standing on her toes to kiss him softly, her smile was his answer.

Tom heard laughter and music as he approached Carol's apartment door that evening. Curious, he used his key entering only to be greeted by a blast of music and the visual of her dancing around the living room.

"Tom! You're Here!" she screamed. "Jon, Tom's Here!" Whirling around, she stumbled over the coffee table as she tried to make her way to him. Jon attempted to grab her, but Tom snagged her first before she fell headlong onto the floor.

Tom eyed the empty wine bottles on the table, then directed his glare on Jon. "What the hell, man?" he barked as he attempted to hold Carol upright as she went limp in his arms. Unable to keep her standing, he scooped her up into his arms. Giggling, she threw her arms around his neck.

"I jus' knew you'd come. I tol' Jon you'd come and to hide the wine. Jon, did you hide the wine?" she slurred.

Jon laughed at the sight of a drunken Carol in Tom's arms, as Tom was still attempting to glare at him. "Hell, Tom. She suggested some wine, and the next thing I know she was chugging it and we were having a good time."

"From the number of bottles on the table, it looks like you were having too good a time."

"Hey, it kept her mind off of some whacko stalking her. Thought you'd be grateful."

Carol wiggled in Tom's arms, pressing her breasts against his chest, making the blood rush to his dick. Jon just laughed again, saying, "Got my ride coming, so I'll see you two later." He headed out of the apartment, leaving Tom to figure out how to sober up Carol.

After he managed to get her to drink several glasses of water and helped her with the shower, he finally tucked her in. She slept through the night never knowing he lay awake the whole time. *Someone's after my girl. Someone's terrifying her. Someone. Is. Going. To. Pay.*

Tom had checked out Carol's new roommate before she moved to Fairfield. She came up clean. Not even a traffic violation. Nothing to make him suspicious. Carol was delighted to be getting a roommate again. Her previous roommate had only lived with her for a few months before moving out to get married. While they had no problems, they also had never developed a true friendship. Carol and the new girl, Laurie, had been emailing and Skyping for a few weeks, already finding many things in common. Laurie was moving to town to become a teacher at the elementary school. Carol was determined to make her feel welcome.

The day Laurie was arriving in town, Carol headed to the Fairfield Hotel to meet with the owners. Laurie had decided to spend the first night in town at the hotel since Carol was going to be working the graveyard shift that evening.

Walking into the hotel's office, Carol greeted Roger, the owner.

"Carol, my dear. How nice to see you again," he said, sitting behind the counter peering up at her over his rimmed glasses. "Helen," he yelled. "Carol's here."

Helen came out from the office. "Roger, I'm not deaf! I heard the bell over the door and was already on my way out." Greeting Carol with a hug, she whispered, "I'm not the one going deaf, but I surely think Roger is!" With a conspiratorial wink at Carol, she walked back behind the counter. "Are you checking on things for your new roommate?"

"Oh, please don't think I'm checking on you. I just want to make sure her reservation is in order. I thought I might have some of Bernie's treats for her."

"Don't worry about that dear. Roger goes every morning to get muffins, so she will have them here when she gets up," Helen assured her. "By the way, how's that handsome detective you've been seeing?"

"Tom? Oh, he is fine," Carol replied, a smile bursting across her face. "We're fine."

"Can't think of a nicer, prettier girl for that rogue," Roger said.

Helen looking over at her husband and rolled her eyes. "You old man. You wouldn't know a rogue if it jumped up and bit you."

Roger, pretending to be hurt, placed his hand over his heart. "I'll have you ladies know that I was somewhat of a rogue back in my day."

Carol couldn't contain her laughter while Roger continued to look hurt.

Helen gently slapped her husband of many

years on the arm, saying, "Well, then I guess I'm just lucky to have tamed such a rogue."

Carol, still giggling, moved to the counter to hug Helen. "All right, then. I guess we are all set. I'm glad I stopped by. It was really nice to see you again, and I'll see you tomorrow morning when I get off work. I'll come by and show her the way to the apartment," she added.

Taking Carol's hand in hers, Helen looked at her beautiful, angelic face. "You're strong my dear. Strong on your own, whether you know it or not. But don't be afraid to lean on others when needed." Continuing to hold Carol's hand tightly, she said, "You'll have pain before joy. You will have danger before safety. But love will prevail. It always does."

Releasing her hand, Helen turned to walk back into the office. Carol, rooted to the spot, just stared down at the hand Helen had held. Roger walked over, patting Carol on the shoulder. "She's always right, you know? She sees things. So you stay strong. If Helen says love will prevail, then it will."

❧

That night Carol could hardly contain her excitement about her new roommate arriving in town. She joined Sofia and Jon in the break room wishing the night was already over.

"As excited as you're, I hope she works out," Jon commented.

"Oh, she'll be fine," Carol added. "And who knows, I just might be able to hook her up with one of Tom's single friends. Lord knows, there are enough of them running around."

"Yeah, well what I want to know is, how does Mr. Sex Pistol Detective feel about you having a roommate? After all, he can't just whip out his revolver whenever he's over at your place with a roommate around."

Jon and Carol burst into laughter at Sofia's newest name for Tom. "Lordy, I hope Tom never hears these nicknames!" Carol exclaimed. "Anyway, we spend a lot of time at his place anyway. I'll have the best of both worlds. I'll have a roommate that I'm already becoming friends with and still have privacy at Tom's place when we need it."

Hugging her friends, Carol headed off to meet Laurie.

❧

Meeting Laurie was everything Carol hoped it would be. She was gorgeous, with the longest hair Carol had seen. Dark, thick, hanging in waves down her back. Laurie's eyes were stormy grey and her flawless complexion framed them perfectly. She was a few inches shorter than Carol and had a drop-dead figure. But it was her smile that captured Carol. It was open, freely given, and utterly sincere.

She met her at the hotel and then showed her the apartment. Carol so wanted Laurie to like it. She found herself almost desperately wanting Laurie to become a real friend, not just a roommate. Having stayed emotionally closed for so many years, Carol realized how freeing it had been to finally open up about her past. Not just to the therapist, but to Tom.

Laurie loved the apartment and they quickly got her settled in. Carol slept during the day, but that night she and Laurie had their first dinner together before Carol went to work. They laughed, talked, shared, and much to Carol's delight, the friendship began.

As she drove to work that night, she called Tom. "Honey, she's so sweet! She's sweet and pretty and caring and she loves the apartment and…"

"Whoa, slow down, sweetheart," Tom laughed. He realized how glad he was to hear that excitement in Carol's voice.

"I thought that we could have the gang over at Smokey's soon. She needs to meet people, and maybe Jake or Rob would be interested."

Oh hell, Tom thought. *Jake's not looking for a young thing, and Rob is the quintessential man whore.*

"Angel, I'd love to help her meet people, but don't know that my friends are gonna be what she needs."

Huffing, she asked, "Why? Because you all are such horndogs? Well, you settled down, why can't they?"

"Did you seriously just call me a horndog?" he asked incredulously.

Giggling, she wondered what he would think if he heard what Sofia called him. "Well, that sounds better than some things you could have been called," she retorted.

"Carol, you just go to work, concentrate on being safe, and I'll get the gang to have a night at Smokey's. But no promises on meetin' anyone. Deal?"

"Okay, honey. Deal. I love you, Tom."

"All my heart, Carol. All my heart."

∾

Tom sat with Jake at their desks working on the Calvin case. The chief strolled over to their desks before plopping down heavily in one of the chairs nearby. Tom and Jake shared a quick look between them before turning their attention back to the chief.

"What's up, sir?" Tom asked.

"Looks like Calvin Penski might make bail unless the DA can convince the judge that he is a flight risk."

"What the hell?" Tom cursed. "Of course he is a goddamn flight risk. Drugs for sure. Big time. Now the cops in Richland are starting to see ties to prostitution. And not the kind where the woman is willing. My buddies on the force there say they are trying to connect the dots with him drugging girls then using them in a sex slavery prostitution ring."

"I know, gentlemen. I just thought I would share this tidbit of information. Know you two have been working hard. Keep it going. We'll get something nailed down." He pulled himself up out of the chair and walked back to his office. Calling over his shoulder, he added, "Keep checking that brother of his. Don't trust the man."

Jake tossed his files on his desk and rubbed his eyes, shaking his head. "Sometimes this job is like ramming my head against a brick wall."

Tom agreed. "Let's head to Smokey's this weekend for a break. Carol's been wantin' to get everyone together so her new roommate can meet some people. Who knows? Maybe you'll be interested."

Jake eyed him suspiciously. "Oh, no, man. Not me. Not lookin' for a sweet young thing. Don't know who it will take to fall for me and my situation, but I doubt I find it in Carol's roommate." Looking away for a moment, he began to chuckle. "What about Rob? Now, that boy's in desperate need for getting knocked on his ass by love."

"Oh, no. The last thing I need is for Rob to fuck-and-run with Carol's roommate. That would piss off the roommate, which would piss off Carol, which would piss off me. Hell, I can just see the disaster now."

The chuckling died down as the partners and long-time friends looked back at the files in front of them.

"Do you still think the brother is the one sending Carol those flowers and notes?" Jake asked.

"He's gotta be. I mean, who else has acted infatuated? Well, other than that dick she used to date in college, Ronald Harriston. But hell, he's rich enough to get any woman. I can't see him sneakin' around leaving notes and shit."

"All right. Well, since we are diggin' into the brother about Cal's case, we've got a legal reason to keep an eye on Bert."

Tom looked over at Jake with a smirk on his face. Jake knew that look. He knew Tom was going to be keeping an eye on Bert, whether legal or not. *Hell, if it were my girl, I'd do the same.*

∽

Tom wanted to pick up Carol and Laurie for their evening at Smokey's, but Carol said it was important for Laurie to drive. Since Carol knew she was going home with Tom, Laurie would be able to have a car there so that she could leave whenever she wanted.

As Tom strolled into the bar, he saw Jake and Rob already there. Warning them to be on their best behavior, he stared directly at Rob.

"Just how pussy-whipped are you, man? Rob asked.

"Fuck you, Rob," Tom scowled. "It's just that for once, try to be a gentleman, for the girl's sake."

Rob walked over to the pool tables while Tom and Jake claimed a table large enough for their group. Several more of their friends joined them, and Wendy started serving the beers.

Carol, with Laurie in tow, entered the cozy bar. Laurie's pace slowed as she was entranced by the beauty of the restored bar. Carol waved at Wendy standing behind the counter and nodded as Wendy pointed to the table near the back where the men were. Pulling on Laurie's arm, she led her to the table.

Carol's eyes found Tom's immediately. Wearing a blue button-up shirt that stretched across his muscular chest, it was enough to get her heart pounding. Paired with the tight jeans, hugging his thighs, ass, and especially his crotch just made her pounding heart begin to beat erratically. Carol could feel her sex clench and her nipples bead as she walked toward him.

He was looking her way, drinking her in as always. Her blonde locks framed her porcelain face. Her pink mouth, made just for kissing, was slightly open, and the thought of it sliding around his dick made his pants uncomfortably tight. *Get a grip. Sporting a hard-on right now is not the way I want to greet the girls.*

His eyes did a quick body sweep. He frowned as he took in her pink top as it draped in front, showing just a hint of cleavage. Her skinny jeans fit her ass and legs like a second skin and her short stature was assisted by heels on her tiny feet. His eyes swept back to her face. Her wide blue eyes captured his.

Carol and Laurie were standing in front of him before he could even take a breath. Jumping to his feet, the other men followed suit, standing to greet the women. Placing his large hand on Carol's tiny waist, he leaned down for a chaste kiss. Smiling down at her, he pulled her to his side. Looking over her head, he greeted Laurie. "Nice to see you again, Laurie. Let me introduce you to some of our friends." He began the rounds of introductions, then they all sat while he began ordering the food.

Carol, tucked into Tom side as they were seated, noticed that Rob wasn't present. Leaning up to whisper in his ear, she asked, "Where's Rob?"

"Over by the pool tables," he whispered back, his lips barely touching her ear. He felt her breath gently wash over his face, and he suddenly wished they were back at his place already. It took all of his self-control to keep the blood from rushing to his dick.

Carol rolled her eyes at hearing that Rob was over by the pool tables. *No doubt finding some big-boobed barfly to take home.* Carol noticed that Laurie's eyes roved around their table before settling on the back of the bar where the pool tables were.

Carol saw Rob staring back at Laurie as though she were the only woman in the room. *Interesting.* Glancing between the two of them, she could almost feel the sparks herself.

"Leave it alone," came the whisper in her ear. Carol's eyes shot up to Tom's, with an innocent look on her face. He just smirked. "That innocent look doesn't work for me, babe. I can see you plotting and planning already."

Carol smiled, ducking her head. Tom lifted her chin with two fingers, raising it to just the right level for him to take her lips in a soft kiss. Gentle. Chaste. But with the promise of passion later to come. Carol's breath caught in her throat as she felt the lust spear her from her lips right to her sex.

"That's better," Tom stated. "Want you with me. Not off in your mind, planning romance for my friends. Whatever happens, happens. No interfering. Okay?"

Carol smiled, and Tom felt the air rush out of his body. *Who the hell am I kiddin'? I'd give this woman my soul if she asked.*

"Sure, honey. Whatever happens, happens," Carol agreed and Tom relaxed, pulling her to his side again.

Laurie seemed to have a good time and much to Carol's surprise Rob appeared infatuated with her. Rob sat closely to her, with his arm resting on Laurie's chair. Just as Carol and Tom were getting ready to leave, the barfly came over to Rob causing a scene. Laurie decided to quickly leave after giving Carol a goodbye hug.

"Are you going to be all right?" Carol asked, concerned for her new friend.

"Oh yeah. This," glancing back at Rob dealing with the drunken woman, "is nothing to me. I really had a good time, though. Thanks, Carol. I'll see you tomorrow."

Carol watched Laurie walk out of the bar alone. Rob turned back to see Laurie leaving, but Tom grabbed his arm when Rob tried to follow her.

"Rob, let her go, man. I think enough damage has been done tonight," Tom said.

Rob cursed, then looked down at Carol. Apologizing to her, he ran out of the bar after Laurie.

Tom leaned down, kissing Carol the way he had wanted to all night. Licking her lips, she opened her mouth, and he took the invitation. Plunging his tongue in, he sucked on her tongue until he could feel her moan into his mouth. Blood rushing to his dick, he fought the urge to press his cock onto her body that he held tightly.

Carol pulled away slightly to look up into his face. Seeing an uncertain look in her eyes, he asked, "What's wrong, Angel?"

"Do you think Laurie will be all right?" she

asked tentatively.

"She'll be okay. Rob will make sure she gets home safely. Even if he has to follow her in secret."

"She doesn't seem to trust men, Tom. I don't want to see her hurt."

Tom leaned down for another kiss. This one gentle again. Soft. Reassuring. Comforting. "I know. But I think maybe they both just need to find their way." With that, he threw his arm around her shoulders, escorting her to his truck.

"Can't wait to get you home, babe."

Carol just smiled. She had a surprise and could not wait to get home either.

❧

Tom and Carol barely made into his house before they began undressing.

"Wait. Hold on," she said breathlessly. "I want to go slower."

Surprised, he readily agreed. He never wanted her to feel rushed or out of control. Even though his dick was begging to be released from his pants, he vowed to take it as slow as she needed.

Smiling smugly, she took him by the hand, leading him up the stairs toward his bedroom. Once they entered, she walked him backward until his legs hit the mattress. Placing her hand on his chest, she gave a gentle push sending him falling back onto the bed.

Watching in awe as she stepped away from the bed sliding her hands to the button of her jeans. As she unbuttoned them and slid the zipper down, she turned her back to him. Hooking her thumbs into the waistband, she began to shimmy them down her legs. Bending over, presenting her ass to him as she pulled them off of her feet had him holding his breath. She was wearing a light blue, silky thong, showing off her ass to perfection.

He started to lift himself off of the bed, but she turned back to him quickly and put her hand out.

"Oh, no, big boy. This is my show. You just sit back and enjoy the view," she said, tossing her blonde tresses over her shoulder.

Crossing her arms in front of her she grasped the bottom edge of her pink shirt. Slowly, tortuously, she lifted the shirt up. Tom could see that her thong did not end. The silky blue, transparent material continued up her abdomen. Waiting, watching, he felt as though he saw the greatest present in the world be unwrapped.

Carol halted momentarily at her breasts,

piercing him with her look. Smiling, she continued to raise the shirt over her breasts and over her head, tossing it to the floor.

Tom stared at the vision in front of him, his dick aching for release. *Hell, if this is what angels look like, take me now!*

Carol stood before him in a light blue, silky teddy; the sheer material left nothing to the imagination showcasing her assets. The lacy cups of the teddy pushed her breasts together, as though they were presenting themselves to him. He could see through the material, her nipples prominent, beaded, ready for his mouth. As his eyes scanned downward, he noticed her pressing her legs tightly together. *Oh yeah. She's ready.*

Before she could protest, Tom was up and off the bed in a flash. Towering before her, he placed his hands on her shoulders. Her skin was warm and soft. Her eyes raised to his, her mouth slightly open, waiting to be plundered.

Carol unbuttoned his shirt, pulling it out of his jeans and sliding it down his massive arms and into the floor to join her clothes. Her hands reached out to his jean's button as his thumbs slipped under her teddy straps. He slid the straps off her shoulders as she undid his jeans. Smoothing his hands up and down her arms, he continued to pull the top of the teddy off of her shoulders and down to expose her delectable breasts.

Dipping, he picked her up so that her breasts were at his face. Sucking one nipple deeply into his mouth, his tongue rolling the pearl, he felt her head throw back as she moaned. Nipping at the bud before soothing it with his tongue, he felt her begin to press her mound against his waist, seeking to relieve the pressure.

Sliding his mouth over, he gave the other breast the same attention, feeling her undulations growing in frequency. Chuckling, he raised his head up to look at her face. "Want something, sweetheart?"

Her lust filled eyes peered back at him. Setting her down on the edge of the bed, he reversed their earlier position. He placed his hand on her chest and gently pushed her backward. Continuing to pull the blue silk off of her body, he fought the urge to rip it. *Gotta see her in this again.*

Tom stood and stared at the gift laid out in front of him. Naked. Perky breasts tipped with rosy nipples. Trim waist leading down to the prize. Her beautiful sex. Moist. Gleaming. Ready.

Tom dropped to his knees by the side of the bed. Spreading her legs with his hands, he dove in for a taste. "Been wantin' this all night." He slowly licked her wet folds. Moving his tongue expertly around her clit before sucking it into his mouth, he then nipped at it, eliciting the most enticing noises from Carol. She began to undulate on the bed, raising her hips trying to press her mound closer to his mouth.

"Still, Angel. Lie still. Don't move, or I'll stop." He pressed his hand to her stomach to still her movements. He heard her mewl in protest, but he just grinned.

Plunging his tongue deep into her, he reached up with his free hand and grabbed her breast, fondling and squeezing.

Her head thrashed back and forth on the bed as she tried to hold her hips still. She felt as though she were running on the track toward a goal but couldn't see the end, couldn't find the finish. The pressure built until she thought she would explode.

Watching her in the throes of ecstasy, he kept his head between her legs. Just as it looked as though she could take no more, he tweaked her nipple as he suck hard on her clit.

She screamed out his name as she burst into a million pieces, her body trembling with the force of the orgasm. Panting, feeling boneless, she lay unmoving on the bed.

Tom stayed between her legs lapping at her juices. *Goddamn, she is sweet. And she's mine.* Standing, he quickly pulled off his jeans, toeing his shoes off in the process. Joining her on the bed before she could lift her head, he lay beside her, pulling her in tightly to his front.

Sated, she felt as though she couldn't move until she felt Tom lift himself over her body, pressing his enormous cock between her legs. Suddenly, needing the feel of him inside overrode the necessity of rest.

Spreading her legs as wide as she could, she welcomed his cock into her waiting sex. He entered slowly as always, giving her tight vessel a chance to acclimate to his size.

"More. Faster. Harder," she panted.

"You sure?" he asked, wanting desperately to slam into her.

"Tom, now!" she ordered.

"Yes, ma'am," he replied, grinning as he pushed to the hilt. Her wet, slick channel grabbed at his cock as he began pounding into her. Resting his upper body on his arms, he watched her breasts bounce with each thrust. Torn between not wanting to hurt her and wanting to pound her into the bed, he watched her face for a moment to gauge her comfort.

Showing no signs of discomfort, her eyes were closed in ecstasy as the feelings of her core grabbing his cock washed over her. The mouth job from earlier was exquisite, but the friction of his cock sliding in and out of her was going to be her undoing. She threw her arms back, grabbing the rails of the headboard as he continued to thrust. Higher and higher she climbed, reaching for something that was just outside of her grasp.

Leaning down to grasp a nipple in his mouth, he sucked it in deeply. Using his tongue to swirl around the beaded nipple, he then used his teeth to bite gently at the swollen tip.

That was all it took for her to go over the edge once again. The orgasm swept her over the precipice, taking her flying. Once again, screaming out his name, she could feel her inner muscles pulling at his cock.

Tom, so close himself, did not want it to end too quickly. Pulling out quickly, he heard her cry out as he left her willing body. He flipped her over onto her stomach, pulling up on her hips.

"Up on your knees, babe. Grab the headboard and hang on," he ordered.

She allowed him to take complete control, bringing her hips up and wrapping her fingers around the rails again.

Tom slammed into her soaking wet sex once again. The force moved her forward on the bed. He grabbed her hips firmly to hold her still, pounding in and out. For a fleeting second, the sexual exploits Tom had had over the years with many partners flew through his mind. *Never. It's never felt like this. Perfect. Right. Connected.*

All thoughts left his mind at that moment as her tight sex continued to pull at his cock. Feeling his balls tighten, he knew his release was imminent. Reaching around her body, he grabbed her clit with two fingers, tweaking just enough to bring her to an orgasm again. Screaming out a third time, Carol came harder than she had ever come before. Still holding onto the bed rails, she was pounded several more times from behind until she could feel his release.

Head thrown back, neck straining, he yelled as his seed filled her waiting cunt. Pulsing several more times, he emptied himself. Crashing down on her back, he barely had the energy to roll off of her, pulling her once again into his body.

Both breathing in great gulps of air, bodies sweating, they lay entwined for several moments until their heartbeats slowed.

Massive arms wrapped around her tiny frame, and she felt protected. Safe. Loved. *I want this forever. I want him forever.*

Tom cradled her body to his, willing her to be as close as possible. *Knew this felt different. Know this is different. This woman is it. This woman is forever.*

Leaning down to grab the covers, he pulled them up over their cooling bodies. Tucking the sheet and blankets over her, he then tucked her body in tightly to his. Kissing the top of her head, he began to drift off to sleep.

"I feel your heart beat."

Smiling as sleep overtook him, he replied, "It beats for you."

Chapter 17

C arol and Laurie's friendship grew as they got to know each other slowly. It took several weeks, but Rob's persistence had paid off and he and Laurie were dating. Laurie was understandably cautious given Rob's reputation, but Carol was convinced that Rob was in love with Laurie, and she couldn't be happier.

She and Laurie's shared more and more of their past. Laurie opened up about her childhood and becoming an orphan at the age of twelve. She admitted that she did not know anything about her father since she was the product of a one-night stand. Carol revealed her eating disorder and some of her childhood tales.

Their schedules were slightly similar, so they had time off of work to enjoy each other's company. After a couple of years working the graveyard shift, Carol found that she liked working days. Instead of running or exercising in the afternoons, she switched to running in the early morning. An early riser by nature, she would begin her runs as the sun was coming up. Seeing the sun rise over the mountains in the background was the perfect start to her day. With a park next to her apartment building, she had a great place to run and still be close to home. She could run and be back in time for her and Laurie to share breakfast before they headed off to work.

Carol followed this routine for several weeks, starting to notice the same early morning runners out with her. There was an instant camaraderie amongst runners. Each would wave as they passed on the trails. Runners just seem to understand and respect other runners.

Carol began her run as usual; stretching, then slow jogging, working her way up to a run as she followed the trails. After a while, she could hear the pounding of feet coming up behind her. Moving over to the right side of the path, she made room for the runner to pass her. The footsteps got closer but never overtook her. She could feel the hairs on her neck prickle as she realized that the runner had come up right behind her and was just staying there. Deciding to slow her pace to encourage them to move on around, she slowed down just a little and then more. The footsteps pounding the pavement behind her kept pace with her.

Unnerved, she spared a glance over her shoulder. A mid-sized man with dark hair underneath a ball cap was running about five feet behind. She could not see his eyes since they were behind dark sunglasses. He did not wave. He did not smile. He stared straight ahead at her.

Speeding up, she could feel panic set in when she realized that he kept pace with her at whatever speed she was running. *Almost home. Almost home.* Coming around the last curve of the trail, her apartment building loomed in front of her. *Thank you, Jesus.*

She veered off quickly, breaking her regular routine. Instead of slowing down, then walking, then stretching, she barreled through the door and up three flights of stairs flying through the front door, collapsing on the floor, gasping for breath, frightening Laurie.

"Oh, my God. What's wrong?" Laurie yelled, crouching by Carol on the floor.

Between pants, Carol tried to explain. "Man was...following...couldn't   lose him...wouldn't...pass." Carol turned on her side, rubbing her cramping legs.

Laurie grabbed Carol's cell phone, finding Tom's number.

"Mornin', Angel. Wishin' it was your body I

was waking up to and not just a phone call," Tom answered sleepily.

"Tom, it's Laurie."

Tom woke immediately. "What's wrong?"

"Carol just came in from running. She's on the floor right now. She says a man followed her on the trails."

"Be there in ten."

In exactly ten minutes, Tom was pounding up the stairs to the apartment, with Jake and Rob close behind. Tom had called Jake as soon as he got off the phone with Laurie, and she had called Rob. Bursting through the door, Tom found Carol still lying on the floor with ice packs on her calves and dried tear streaks down her cheeks.

Falling to the floor, he scooped her up, cradling her against his massive chest. Her breathing had slowed, but her leg muscles were still slightly cramping. Rob hugged Laurie, then walked over to Carol and knelt next to her. Feeling her calves, he slowly stretched them out as he massaged them. With a background in sports medicine, Rob was able to ascertain that she was not injured, just in pain.

Jake calmly walked over looking into Carol's face. "Honey, can you give us a description and tell us what happened?"

Tom could not believe that he had not thought of that, then realized that Jake was taking charge as the detective since he knew Tom wasn't thinking clearly at the moment.

"Tom, can you help me to the sofa? I feel rather undignified here on the floor," Carol mentioned.

He stood, carrying her slight weight over to the sofa but did not place her on it. Instead, he turned and sat down himself, continuing to cradle her in his lap.

If this seemed unusual to his friends, they did not show it. Once Rob replaced the ice packs, he moved back to wrap his arms around Laurie. Jake sat on the coffee table, facing Carol with his notebook and pencil ready. "Start at the beginning, Carol. Just tell us what happened in your own words."

"I was running on the trail that I have been running every morning before work, and…"

"You run the same path at the same time every morning?" Tom interrupted, eyes wide, brow furrowed. "Do you know how dangerous that is for a woman?" His voice rose with each word.

"Tom," Jake warned. "Not now. This isn't the time."

Carol's breathing hitched as though the tears

might begin again. Tom placed his hand on the back of her head, pulling her toward him so he could place a kiss on her forehead. "Sorry, sweetheart."

Nodding, Carol composed herself and began again. "There are always runners out. We're a friendly group; people wave, move to the side if someone is running faster. I heard someone coming up behind me. I moved to the side, but they fell into step behind me and just stayed there. I tried moving to the side, then I tried slowing down. They just stayed with me."

Carol had been looking at Jake as she spoke, but she spared a glance up at Tom's face. His fury was palpable, and she wished she hadn't looked. Swinging her eyes back to Jake, she continued. "I finally glanced over my shoulder and that was when I saw him. He stayed about five feet behind me the rest of the way. I finally sped up when I came around the corner and saw the building. I just ran here as fast as I could."

Tom's arms had tightened with each sentence out of Carol's mouth until his grip was uncomfortable.

"Tom," she murmured. "You're hurting me."

Quickly loosening his grip, he apologized as

he kissed her head once again. Cutting his eyes to Jake, he willed Jake to continue. Knowing he lacked the control right now to ask her about the stalker, he needed Jake to take control.

"Honey," Jake continued. "We need to know what he looked like. Can you give us a description?"

"He was medium build. Not as tall as you."

"How tall, Carol?" Jake prodded.

Carol scrunched up her nose in thought. "Well, I'm five foot five and he was probably about five or six inches taller than me. He was thin, though, with a lean runners build."

Jake and Tom read each other's minds; there was no way this could be Bert. Jake continued, "What was he wearing? What did he look like?"

"He was wearing a black hoodie, but it had no writing on it at all. Black sweat pants. I don't know about his shoes. He had dark hair and was wearing a black ball cap, but it also didn't have any writing on it. I couldn't see his face very well. He was wearing reflector sunglasses, so all I could see was myself."

Thinking it over, her shoulders slumped. "That's not very much to go on, is it?" Sighing deeply, she looked up. Glancing at the clock, she jumped up. "Oh, my God. I'm going to be late for my shift. Laurie, you have to leave too!"

Laurie hugged her and assured her that she had time to get to school. Rob hugged Carol also as he walked Laurie out.

"Angel, why don't you call in sick today and stay home?"

Carol turned and looked at Tom incredulously. "Tom, I can't miss work and Laurie gets home about the same time that I do."

Wanting to diffuse the conversation, Jake interjected, "Carol, do you have any idea who'd want to follow you?"

Shaking her head, Carol simply replied, "No. No one. I know you all thought Bert was sending the flowers and note, but it wasn't him running behind me today for sure."

Jake crossed over to her in a couple of steps, stopping directly in front of her. Leaning over, he kissed the top of her head and said, "Be safe. Be smart, keep your phone with you, and don't go anywhere alone." Nodding to his partner, he walked out of the apartment.

"We need to talk, babe," Tom stated.

"Tom, I get you're pissed about me running in the early morning, but we don't have time to argue about it now," she said walking to her bedroom. "I have to shower and get to work."

"Oh, we're not gonna argue 'bout it. It's as simple as this. You don't run same time, same place, every day. In fact, until we know who this guy is, you don't run period."

Carol shouting over the running water answered, "Tom, don't you dare tell me what I can't do."

Tom, standing in the bedroom instead of the bathroom, felt at a distinct disadvantage. What he really wanted to do was join her in the shower, hoist up her soaking wet body and fuck her until she was too sated to argue. His dick was imagining that scenario, but his head knew that if he did that, neither of them would get to work.

The water stopped, and he heard drawers opening and slamming quickly. In ten minutes, Carol came out dressed in navy scrubs. Her hair was pulled back into a sleek, still damp ponytail. Her minimal makeup only enhanced her angelic features.

Feeling his resolve, as well as his dick, stiffen, Tom continued. "Angel, I need you to at least promise me no more morning runs until we have this situation under control."

Stopping in the middle of grabbing her bag, Carol looked up at his handsome face. Her Nordic God. Her Viking. He ran over from an early morning sleep just to make sure she was safe. *I have friends who care. And a man who loves me and wants me protected.* The realization that life is now different swept over her – a warm feeling that filled every empty crevice.

Walking over, she lifted her hands to cup his face, pulling him down for a kiss. The kiss started chastely, but she continued to move her lips over his, willing him to feel her complacency.

Tom slanted his mouth and took control of the kiss. What began as soft become demanding, possessive, unyielding. Plunging his tongue into her sweet opening, he explored every crevice of her mouth. Sucking her tongue into his mouth, he captured her moans. Tongues tangled, breaths mingled, Carol felt sucked in, as though she couldn't tell where she ended and Tom began.

He raised his knee up so that she was riding his thigh. Rubbing herself on his jean-clad thigh, she felt the friction and pressure on her clit that she desperately needed. Sliding his hand under her scrub top, he yanked her bra cup down and pulled on her nipple. Carol threw her head back as the orgasm washed over her, causing her inner core to clench as she rode it out on his leg.

Lowering her back down, Tom looked down into her lust filled eyes with a smug look of his own.

"Why are you so smug?" she asked.

"Man's gotta feel proud, knowin' he can make his woman come just by letting her rub up on him."

Carol, glancing at the clock, knew she only had a few minutes before she had to leave for work. Unzipping his pants, she freed his swollen cock. Grasping it in her hands, she began to slide her hand up and down its length, feeling the silk over steel texture. Always amazed at the size, she wondered once again how it ever fit inside. *But I'm sure glad it does!*

Sliding down to her knees, she looked up coyly, saying, "Let's see who's smug now."

And with that, she took him in her mouth. Using one hand to fondle his balls and the other hand to move at the bottom of his shaft, she took him as deeply as she could. Using her tongue, she swirled it around his cock, moving from the tip, down the side and back up again. Tonguing his slit, she heard him growl as he grabbed her ponytail, moving her slowly up and down.

Carol slid her mouth down over his cock as far as she could take him, then began sucking gently. Glancing up at him she saw him throw his head back, eyes shut, mouth working as if in silent prayer. Continuing to slide her tongue around him as she worked her lips over his shaft, his breathing increased with the pace that she kept, as though his lungs had a direct connection to his dick.

"Fuuuuuuck," Tom yelled out. "Gonna come, babe. You gotta stop." As hard as it was to let go of her hair, the last thing Tom wanted was for Carol to feel forced. He should have known she was still in control.

Continuing to suck as she took him quickly in and out of her mouth, she felt his balls tighten right before he came into her mouth. Sucking him off completely, she looked up in satisfaction as she wiped her lips.

"Goddamn!" Tom cursed, as the thick muscles in his neck strained with the force of his orgasm. Reaching down, he grasped her under her arms, hauling her up the front of his body. His breathing ragged, he held her tightly as though if he let go, she would disappear.

They stood there for a few minutes, saying nothing, letting the power of their orgasms take hold. Slowly, they both floated back to reality as she looked over at the clock beside of her bed.

"Tom," she shouted, as she pulled away from his embrace. "I have got to get to work now." Then looking down at his cock, standing at half mast, she smirked. "But, you might want to tuck that back in your pants before you leave."

Laughing, she tried to run out of the bedroom, but Tom managed to swat her ass before she made it out of the door. Tom grabbed her just as she made it to the front door, twirling her around in his arms so that she was pressed against him from chest to knee.

Walking her out to make sure she was safe, he leaned down as she was getting into her car.

"Love you...be safe today," Tom whispered against her blonde hair.

"Love you too," was the heartfelt reply.

Carol found that working straight days were great for connecting with Laurie and for dating, but she did not get to see Sofia and Jon as much. She was used to eating in the nurses' lounge in the middle of the night, so finding herself in the crowded cafeteria was sometimes lonely. Sitting alone while eating lunch, she would often take her Kindle so that she could read.

"I thought you were on days now. Good, I have someone to eat with," said a voice from directly behind her. Turning her head, she saw Dr. Driscoll placing his tray next to hers.

"Actually, I'm almost finished, Dr. Driscoll,"

Carol replied.

"Please stay," he begged, placing his hand on her arm. "We haven't had a chance to talk in a while. And call me Harry."

Forcing a smile, Carol stayed in her seat but kept her eyes on her Kindle.

"So, if you're working days now, you must have a lot of evenings free?" Harry asked, in a not so subtle way.

"Not really," Carol replied, not wanting to continue the conversation.

"Well, surely you have an occasional evening free? I'd love to take you out sometime."

"Actually, my free evenings are spent with my boyfriend," Carol stated. Having spent so many years trying to be as private as possible, Carol hated giving out any information. Feeling uncomfortable, she rose from her seat grabbing her trash to leave.

"Your boyfriend? You're still seeing that policeman?" Harry asked in surprise.

Carol whipped her head around, glaring at the impertinence of her tablemate. *Who the hell does he think he is?* "Yes, I'm still seeing him. If you'll excuse me, I have to get back on the floor." With that, she turned, tossed her trash in the nearest receptacle, and stalked back to the ER.

Storming into the nurses' lounge, she almost ran over Sofia.

"Slow down girl. You almost bowled me over," Sofia cried out as she grabbed Carol's arms.

In an uncharacteristic show of emotion, Carol threw her arms around Sofia in a hug. "I'm so glad to see you!"

"What's up, girl? You and Mr. Tight Ass having problems?"

Carol smiled, Sofia's nicknames always catching her by surprise. "No. We're fine. I just feel a little lonely on days without you and Jon always around. By the way, what are you doing here now?"

"I picked up a couple of hours today since the kids are with their grandmother right now. So at least, you will see me some in the afternoons. But you still haven't answered my earlier questions. Why the hell did you come blastin' in here?"

"Dr. Driscoll. Need I say more?" Carol replied.

"That toad still after you? I'd have thought by now he would have realized that he can't complete with your Dick," Sofia added.

Carol, raising her eyebrows at Sofia, replied, "My Dick?"

"Yeah, you know? Detective…Dick? Well, it sounded better in my head at the time I said it," Sofia confessed.

Laughing, Carol said, "Yeah, well now Dr. Driscoll wants me to call him Harry. I mean he hasn't done anything wrong, he just gives me the creeps."

"Hmmm. Between Bart, who epitomizes creepy, and Harry, the doctor who can't take no for an answer, you've certainly got more than your share of stalkers," Sofia stated as she walked out of the room.

At the word, "stalkers", Carol became still. *Bart. Harry Driscoll. Even Ronald, with that stunt he pulled at the dinner. Could one of them have sent the flowers? Left the note? But none of them looked like the runner behind her.*

Shaking her head to clear out the musing, she followed Sofia out to the ER floor.

After a long day, involving numerous influenza cases, injuries from two car accidents, and an elderly man having a heart attack, Carol was ready to head home. Tom had plans for the night, and she was nervous. Sofia had volunteered to walk Carol to her car, so the two women waved goodbye to Marcus. Sofia picked up on Carol's quietness as they walked.

"You seem pre-occupied, girl. You still worried about Dr. Harry?"

"No, I was thinking about tonight. Tom made plans and well...it's difficult for me," Carol confessed. Seeing Sofia's confused look, she continued. "Tom lives in the house he grew up in; he got it from his parents when they moved away. And there's a hot tub on the back patio."

"So. Not seeing anything wrong with this picture so far," Sofia said. "In fact, my imagination is starting to run wild about now!"

"We've been in it by ourselves, but tonight he invited Rob and my new roommate Laurie over." Carol glanced sideways at Sofia to see her reaction.

"Uh huh." Sofia stopped in the parking lot, cocked her hip and put her fists on her waist. "And you got some cockamamie idea that your body ain't good enough, right?"

Carol stood, biting her lip. "I know. I know. But Laurie is gorgeous. Long hair, great curves. I mean she'll be a knockout in a bikini. And me? I look in the mirror—"

"Girl, what the hell do you see when you look in the mirror?" Sofia asked gently.

Carol looked into the distance, pulling her

thoughts together. "Sometimes, I see pretty. Sometimes I see cellulite. Sometimes I think my boobs are too small. Sometimes I see someone who is still trying to find the perfect image. Most of the time, it's not so bad. But bathing suits? Jesus, that makes it horrible!"

"Do you get this anxious at the beach?"

Carol just sucked her lips in and didn't reply.

"You think Jon and I don't know you're bulimic?" Sofia whispered as she pulled Carol in for a hug.

"You know?" Carol asked incredulously. "But how?"

"Honey, we took the same nursing psych classes you did! But we could tell you were getting counseling, and you're so healthy now. So we just decided to support you without getting in your face."

Tears threatened to spill over as Carol hugged Sofia. Then the tears won out and ran down her face uncontained.

"It feels good to let that shit out, doesn't it, girl?" Sofia asked.

Carol nodded, silent tears still falling. Sniffling, she wiped her eyes, looking into the soft brown eyes of her friend. "I know what you're going to say," she said, smiling through her tears. "You're going to tell me that I'm pretty and that Tom is lucky to have me, and that I'm healthy, and that I need to feel good about myself."

"Yeah, and on top of that…if I could rock your body in a bikini, hell girl, you wouldn't get me out of the hot tub!"

By this time, the women reached Carol's car. She breathed a sigh of relief as it appeared unaltered. With a goodbye hug, Carol climbed in as Sofia sashayed over to her car. Gazing at her face in the rearview mirror, Carol could not help but smile. *I can do this. Tom loves me. Tom thinks I'm beautiful.* Pausing to stare at her reflection for a moment, she continued. *I'm beautiful. Just me.*

Chapter 18

Carol and Laurie arrived at Tom's house in Laurie's little yellow VW bug, knowing that Carol would be spending the night. Walking through the kitchen and out onto the patio, they found Tom already cooking steaks on the grill and Rob lounging with a beer in his hand.

Both men greeted their women enthusiastically, although Tom felt cheated on his hello kiss since he had to rush back over to the grill. Flipping the steaks, he glanced over his shoulder at Carol, winked and mouthed, "To be continued later."

Carol grinned in return and headed into the kitchen to grab the rest of the meal. The four friends were soon sitting down to grilled steaks with all the fixings.

Carol tried to fight the feelings of counting calories. Knowing she was going to be getting into a bikini later made her feel less in control. She began to eat slowly, pushing her food around on her plate instead of eating it.

Tom noticed. He said nothing for a few minutes, but then realized he did not want to embarrass her but wasn't going to let her not enjoy her meal.

"Hey Angel, I'm gonna grab some more beers. Can you come help me?" he asked casually.

"Sure," was Carol's quick response, already rising from the table.

Once inside the house with the patio door closed, he rounded on her, moving her backward until her back hit the counter.

"You gonna tell me what's going on in that pretty head of yours? 'Cause I get the feelin' you're being clueless again, and we're not going back out until we get this out and deal with it."

Carol opened her mouth to reply, but Tom put his fingers on her lips.

"And don't you dare try to tell me nothing is going on."

Huffing, Carol looked down at their feet for a moment, hating to admit that he was right. *Deal with this. Get it out in the open. Don't hold these feelings in.*

Carol admitted, "I hate eating right before I'm going to be in a bathing suit. I know I'm not overweight—"

Tom interrupted with a rude sound.

Flashing her eyes at him in exasperation, she agreed. "Okay fine. I may even be a little underweight. But I don't want to purge right before going to the pool. So I just figured that if I don't eat much, I won't be tempted."

Tom hung his head for a moment, saying nothing.

"You're angry," Carol whispered.

Tom's head snapped up, his eyes latching onto hers. "I'm not mad, but I'm kinda pissed you think I would be." Taking a deep breath, he continued. "Was gonna say you were clueless again, but when I asked you what was going on, you told me. You laid it out clear. I'm proud of that, and I'm proud of you. I never want you to hide shit from me. Told you before, we get it out, we deal, and then we lay it to rest."

She stared into his beautiful face; the face that captured her heart the first time she saw him.

Tom reached up to cup her face, holding her gaze. "So you got it out. Now let's deal."

Nodding, Carol agreed. "I'll eat, but just don't expect me to shovel it all in. That's too much and I won't enjoy myself. Laurie is so beautiful and compared to her…"

Tom interrupted her again. "Whoa, Angel. Stop right there. Now you're about to piss me off by going clueless again. Yes, Laurie is a beautiful woman, but she doesn't hold a candle to you. I feel nothin' when I see her other than I'm glad Rob decided to pull his head outta his ass and find a great woman. But you. Carol, when I look at you, I see everything. Beauty. Brains. Sweetness. Care. Love. I see everything I could ever want and everything I could ever need. That's what I see. That's my image of you."

Carol felt a lightness that had escaped her for years. She knew deep inside she would always battle her own image, but hearing what Tom saw made her feel truly beautiful. Just as she was.

Sliding her arms around his waist, she pulled herself into his chest and held tight, letting his heartbeat echo throughout her being. *He sees me. He loves me. Just me.*

Wrapping his arms around her in his powerful embrace, he pulled her even tighter. "Okay, sweetheart?"

Nodding, Carol answered softly, "Okay."

Kissing the top of her head, Tom released her to grab some beers before they headed back out.

True to her word, Carol ate some of her dinner and then the four friends settled into the hot tub. Laurie's curves were lusher than Carol's, and Tom realized that in the past, that may have been what would have attracted him to a woman. But now? Looking at Carol's toned, perfect figure and angelic face, he knew he had exactly what he could have ever wanted. Shifting her weightless body through the water, he maneuvered her to sit between his legs. She fit perfectly. Her slender body was entirely framed by his massive one. Wrapping his arms around her front, he pulled her back into his chest and rested his chin on her head.

Rob followed suit, positioning Laurie in much the same way, and Carol could not help but notice how good they looked together. Smiling, she was pleased with her part in getting them together. *Friends. This is what it is like to have real friends.* Other than Sofia and Jon from work, Carol realized that she had never allowed herself to have friends.

Tom leaned down to whisper in her ear, "What are you smiling about?"

Carol could feel his breath against her ear, and she shivered even in the warm water. Twisting around so that she could look in his face, she answered, "I'm just enjoying friendship. I never really had that before."

Tom held her gaze for a moment, allowing

himself to peek inside of Carol's past. No friends meant never having to disappoint someone. Never having to live up to their expectations. But is also meant never knowing the fun, the camaraderie, the joy of spending time with others. Leaning down, he placed a gentle kiss on her lips before turning her back around to face the others.

For a long time, the four friends talked and laughed as the men regaled the women with tales of their growing up on this very street.

Rob looked around the backyard, noting that Tom had not changed the house or yard much since he had taken it over from his parents. "Are your parents gonna be surprised when they come next week?"

Before Tom could answer, Carol tried to stand and turn quickly in the hot tub, slipping instead and falling backward. Water splashed all around as Tom tried to grab her.

"Damn, Angel. What the hell are you doing? Trying to drown yourself and us too?" he said as he finally got his hands on her slippery body and hauled her up out of the water.

"Your parents?" Carol spluttered. "You didn't tell me your parents were coming!"

"It's no big deal. They come for Thanksgiving every year, and we always have it with Rob's family."

"Tom, it is a big deal. Do you expect me to meet them?" Carol asked her voice raising.

Looking confused, he said, "Of course I expect them to meet my girlfriend. You'll be eating with us."

"Well, you could have warned me. You could have told me."

Rob and Laurie shared a look then Rob stood pulling Laurie up in his arms. "Well you two," he said, looking over at Tom and Carol, "looks like you all need to talk and I have been dyin' to get this gorgeous girl of mine home and in my bed."

"Rob!" Laurie exclaimed, slapping him on his arm. "You shouldn't say that!"

"Babe, I say what I feel and right now, I'm wantin' to be feelin' you!" Rob retorted with a leer. Grabbing Laurie around the waist, he hoisted her out of the hot tub before pulling himself out. He grabbed their towels, and they said their goodnights as they headed off to his truck.

Tom looked down at Carol, water still dripping from her face and hair, but just as beautiful as always. "Don't get clueless on me now."

Carol's eyes snapped to his, but he put his fingers gently on her lips before she could respond.

"Are you my girl? Yes or no?" Tom asked.

Carol nodded.

"Do we love each other? Yes or no?" he continued.

Carol, with his fingers still on her lips, nodded again. This time, though, she could feel his fingers slowly moving over her lips, caressing them. Her irritation fled as the feelings spread from her lips throughout her body.

He leaned close, bending so that his face was just a breath away from hers. "And isn't it appropriate for adults who are in love to meet the families of their partners? Yes or no?"

Carol nodded, but by this time, she would have agreed to anything as long as he kept touching her lips. Needing more contact, she stepped forward so that they were standing chest to chest.

"So, you're gonna to meet my parents next week at Thanksgiving. They're gonna love you. You're gonna be fine. I know it's a big crowd, and I know there will be a lot of food, mixed with stress. But I'll be right there with you every moment, I promise."

With those words, Carol melted into Tom. *He gets it. He gets me. He understands.* Placing her hands on his chest, she slid her tongue out and pulled his fingers into her mouth, sucking gently.

Lust speared through his eyes as he pulled his fingers out and slammed his mouth onto hers. Picking her up, he felt her wrap her legs around his waist. He then settled back down into the hot tub, sitting with her facing him on his lap.

She could feel his erection pressing directly on her clit. Immediately she began rubbing herself on him to relieve the pressure building.

He gave into the lust that threatened his sanity at the moment. His hands slid from her ass to her back, releasing the bikini strap knot. Pushing the nothing material up and over her head, he pulled his lips away from hers just long enough to take in her naked breasts. *Perfect.* He was always amazed at her body. Almost fragile looking and yet, she was one of the strongest women he knew.

His large hands covered her breasts, feeling their weight as his thumb rubbed over her nipples. Pebbled and hardened, he had to taste one. Dipping his head, he captured a nipple in his mouth, sucking it in deeply. One hand slid to her back to support her, and the other hand slipped down the back of her bikini bottoms, tugging them down.

As his mouth devoured her nipple, Carol felt her weightless body rising in the water as she maneuvered her legs around to get rid of the bikini bottoms. Completely naked in the water, she straddled his body again as she settled on his lap, feeling his erection once again pressing into her body.

Tugging on her nipple gently with his teeth, he eliciting a moan from Carol as she threw her head back, eyes tightly closed. He moved his free hand down to her folds, fondling her clit. She settled down slowly on his cock, gradually taking him entirely into her waiting body. His head tilted back as he looked up to the heavens for a moment as the delicious feel of her surrounding him tightly wrestled with his control. Wanting to pound up into her, he forced himself to let her take it at her pace. With her hands on his shoulders, she lifted herself up and down, slowly at first then faster as the sparks between her breasts and her core began building.

Tom watched her, fascinated as the emotions danced across her face. Her eyes were closed, a smile curved her lips. She began to pant as she came to the edge, moving faster and faster.

Crying out his name as her eyes sought his, she powered through her orgasm, fingers grasping at his arms. As she slowed down, Tom placed his hands on her hips and took control. Lifting her slightly, he used his hips to continually thrust up, giving in to the desire to bury himself as deeply as he could. Pounding, he held her lightweight body, almost afraid of bruising her hips from holding on too tightly. Finally, with his last few thrusts, he threw his head back and roared as his release came and he emptied himself into her.

"You okay?" he asked, his voice rough.

"Mmmm," was the only answer that came in return. Carol buried her face in his neck as he stood and carried her out of the tub.

Aware of her nudity, he bent and grabbed a towel to hold over her ass since her front was completely plastered against his chest. The walk to the back door was only a few feet and he quickly had her inside, where he carried her to the bedroom. Not wanting her to chill, he deposited her gently on his bed, pulling the covers up.

"Gonna lock up, Angel. Stay here and stay warm. I'll be back in just a few minutes."

She looked up through her satisfied haze, smiling as he turned and left the room. I could stare at that ass forever. Giggling to herself, she let the warmth of the hot tub sex and bed covers lull her to sleep. Later, she felt the bed move and her body was pulled over against his hard front. Snuggling deeper, she drifted back to sleep, unaware of his tight hold on her, but instinctively knowing she was safe in his arms.

Chapter 19

E arly Thanksgiving morning found Carol in the kitchen making a sweet potato casserole. Laurie stumbled from the bedroom rubbing her eyes, staring at Carol, who was already dressed.

"What are you doing up so early?" Laurie asked.

Carol whirled around, immediately contrite. "I'm so sorry. Did I wake you? Did I make too much noise?"

Laurie walked over, embracing Carol in a hug. "Honey, calm down. No, you did not wake me and no, you were not making too much noise. But you're definitely jazzed up about today. Are you nervous?"

"Laurie, don't you remember how stressed you were when you first had dinner with Rob's parents? You had every outfit in your closet tossed all over your room!"

Laughing, Laurie agreed. "Yeah, you're right. I guess I keep thinking about today just being with friends and family, having Thanksgiving meal. But for you, it is meeting Tom's parents for the first time." She looked at Carol's face, seeing the doubt and concern. "Carol, you have nothing to worry about. From everything I've heard, Tom's parents are great. They're just like Bernie and Mac are to me."

"I'm sure they are nice. I just...I just... well, it's just stressful." Carol looked over at the casserole sitting on the stove.

Laurie quietly asked, "Are you going to be okay?"

Looking into Laurie's face, Carol felt the warm emotion flow over her, knowing that she had real friends who were concerned. Smiling, she returned Laurie's hug. "Yeah. I'm going to be fine. I hope they like me, but as long as I'm happy with who I'm, then right now, that is all that matters."

Just then the doorbell rang, and Laurie ran to answer it. Swinging the door open wide, she was greeted with a wall of gorgeous. "Rob," she yelled, jumping into his arms, wrapping her legs around his waist.

Rob greeted her enthusiastically, carrying her down the hall toward her bedroom so she could get ready.

Carol waved at them as they walked by, then

turned her attention to the man left standing at the door. Her heart caught in her throat as she stared at him. Her eyes traveled from his neatly trimmed blond hair, strong jaw, navy sweater pulled tightly over his muscular chest and arms, down to his trim waist and jean clad thighs. As her eyes made it down to his cowboy boots, she realized she was holding her breath. *I can't believe all this man is mine.* Eyes traveling back, they landed on his eyes and she saw that he was doing his own perusing.

Tom stood still, seeing her scan him from head to toe and masculine pride had him noticing the flush on her face as she unconsciously licked her lips. He stared at her lips momentarily, finding the blood rushing from his head downward as he envisioned those luscious lips around his dick.

"Carol, you keep staring at me like I'm on the Thanksgiving menu, and we're never gonna get to the McDonalds' house."

Smiling, Carol turned back to the stove to pack up her casserole.

Behind her, Tom was doing his own devouring. Carol's blonde tresses were tucked behind her ears and flowing across her shoulders, framing her angelic face. Her deep green tunic sweater set off her hair and eyes. Her toned legs, covered in black leggings paired with boots. The leggings cupped her ass and Tom found his blood rushing back to his dick again. *Stop looking. Think of anything besides her ass.* He knew she was nervous about meeting his parents, and the last thing he wanted to do was embarrass her by walking in with a hard-on.

Carol, with the casserole in her hands, turned around and lifted her eyebrow. "Staring at my ass, Mr. Rivers?"

Smirking, he crossed the room in two long steps and took the casserole from her. Cocking out his elbow for her to take, he drawled, "Come on, darlin'. Let's get to this shindig."

Carol slipped her small hand through his arm as they headed out of the door. Tom put the casserole in a box in the space behind their seats then settled Carol into his truck.

"Honey, I could have just held the dish in my lap," she said.

Tom shook his head as he slid into the driver's seat. "Not taking a chance that a sudden stop could have that hot dish burn you."

He backed out of the parking lot and started driving down the road. Looking over at his beautiful girl, he asked, "What are you smilin' about?"

Carol shifted in her seat so that she was facing him. "I was just thinking about how you make me feel safe. I have never had anyone who made me feel that way. You're always making sure that I'm okay." Looking down at her hands in her lap, she was suddenly overcome with emotion, and a tear escaped down her cheek.

Tom pulled the car to the side of the road and brought it to a stop. "Angel, eyes on me," Tom ordered gently. Her eyes went back to his. Blue eyes gazed at blue eyes. "Whenever you have anything you need to say to me, good or bad, I want you lookin' at me so I can tell exactly how you're."

Another tear slid down Carol's face, but she kept her gaze on him. "Just like now. You want me to look at you so that you can see what's going on with me. I have never had that." She paused for a moment, gathering her thoughts. "I know I'm a strong person. I have had to become one. But you still make me feel safe."

Tom pushed his seat back, unbuckled her seatbelt, then leaned over to grab her. Hauling her over the console, he planted her in his lap. Face to face. Eyes to eyes. "Carol, you're so strong. You overcame your parent's shit, became your own person, have your own career. But I'll always take care of you. You're mine just like I'm yours. Mine to care for. Mine to love.

For a man like me, that's just how it's done, babe."

As he spoke, she leaned closer and closer until his final words were said against her lips. Moving in the rest of the way, she gently moved her lips over his. The kiss told of fears that had been faced, wounds that had been healed, futures that had been rewritten. Soft. Gentle. Slow. The kind of kiss that takes your heart and gives it out, trusting the other person to hold it close.

The loud sound of honking startled them both, jerking them apart. Looking up, they saw Rob's truck pull by them with Rob and Laurie laughing and waving.

"I feel just like a teenager that got caught parking," Carol laughed, as she climbed back over to her side of the truck.

Tom stretched his legs as he adjusted his swollen dick once again. "Damn, this day so far is one cock-blocker after another." Looking back over at her, he asked, "You okay?"

Smiling, she nodded. "Yeah. Let's go meet your parents."

It did not take Carol long to realize that she had been worried for nothing. Tom's parents were very much like Rob's parents, Bernie, and Mac. Easy going. Down to earth. Friendly. And seemed very much taken with her.

As they pulled into the crowded driveway at the MacDonald's home, Tom warned Carol to stay in the truck until he came around to get her. As he lifted her from her seat and set her gently on the ground, they could hear the sounds of running feet and the call of, "Tom, Tom." He turned just in time to catch his mother rushing into his arms. Mrs. Rivers was tall, thin, blonde and looked much younger than her years. Before she could let her son go, Mr. Rivers grabbed his son and wife in his embrace. An older version of Tom, Carol could easily see where Tom got his looks.

She stood to the side for a moment letting Tom have his greeting with his parents, awed at the familiarity and openness of it. She almost giggled trying to imagine her mother running across a yard. *Nope. Never happen.*

Tom disentangled himself from his parents, stepping back to Carol, drawing her close to him. "Mom, Dad, I would like you to meet my girlfriend, Carol Fletcher. Carol, these are my parents, Charles and Nancy Rivers."

Carol moved her arm up to shake their hands when she was suddenly engulfed in a massive hug by first his mother, and then his father joined in.

"Oh my dear, we have been dying to meet you. Tom has told us so much about you, and we're just so thrilled to finally be able to meet this wonderful woman we keep hearing about."

"Didn't think my Tom would ever settle down," Charles said, "but one look at you, and I can see why my son is off the market."

"Mom, Dad," Tom admonished, gently pulling Carol back into his embrace. Tucking her safely into his side with his arm protectively around her, he quickly looked down to see how she was handling the attention.

Carol's smile lit up his heart. She was absolutely beaming. "It's so nice to meet you, Mr. and Mrs. Rivers."

Tom's handsome father beamed down at the angelic woman tucked into his son's embrace. "Oh, none of that. We insist you call us Charles and Nancy."

"At least, until mom and dad will work," Tom's mother added.

"Mom!" Tom interjected, not wanting her to scare Carol off.

Laughing, Nancy just looped her arm through Carol's, pulling her away from Tom. "Well, a mom can hope, right?" The two women walked arm in arm toward the big house.

"She'll be fine, son," Charles said. "Your mom will charm her socks off, just like she does everyone." Seeing Tom's gaze following the angelic creature walking with his wife, he added, "But are you going to be fine? Looks like you're smitten."

Tom looked back over at his dad. "Smitten? Who says smitten any more, dad?"

Charles chuckled as he slapped Tom on the back. "Don't mind being old fashioned, son. Nothing's wrong with a man being smitten. I have been smitten with your mother for thirty-five years now."

Tom looked back as his mom and Carol entered the MacDonald's house. "Yeah, dad, I guess I'm smitten. From the moment I looked at that face, she is all I see. I see that face wherever I go. Even when she's not with me, I can just feel her."

Charles watched his son reach up and rub his chest, right over his heart, and not even realize he was doing it. "So, what are you gonna do about that, son?"

Tom's eyes snapped back over to his father's face in question.

Charles continued, "You gonna waste time or you gonna put a ring on that girl's finger?

Make it permanent?"

"Dad, we've only been dating since last summer."

"So? You love her? You want to spend the rest of your life with her? You want to be with her always? You want children with her?"

Tom continued to rub his chest over his heart as his father spoke. Nodding slowly, he answered, "Yeah. Yeah, I do."

"Well then, I think you have your answer. I have lived a good life son, with a good woman. Want that for you too."

Smiling, Tom just nodded again as the two men followed the women into the house.

ॐ

The Thanksgiving meal at the McDonald's was nothing like Carol had ever experienced. Growing up, holiday meals were very formal events with no fun involved at all. Here, Bernie and Mac invited everyone they could think of to celebrate with them. They had converted an old barn on their property to a large family rec room that could be used to host large events. Several picnic tables were pushed together, along with some folding tables and chairs to make seating for everyone.

Rob and his dad Mac, along with Roger, Bill,

and Jake, set up most of the heavy food items. Bernie provided the cakes and bread, while Bill and Wendy brought the beer and wine. Jake's mother, Mary, took care of the turkeys. Laurie, Carol, and Nancy brought side dishes. Rob's teenage sister, Suzy, helped her mom while secretively keeping an eye on Wendy's teenage son, Brad, as he helped his dad. Bernie and Mac always invited several single firemen and policemen who did not have family in the area to join them, so the group was large and lively.

Carol was so at ease during the meal. She listened to stories of Tom, Jake, and Rob growing up and playing football together. She watched the simple camaraderie between Bernie, Mac, Charles, Nancy, and Mary, knowing they had years of shared memories as neighbors with three little boys to raise. Everyone included her in their conversations, especially wanting to know the story of how they met when Tom was hit with the car.

During it all, Carol found herself eating the food without once counting calories or worrying about how much she was eating. She enjoyed the taste of the food, something she realized she hadn't done in a long time.

Looking around the table, she was suddenly struck with the realization that this was what she wanted and what she had missed. *Friends. Family. Laughter. Joy with others. Comfort. Sharing good times as well as heartbreak. Acceptance.* She spared a glance sideways at Tom's handsome face. *Desire. Love. Forever.*

Tom had been watching Carol throughout the meal without her noticing. He saw the ease of her laughter, the way she ate without fear. He saw the smiles she bestowed on everyone around as she listened to their stories and joined in with tales of her own. His hand found its way up to his chest rubbing over his heart. As he looked around, he saw his dad staring at him, smiling. Smiling back, Tom just nodded. *I have called her mine. It's time to make it real.*

As the meal came to a close, the women took the leftovers to the kitchen while the men began taking down the table and chairs. Rob walked over to Tom asking, "Hate to bring up a sore subject, but has anything else recently happened to Carol?"

Sighing, Tom answered, "Not since the running incident. She has convinced herself that it was a single incident, having nothing to do with the notes or flowers, but Jake and I aren't convinced."

Jake agreed saying, "Don't believe in coincidences. It's almost like someone's just trying to let her know they're around. Not too often, not to have her totally scared, but just enough to throw her off balance."

Charles and Mac joined in the conversation, wanting to know what was going on. Tom explained, then added, "The trouble is, we've got no leads. The flower delivery guy took special precautions to keep his face from the cameras. The note on the car could have been anyone, and the runner was definitely not who we thought."

"Who do you think is behind this, son?" Charles asked Tom, concern on his face.

"Thought it was the brother of a criminal she treated at the hospital. He got taken with her, and it seemed inappropriate. I actually want it to be him, 'cause I'd be able to get my hands on him. Gotta admit, she has a slimy ex-boyfriend from years ago that her parents keep pushing on her even now. Don't trust that slick piece of shit. But got nothin' to even go looking at him right now, and I don't know that he'd risk his cushy career."

By this time, the women had returned to the barn looking for the men, who quickly changed the subject. Hugs, thank you's, and goodbyes were said all around. Rob and Laurie were going to stay for a while with Bernie and Mac, and

Tom's parents were heading back to his house.

Nancy turned to Carol as they were walking toward their cars. "I hope you will come over as well. I really want more time to get to know you."

"I don't want to intrude, Nancy. You don't get to see Tom very much anymore, and I want you to have plenty of time with him," Carol answered.

"Oh my dear, we'll have plenty of time with Tom. I know you're now a very important person in his life, and I want us all to have time together. Please say you'll come back to the house with us," Nancy pleaded. "Plus you'll be doing me a huge favor. You'll give me someone to talk to while the men pile up on the couch and watch football all afternoon!"

Laughing, Carol agreed, "I would love to." Glancing behind her, she saw Tom walking with his dad a few feet back. Catching his grin, she returned his smile. In two strides, Tom caught up to her, grabbing her hand, linking their fingers.

"We'll meet you back at the house, mom," he assured. Getting Carol settled into his truck, he leaned in before closing her door. "You okay with all this? I want you to be comfortable."

Carol placed her hands on either side of

Tom's face, feeling his stubble beneath her fingertips. Pulling him in for a kiss, she confessed, "I have never had a day like this ever. I have never been with such an enormous crowd of people who all genuinely liked each other. Even last year, Sofia had me to her house for Thanksgiving so I wouldn't be alone, but her siblings all hate each other, so it was awful. But this, Tom. This was the most amazing meal I have ever had. And your parents are... everything I could have ever hoped they would be. You're very lucky you know."

With that, she pulled him in for a kiss, molding her lips to his. Starting out soft and slow, she quickly felt when Tom's desire took over.

He slid his tongue inside, dancing with her tongue, exploring the mouth that he knew so well. Sucking on her tongue, he captured her moan in his mouth, feeling his dick swelling uncomfortably in his jeans. Pulling back, he stared into her eyes. *Yep, time to make this official.*

"Let's go back to my place and visit with my parents for a while. Then we'll head to your apartment. Rob and Laurie will be at his place tonight." He leaned back in for a chaste kiss. "So tonight, we'll continue this. And you will feel all of me, babe, buried deep in you. That's a promise."

Carol felt the loss immediately as he pulled back again and closed the truck door. She noticed him discreetly adjusting his dick in his jeans as he rounded the front of the truck. Smiling to herself, she leaned back, ready for the day to continue at Tom's house with his parents.

Tom and his father did watch football until they both fell asleep on the couch while she and Nancy continued to get to know each other. After a while, Nancy also drifted off to sleep in the easy chair. Carol, not feeling sleepy, stepped out onto the front porch and sat on the swing. The late November day was still sunny, but cool. The warmth of the afternoon sun fell on the porch, so she was very comfortable with her sweater and using her foot, she pushed herself gently in the swing, allowing her thoughts to wander.

Thinking back to the lessons learned in her many counseling sessions, she thought about the day and began to put it in perspective. She knew that she had never had actual acceptance from her parents, simply because she did not fit the image of the daughter that they wanted. And that colored everything she thought about herself. *Never good enough. Never pretty enough. Never clever enough. Never thin enough. Not the right career. Not the right path.*

In comparison, she thought about the events of the day. *Friends who accepted her. Friends who enjoyed being with her. Tom's parents accepting her. Tom's love.* Smiling, she brought her legs up on the swing and wrapped her arms around them. Leaning her head back so that the fall sun fell directly on her face, she felt its warmth seep into the crevices that she tried to hide. The cracks that never seemed filled. *I'm really okay. Who I'm and what I'm, is actually good,* she admitted to herself.

Tom had risen from his nap on the sofa and went in search of Carol. Hearing the porch swing creak, he looked out of the window at her. Beautiful face turned up toward the afternoon sun, eyes closed, a smile on her face. The sunlight on her blonde hair created a halo effect as he stood staring at this tiny beauty that he loved. He saw everything. *Beauty. Fragility. Strength.*

Tom walked through the front door, the sound had her opening her eyes as she turned her face toward his. Her smile grew wider, and its warmth penetrated his soul more than the afternoon sun. He sat down on the swing, pulling her back into his chest, wrapping his arms tightly around her in a cocoon of protection.

Twisting her head, she looked up into his face. Blue eyes gazing at blue eyes. Tom touched his mouth to hers. Keeping it light, this time, the kiss was more of a promise between two souls.

Pulling away, she leaned her face against his chest, as the sun continued its path down toward the trees across the road. "I hear your heartbeat," she whispered.

"It beats for you," was the familiar reply.

Chapter 20

Tom and Carol arrived at her apartment late that evening, having spent more time with Tom's parents. Charles and Nancy were leaving the next day, but since Carol was working, she said her goodbyes when they left.

Barely making it in, Tom rounded on her pushing her gently up against the door. Sealing his mouth over hers, he took command of the kiss. Not gentle. Not soft. This kiss was demanding and unyielding. His tongue invaded her mouth, searching every crevice, tangling with her tongue, dueling for dominance. He leaned his massive body in, touching every inch of the front of hers, chest to knees.

Sliding his hand under her sweater, it continued its upward path, coming to rest on her breast. Using his other hand under her ass, he lifted her easily and she wrapped her legs around his waist. His swollen cock, which had been pressing into her stomach, was now deliciously pressing into her aching folds.

Capturing her moans in his mouths, he continued to devour her lips. Pushing her back against the door and lifting his leg slightly so that she was seated on him, he continued to fondle her breasts then pulled her sweater up and over her head. Lifting her arms only long enough to have the sweater pass, she immediately reached back to him, clutching his shoulders as though she were hanging on for her life.

Tom pulled the tops of her bra cups down, freeing her breasts. He hoisted her a little higher so that her breasts were at his face level, and he continued his assault on them with his mouth. Sucking first one nipple in and then moving to the other, he felt her begin to move her crotch against his leg, trying to create the friction that she needed.

Lowering his leg, he settled her feet back down on the floor so that he could divest himself of his shirt. Jerking it off, he leaned back, in pressing her against the door once more, recapturing her mouth with his. This time, flesh against flesh, breasts against chest. *Jesus, she feels so good.*

His hands went to the top of her jeans, but her hands were already there. She broke the kiss long enough to slide her pants down and pull her boots off. Before moving in for another kiss, he stopped for a moment just to stare at the naked beauty presented in front of him. He had seen many naked women's bodies over the years, but none of them came to mind. He could not recall their features, their faces, their shapes. All he could see in his mind was the angelic perfection that was standing in front of him, staring at him with her big blue eyes. Eyes that were not just shining with lust, but with love.

Her hands moved quickly to the button of his jeans. Chuckling, he allowed her to slide the zipper down over his impressive cock. "In a hurry, babe?"

Carol's sparkling eyes looked up to his. "Yeah," she whispered. "Aren't you?"

Shoving his jeans and boots off quickly, he stood in front of her just as naked, his cock jutting out toward her. He saw her look down and watched as she sucked her lips in momentarily before licking them. His cock twitched as though anxious to be seated in her. Seeing her eyes come back up to his, he laughed. "It's got a mind of its own and right now, it knows what it wants."

Picking her back up, she wrapped her legs around his waist again, this time her sex directly on his dick. Wanting to make sure she was ready, he slid his finger into her wet folds, moving it deeper and deeper, looking for just the right spot to make her scream. "So damn tight, babe. So Goddamn wet."

Carol could feel the pressure building, knowing that she was close. She knew she could have come just dry humping his jean clad leg, but the feel of his fingers deep inside of her, tweaking just the right spot was making her crazy. She felt him suck her nipple into his mouth, biting down just enough to give a sharp pain then smoothing it with his tongue. That was all it took as she felt her inner muscles clamping down on his fingers as the orgasm washed over her.

Tom looked at the beauty in his arms. Head thrown back against the door in ecstasy, eyes tightly shut, and that smile. *Jesus, I'd walk through hell to see that smile every day.*

Placing his aching cock at her entrance he rasped, "Ready, Angel?" A nod was all the answer he received and all the answer he needed. Her body impaled on his cock, balls deep, he began thrusting. One hand under her ass for support, the other pressed against the door next to her head. Thrust after thrust, he slid in and out of her wet core, the friction nearly taking him over the edge quickly. Forcing his mind to hold back, he wanted her to come again.

Growling, "Mouth," Tom sealed his lips over hers when she brought her mouth back to his. Deep. Demanding. His tongue mimicking the movements of his cock.

Carol felt the pressure building again. The feeling of trying to reach the finish line of a race, knowing that crossing the end would bring the most incredible euphoria. Closer and closer she came. Feeling Tom's hand move between them and tweak her clit was all it took. She finished the race with the feeling of shattering into a million pieces. Shouting out his name, she threw her head back against the door as her inner walls grabbed at his cock.

The feeling of his cock being milked by her sex was all it took for Tom to lose control. His head reared back too as he powered through his orgasm. Neck muscles straining, face red and tight, he felt himself empty into her waiting body. *Never. Never have I come that hard.*

As his lust-filled mind began to clear, he lowered her body to the ground, allowing her legs to steady underneath her. Keeping his large hands on her tiny waist, he leaned over looking into her eyes. "Are you okay? I didn't hurt you did I?" Guilt at the pounding his large body gave to her small one filled him now that his lust was sated.

Smiling up at him, she reached up to cup his face. "I'm fine, Tom. Better than fine, in fact. I'm great."

Pulling back, he reached down to scoop her up in his arms. "Let me take care of you, babe. I'll run the shower."

Just then, her cell phone chimed, showing a message coming through. "You start the shower honey, and I'll check my phone. It might be Laurie, and I don't want any surprises if she has decided to come back here tonight."

Setting her back down on her feet, he gave her a quick kiss before heading back to the bathroom.

Carol walked over to her purse and pulled her phone out. Not recognizing the number, she opened the text.

There, next to a grainy picture of Tom with her against the door of her apartment, was a message.

He has you now, but you should be mine.
You will be mine.

Carol screamed for Tom as she dropped to the floor to get out of sight from the window. Tom came running back into the room to hear her scream, "Get down, get down. He's out there."

Tom had no idea what she was talking about, but he stooped down to gather her shaking form in his arms. "What the hell is happening? Who's out there?"

She shoved the phone in his hands and watched as he looked at the picture and text. The change in his face was frightening. The fury began to pour off of him as he stood and quickly crossed to the door. Throwing on his jeans, he grabbed his cell from his pocket.

"Gotta situation. Need you now, and make it official. At Carol's. Call Rob and tell him to get Laurie here too." With that, he hung up then looked down at the naked, frightened, crouching woman still huddled on the floor. He hurried to the window and pulled the blinds down, inwardly cursing himself that he hadn't thought to close the blinds before taking her up against the door, even if they were in a third-floor apartment. Once the blinds were closed, he crossed back over, gathering her in his arms.

"I know you're scared. Gonna take care of this and someone's gonna pay dearly for this shit. Got Jake and the police coming so we need to get you dressed. Can you do that for me?" Tom recognized the signs of shock, as her face just stared at his momentarily. Pulling her body in closer, he stood with her in his arms, walking back to the bedroom. Placing her on the bed, he helped her into a robe.

Hearing knocking on the door, Tom leaned down to kiss the top of her head. "Be right back, sweetheart."

Opening the door, he let in Jake, followed quickly by Rob and Laurie. "Laurie, she's in the bedroom. She needs you but don't question her right now. Just help her get dressed."

Laurie ran back to Carol's room and disappeared inside.

Tom turned and explained quickly what happened, showing them the text. Jake cursed as he glanced from the window to the door. Turning to Rob, he growled, "I'm heading outside with a couple of patrolmen. Gonna secure the area and see if I can determine where the bastard was standing."

Rob went over and reopened the blinds. Turning back to Tom, he lifted his eyebrow in question. "You're not going down there?"

"Can't. I want this official. I want the bastard, so that means I can't investigate. I gotta let Jake take over so that when we do get the asshole, we can nail his ass." Turning away, he shouted, "Fuck!"

"Tom, this isn't your fault. Some sick asshole is trying to get to Carol – that is not on you, man."

"Not on me? Rob, I took the girl I love, the woman I'm supposed to protect, up against the front door, not even lookin' to see that the blinds were up." Tom threw his head back in frustration. "Jesus, Rob. What have I done?"

Rob stalked across the room in a couple of steps, stopping directly in front of his longtime friend. Putting his hands on Tom's shoulders, he got right in Tom's line of vision. "Tom. This. Is. Not. On. You. You did nothing wrong. You did nothin' that any of us hasn't done at one time or another. This is all on the asshole that's after her. This is all on him."

By this time Jake had walked back into the room, hearing what Rob was saying and knowing how Tom was beating himself up over the situation.

Tom looked into Jake's face, saying, "Jake, we knew this was gonna escalate. Why the hell didn't I do more to find him?"

Jake joined Rob and Tom in the living room. "Tom, up to now, there's not much to go on. But now we got her cell phone, and we can try to find out where the message came from. I have got someone working on it right now."

The men grew quiet as Laurie and Carol re-entered the room. Tom crossed over to Carol, gathering her in his arms. Gently leading her to the sofa, he sat and then pulled her down on his lap determined to cradle her in safety. He noticed she seemed calmer and more in control than earlier.

Jake sat down on the other side of the couch while Rob and Laurie took the loveseat. Jake began his questions, gently so as not to upset her, but pleased when it appeared that Carol was in control of her emotions.

"Carol honey, I need to ask you some questions, and I need you to think carefully about your answers. Don't hold anything back." She nodded and he began. "Besides Bert, who else has shown an interest in you? Could be at work, could have seemed like a joke. Could have seemed innocent."

Licking her lips, she answered, "Well you know about Bert. But I haven't seen him in a long time, so I can't imagine it is him."

Shaking his head, Jake said, "Carol, you can't analyze. You can't put rational thoughts onto someone who may be irrational. Some people sit on infatuations for years before acting on them."

"Jake, honestly, I'm a boring person. I do work at a hospital, and there have been lots of grateful patients over the years, but no one that ever made me feel weird." Turning her head to look at Tom, she saw the tightness in his jaw and knew that he hated taking a subordinate role in this. Sighing deeply, she turned back to Jake.

"I know Tom doesn't trust Ronald." Seeing Jake writing his name down, she continued. "Ronald Harriston. His dad and my dad are law partners. They assumed I would go into law, marry Ronald, and continue their empire. Ronald was my escort when I was a teenager and first into college. That was always arranged by our parents because it looked good. Fit their image and all that. I suppose we even dated, per se, but he was never that into me. Don't get me wrong, he wanted us to be together because that would solidify his dynasty, but we were never...um..." Feeling Tom's fingers tightening on her, she twisted in his arms, looking directly into his face.

"Tom, you don't get to be jealous. You set me straight about the women you had been with, so just deal with this!"

Rob and Jake chuckled, seeing their friend put in his place by his tiny sprite of a girlfriend.

Tom clenched his jaw so tightly for a moment he was sure his teeth would crack.

Looking into Carol's eyes, he realized she was right. He'd been with a helluva lot of women and had a lot of experience before meeting Carol, so he had no right to get upset at her past. *But shit! I hate thinking of anyone with her but me.*

Breathing deeply, he just nodded for her to continue.

Carol stroking Tom's arm gently, turned back to Jake. "Ronald and I were never sexually active. He always said that he wanted to wait until we were married, but I knew he had other women. By the time I found out, I'd changed my major to nursing and knew I wasn't going to marry Ronald, so I just didn't care. He was angry when I broke it off with him, but he never pursued me. I moved to Fairfield after college and didn't even see him until a couple of months ago."

Looking back at Tom, she questioned, "Honey, why would you even suspect Ronald? What could he possibly gain?"

Tom answered, "Lots of things. He proves to you that your police boyfriend can't protect you, you might come back to him. You get scared of being in Fairfield, you might run back to your parents. Maybe his becoming partner in the firm is dependent on getting you back. He certainly cozied up with your mother's plans to get with him at the dinner. Who the hell knows, babe. Maybe he simply got tired of waiting and decided to up his game?"

Jake nodded. "He's right, Carol. He is definitely a suspect, and we're gonna check him out, although I doubt he does his own dirty work. If it is him, he probably hires it out." Looking at her again, he continued, "Anyone else?"

The room grew silent as Carol sat very still. It was apparent that she wasn't thinking but that she was holding back.

"Angel," came a growl from behind her. "What are you not sayin'?"

Carol licked her lips again, trying to figure out how to express her concerns.

Jake, knowing how to coax a witness, just said, "Carol, any information you give us will just help us keep you safe. Now that the person knows where you live and what apartment you live in, you need to look at all possibilities."

Carol just shook her head. "But it seems so silly."

"Doesn't matter, Carol," Jake prodded.

"Well, there's a doctor at the hospital that has liked me for a while," she admitted.

Tom's hands jerked again, and she could feel the growl deep in his chest before it came roaring out. "What the hell are you talking about?"

"Tom, shut the hell up. Give her a chance to speak," Jake said.

Tom glared at him but knew he was right. *Who the hell was she talking about?*

"Well, there's a doctor that I have worked with for about a year. He asked me out a couple of times, but I was never interested. I tried to let him down easy, so I just said that I didn't date people from work. Anyway, that worked for a while, but he was a bit persistent."

"Define persistent," Tom rumbled.

Glaring at Tom, she then turned her attention back to Jake. "He would try to eat at the same time that I did. He would walk me to my car occasionally if we got off at the same time."

"So he knows what your car looks like?" Jake pursued.

"Well, yeah. I guess. I never thought about it. But then I park in the hospital employee's lot, so many people see me coming and going."

"Okay," Jake prodded. "What else?"

"Oh, damn," Tom cursed. "He was that prick who tried to get in your examining room when you got hurt."

Sighing deeply, Carol nodded. "His name is Dr. Harry Driscoll. The day that Tom is referring to, he was a bit pushy again, and Tom informed him that I was his girlfriend. Our shifts weren't the same for a long time, but a few weeks back he sat with me for a meal and tried to see if I was available. He wasn't too happy when I said I was with Tom," Carol looked at Jake pleadingly, "but honestly, he's not the sort to do something like tonight."

Jake, still taking notes, looked back up. "What about other friends?"

"I don't really have many friends. I always preferred to be mostly by myself, since I left college. I just…well, it was hard to trust people."

Suddenly wanting to unburden herself to her new friends, she confessed, "Tom already knows, and Laurie probably suspects. You see, I'm bulimic. I have had an eating disorder since I was a pre-teen. I see a therapist, and it's under control, but when I'm stressed and around food, well it is a struggle."

"Stress? With your job?" Jake asked.

"Not that type of stress. I can handle anything that comes in the ER. But personal stress. When I feel out of control. When there are too many people around especially when food is involved."

"But Carol, you seemed fine today at my parent's place," Rob interjected.

Smiling, she looked over at Rob and Laurie. "I know. Wasn't it great? It was the first time that I felt fine with a bunch of new friends and didn't feel like purging afterward." Still beaming at the day's accomplishments, her smile slowly left as she was brought back to the subject at hand.

"That's it, Jake. The only two friends I really have at work are Sofia and Jon."

"Jon?" Jake asked.

"Oh, he's not interested. Well, not that way. He'd be more interested in Tom," she giggled.

Laurie laughed too, and Tom just hung his head.

"That it, Carol?" Jake asked as he snapped his notebook closed.

She nodded and slumped back on Tom's chest, suddenly exhausted.

Recognizing that the adrenaline of the evening had worn off, Tom stood with her in his arms. "I'm gonna settle her in." He carried her down the hall to her room, laying her gently on the bed. "I'm coming right back, sweetheart. Go ahead and get under the covers, and I'll join you as soon as I get rid of everyone." Leaning over to kiss her forehead, he walked back out of the room, closing the door behind him.

Looking at Jake, he asked, "What'd you find

outside?"

Shaking his head, Jake answered, "Nothin' man. Not a Goddamn thing. Not a cigarette butt; the grass is too dry for footprints. Got it cordoned off and guarded overnight. The investigators will take another look in the daylight, but my guess is that this guy is too smart to leave stupid clues."

"A doctor, a lawyer, and a fuckin' criminal's weasely brother. What a collection of suspects."

"Tom, you gotta stay outta this. Let me do my job on this, and you just work the cases piling up on our desks."

Tom nodded his agreement, but he hated it. He wanted to find the one responsible for that picture. He wanted to pound them into the ground until they never threatened Carol again.

Saying goodnight to his friends, he bolted the door behind them. Walking back over to the living room window, he looked out into the darkness. *I'll find you, you bastard. And when I do....*

Closing the blinds, he then walked back to the bedroom. Opening the door gently, he wasn't surprised to see Carol's sleeping form tucked under the covers. Stripping out of his jeans, he slid in next to her. Pulling her body into his, he tucked her back firmly into his front.

Wrapping both arms around her, he willed her to sleep all night peacefully, knowing that sleep was the furthest thing from his mind.

Chapter 21

The next couple of weeks were miserable for Carol. Even the holiday festivities couldn't lift her spirits. The police had questioned Dr. Driscoll about his whereabouts on Thanksgiving evening, and he was furious. His alibi checked out, but Tom still didn't trust him, telling her to stay away from him.

That was difficult since he showed up in the ER after being questioned, threatening to sue for defamation of character and telling her that he was never interested in her but that he had only felt sorry for her.

Sofia and Jon were present during that confrontation. Carol just wanted him to go away, but Sofia wasn't taking the insult lightly. "Oh sure, Dr. Harry. Like she needs your sympathy with Mr. Hot Stuff in his Pants Detective claiming her for his own!"

Sputtering, Dr. Driscoll stalked down the hall away from the trio, while Jon couldn't contain his laughter.

"Guys," Carol admonished, "this isn't funny. He's threatening my job. On top of that, my mother is threatening to disown me because the police questioned Ronald as well."

Jon sobered and asked, "How'd that go?"

Shrugging her shoulders, Carol just answered, "I don't really know. He has an alibi too, but then according to Tom, Ronald wouldn't dirty his hands doing it himself."

Sofia and Jon shared a look over Carol's head. "Honey, I'm worried about you," Jon said. "You need to get out and have some fun! How about we do a night out at Smokey's. We could do it the next time we all have the same night off."

Smiling up at her friends, Carol agreed. "Maybe that would be fun. But there is no way Tom will let me go without him and honestly guys, I wouldn't want to."

"No problem, the more, the merrier!" Sofia claimed.

Just then their pagers went off simultaneously. "Back to work, ladies," Jon called out as they headed back to the ER.

Tom and Jake sat at their desks working several cases. Jake was making it a priority to figure out who was stalking Carol. Tom was talking to his friend from the Richland Police Force about Calvin's case.

"Shane? It's Tom Rivers. Got anything new for me on the Calvin Penski case? He's real close to makin' bail here at his next hearing right after the holidays." The two men talked for several more minutes as Jake made a few more calls trying to get a location on the number that the text came in on Carol's phone.

Hanging up on their calls at about the same time, Tom looked over at his partner saying, "You first."

Sighing, Jake reported, "Looks like it probably came from a disposable cell, and it hasn't been used again. That means the person, or whoever they hired, knows what they are doing."

"Dammit," Tom cursed, running his hand through his hair. "We're getting nowhere, and stalkers tend to escalate. I have got her working days, escorted to and from her car in the lot. Most nights she is either with me at my place or I'm at hers. Won't let her stay alone and honestly, not real happy when it is just her and Laurie there."

Jake looked at his friend, knowing that if their roles were reversed, Tom would do anything to help Jake and his loved one. "I'm not givin' up, man. I'll keep digging."

Tom nodded. "I know you will." Looking down at his notes, he continued. "Okay, for Calvin Penski. Just talked to my friend Shane Douglas."

"Shane? From the Academy?" Jake interrupted. When Tom nodded, Jake added, "I remember him. Real go getter. Real smart. But street smart. Always figured he'd go undercover at some time."

"Yeah, we worked together when I spent a couple of years in Richland before deciding to come back here and keep my parent's house. He's a good cop. Probably will go underground sometime. Anyway, he's working the case pretty carefully, knowing Cal could get out on bail in another couple of weeks. Says if Cal gets out, he'll be right back in Richland and probably dig in deep to keep from being found. They've broken up some prostitution clubs where the girls were drugged, but he is so Goddamn slippery they can't get it pinned to him yet. Shane wants to know if we think the brother is involved."

"Bert?" Jake asked, incredulously. "Hell, Bert couldn't find his way out of a paper bag."

"Shane wondered if it was an act to get everyone to think he was meek."

Jake shook his head. "Naw. Not buyin' it. Bert's not that smart."

"What about being manipulated by his brother?" Tom asked. "Am I so pissed at him trying to connect with Carol that I'm overlooking something?"

"What else does Shane think?" Jake prodded.

Shaking his head, Tom just said, "Not much else now. He's hopin' Cal doesn't make bail, but Shane's ready if he does. He plans on being on his tail the minute Cal gets back in Richland."

∾

One week later, Carol and Laurie were out Christmas shopping. The shops in downtown Fairfield were decorated for the holidays with window displays galore. The weather had turned colder, and light snow had fallen a couple of nights earlier. They watched as people hurried about their shopping, but still shouting out greetings to those they knew.

Stepping carefully over a patch of ice on the sidewalk, Carol grabbed Laurie as she almost slipped.

"We had two broken wrists, a broken leg, and a broken arm yesterday in the ER just from falls on the ice. Don't make it another one," she laughed as she held Laurie up.

"This is a good place to duck into anyway," Laurie said as they neared Bernie's Bakery. Heading inside, the smells of freshly baked bread and cakes assaulted their senses.

"Oh my God, this place smells amazing!" Carol grinned.

Bernie saw the girls as they entered and waved them over to the counter as she came around to greet them. "Laurie, my girl. How are you?" Bernie and Laurie hugged as Carol watched, knowing that Bernie was already considering Laurie to be her daughter-in-law.

Turning next to Carol, Bernie enveloped her as well. "Sit down, sit down and I'll get you all some special coffee and holiday treats." Bustling off, Bernie left them to sit at one of the pink and white tables that lined the wall of the bakery.

Carol looked around at the familiar shop, feeling for the first time in years that she could come in and eat without worrying about the calories. *Free. This feels free.* Smiling, she looked over at Laurie, who had been joined by Suzy, Rob's sister. She was sixteen years old and had the MacDonald's gorgeous genes. Tossing her hair over her shoulder, she casually looked at a group of teenage boys sitting in one of the back booths. Carol recognized Bill and Wendy's son, Brad, as one of the young men. It was evident that Brad and Suzy had eyes for each other while trying not to show it.

Carol thought back to her days in high school and was amazed at how clueless she had been about how much bulimia had ruled her life. Suzy seemed so carefree and happy. Carol smiled indulgently, happy for the young woman.

Suzy headed off to wait on more tables while Carol and Laurie continued their meal.

"So when are you and Tom going to celebrate Christmas?"

Carol, wiping the powdered sugar off of her lips, answered, "We are going to celebrate tonight. I have to work tomorrow on Christmas day so we will exchange gifts at his place this evening." Smiling up at Laurie, she added, "and don't expect me back tonight!"

Laughing, the two women finished their treats and headed back out into the cold.

∾

The night outside was blustery, but inside Tom's living room, the warmth from the fireplace settled in around Carol as she sat next to their little Christmas tree. Tom entered from the kitchen carrying a bottle of wine and a couple of glasses. Smiling up at him, she reached up to take the glasses from him.

"So are you ready for your present?"

Continuing to smile at him, she nodded. She had given Tom his gift before dinner—three tickets to a Washington Redskins game for him, Jake, and Rob. She knew that since they had been dating, his time with his friends had been cut back. So, it only seemed fair to give a gift that he could share with them.

Tom lowered his large frame to the floor next to her in front of the fireplace. The room was lit with only the soft lights from the Christmas tree and the flickering flames of the fire. He looked over at Carol, her beauty taking his breath away. The firelight cast a glow on her porcelain complexion and danced in her large blue eyes. Her blonde tresses caught the lights of the tree, giving her angelic appearance an otherworldly glow. Suddenly nervous, he realized the magnitude of what he was about to do. Nervous? Yes. Fearful? Never.

Maneuvering his body so that he was sitting as close as he could while facing her, he set the wine bottle on the coffee table. She turned her luminescent blue eyes to his, a smile still playing on her lips. All the practiced words flew from his mind. His breath caught in his throat as his heart pounded in his chest. Taking her dainty hand in his much larger one, he realized that the strength of this tiny woman humbled him. He was the one who wanted to protect her but realized that she was the one who saved him.

Lifting her hand to his lips, he softly brushed her knuckles with his kisses. Carol raised her other hand to cup his face, feeling the stubble under her fingertips as she leaned forward to place a gentle kiss on his lips. *Soft. Full of promise. Full of love.*

Leaning back, blue eyes gazed at blue eyes. "Angel, do you remember how we met?"

Her face breaking into a huge smile, she giggled and nodded. "Tom, how could I ever forget seeing you lying on the ground, terrified that you were injured?"

Nodding, he continued, "Carol, I opened my eyes that day in more ways than one. I saw the most beautiful creature leaning over me. The whole world was fuzzy except for your face. I called you an angel, because swear to God, that is what you looked like. That image captured me. Wrapped itself around me. Wouldn't let me go. Everything in my life up to that point lost its importance until I could find you again."

She peered into his face, watching the emotions play across his features. Holding her breath, she reached back over to link her fingers with his, knowing that he needed her strength to say whatever he was trying to say.

"When I finally found you, I discovered that you really were an angel. You care about people with such passion. You're so tiny that I sometimes worry about crushing you and yet you have more strength inside of you than most people I know. I used to call you clueless but realized that you just needed to have someone affirm what was already inside of you. Beauty, intelligence, the heart of an angel."

Sucking in a deep breath, he continued, "I don't want to live without you. I want you with me, every day in every way. I want you to be mine. Mine to hold, cherish, protect and love. And I want to be yours. I want your light to shine on me every day for the rest of my life."

Tears welled in Carol's eyes as she watched the man she loved more than life itself struggle with his emotions. She saw him reach into his pocket and bring out a small jewelry box. Her breath caught in her throat as she began to realize what might be in the box.

Flipping open the lid, Tom held it out to her. Inside was a perfect engagement ring, tiny and delicate. The diamond in the middle of the ring was surrounded by smaller diamonds all around. She watched as his large hands shook as he took the ring out of the box and held it out to her. She lifted her eyes from the ring back up to his expressive face. Blue eyes gazed into blue eyes.

"Carol Fletcher, I don't want to live without you. I need you beside me every day and every night. Will you do me the honor of becoming my wife?"

"Oh, Tom. Yes, yes, yes! I love you so much! I want nothing more than to be with you every day for eternity." Tears streamed down her face as she threw her arms around his neck and felt him pull her in tightly.

Grinning, he gently pushed her back. "Well, let's make this official." He held her hand and slid the perfect ring on her finger.

Carol wiggled her fingers, watching the ring sparkle in the firelight. Her eyes, bright with tears looked back into his face. Grabbing him, she pulled him in for a kiss. The kiss began softly, then quickly burned with passion and love.

Tom pulled her in closer then twisted their bodies so that they were laying together on the rug in front of the fireplace. He took charge of the kiss, his tongue dancing with hers as he explored her mouth, tasting the sweet wine on her lips. Slowly ending the kiss, he pulled her head in tightly to his chest while the other hand slid down to her hips, pulling her in as close as their bodies could be.

Laying there listening to the crackling of the fire, letting their hearts beat in time together, both allowed the emotions of the evening to wash over them.

She lay, tears still sliding down her cheeks, pooling on his shirt. *Safe, accepted, loved.*

He lay, holding her tightly, pressing kisses on the top of her head. *Mine to hold. Mine to care for. Mine to love.*

She listened for a moment to the steady heartbeat of the man who loved her, knowing that somewhere there really was a guardian angel who brought them together.

"I hear your heartbeat," she whispered into the night.

"It beats for you," came the promise.

Chapter 22

C arol and Tom celebrated the news of their engagement with friends and talked with Rob and Laurie about the girls' living arrangements. Tom wanted Carol to move in with him, and Rob thought it was a perfect time for Laurie to move in with him as well.

The next couple of weeks were busy as the girls made arrangements to move out of the apartment. "Can you believe the lease is going to be up right at the time that we decide to move on? No extra payments!" Carol said with glee, filling up boxes with her clothes.

"I know! Thank goodness because Christmas just about wiped me out. I need to save some more money for a while."

"Yeah, I have got the wedding to plan and save for. With Tom's house paid for years ago by his parents, not having to make a rent payment will go a long way for the wedding."

Laurie looked over at her friend, wondering how to ask what was on her mind.

Carol noticed and knew exactly what Laurie was thinking. "You're wondering about my parents, aren't you?"

Laurie laughed and nodded. "Yes, I was. Have you guys talked to them at all?"

"Funny you should ask because we are driving there today to tell them."

Laurie sat down on the bed next to Carol. "How are you with that? How do you think they will respond?"

Looking thoughtful, Carol just shook her head. Sighing deeply and turning to her best friend, seeing the concern in her eyes, she simply said, "I have no idea. I mean it won't go well...certainly not like in the movies where the family all jumps up to congratulate everyone." Laughing ruefully, she continued, "And not even like when we called Tom's parents the other day and I could hear the screaming coming from Tom's phone!"

Wrapping her arms around Carol, Laurie pulled her in for a hug. "I'm sorry, sweetie."

"Oh, don't be. It is what it is. And the most important thing is that they no longer have the power over me to make me doubt myself. I have Tom. I have great friends. I have a great job. And I now have a future with a man I love. If they can't be happy about that, then it is their loss."

Hugging again, the two friends continued to pack until Tom arrived to pick up Carol.

Pulling into the driveway of the Fletcher estate, Tom allowed a moment to envision Carol growing up in the opulence. Everything looked pristine. The lawn, perfectly manicured. The house, palatial. *Cold, unfeeling, no joy.* Glancing to the side, wanting to see her reaction, he noticed her eyes traveling around as though she were seeing it for the first time. "You okay, sweetheart? I won't let anything happen to you, you know?"

Turning her gaze back to his, she smiled. "I know," she replied softly. Reaching out to link her fingers with his, she continued, "Funny, but this place no longer seems to have any hold over me. I don't feel ill…just a little nervous about how this will all go down. But honey," she said, pulling his gaze back to hers. "At the end of the day, I get to go home with the man of my dreams. So whatever their reaction is, it's fine. I'm fine." Inhaling deeply, she glanced back to the house.

The door opened with the butler announcing that they would be received in the family room. Following him, Tom caught Carol rolling her eyes. Smiling, he reached down to link his fingers with hers again. Walking into the family room, he was struck with the difference between this room and the house he grew up in.

The Fletcher's family room was as pristine as the rest of the house. No newspapers or magazines cluttered a coffee table. No TV remotes were seen. In fact, as his eyes quickly scanned the room, there was no TV. There were paintings on the walls, but no family photographs to be seen. The room held no personality. No warmth. No love. His eyes immediately took in Carol's parents sitting formally in two chairs facing the sofa near the massive fireplace. The fireplace that held no fire.

His eyes cut sharply down to Carol, taking a visual pulse of how she was doing. *Not putting up with any shit today. They start something, I'm shuttin' it down.* Her face held a smile that did not reach her eyes, and he could feel the tension radiating off of her body as his hand slid up to her shoulder.

Mr. Fletcher rose from his chair, formerly greeting his daughter. "Carol, you're looking well." Moving forward to shake Tom's hand, he added, "Mr. Rivers."

Carol moved forward to place a kiss on her

father's cheek and then walked over to the chair where her mother sat stiffly, leaning down to kiss her mother's cheek as well.

As she moved back, Tom stepped forward immediately replacing his hand on her shoulder and guided her back toward his embrace. She glanced up at his face smiling, recognizing that he was protecting her. That realization made her smile even more. A real smile. One that reached her eyes and touched his heart.

"Carol. Tom. And what do we owe the pleasure of your company today?" her mother's formal request dripped with sarcasm.

Her father's voice interrupted, "Please, won't you sit down?" He motioned to the sofa across from his chair.

Settling his large frame onto the sofa, Tom wrapped his arm around Carol, giving her his physical support, but hoping that she felt his emotional support as well.

Carol reached over to take his other hand, linking her fingers through his. Together, strong. United. One.

Looking her parents directly in the eyes, Carol spoke softly, but firmly. "Mother, father. We wanted to come by today to tell you that we are formally engaged and plan to marry in May. We, of course, would like your blessing, but will be married regardless."

The momentary silence in the room was deafening. Her mother's eyes cut quickly down to Carol's hand, noting the ring.

"Are you pregnant?" her cool voice asked.

Tom jerked forward, but Carol calmly placed her hand on his leg, giving a little squeeze. "No, mother. I'm not pregnant. We are quite simply in love, want to be together, and have decided not to wait."

Carol's father sat quietly, observing the couple in front of him.

"Well, that certainly isn't enough time to plan a proper wedding. I suppose that's why you're here? To ask for money for the wedding? To ask us to host what should be the event of the season if you were marrying the right kind of man?"

Carol, incensed, answered back. Calmly. Surely. In control. "No, we don't want your money. We simply wanted you to know that your only daughter was getting married. Married, I might say, to precisely the right kind of man. One who doesn't see me as arm-candy. One who doesn't want anything from my parents' position in society. One who sees me for who I am, not what he wants to make me be. Accepts me. Cares for me. Protects me. Treasures me. Loves me. All the things I have never had, ever before."

Standing, she turned to Tom apologetically. "Come on, honey. This was a mistake."

Tom rose from the sofa, more proud of Carol at that moment than he ever could have thought to be. Wrapping his mighty arm around her, he pulled her into his warm embrace. Kissing the top of her head, he hugged her tightly. "This was not a mistake. You came to make an announcement, and you've done that. You came to show your parents that you're happy, and you've done that too. Proud of you, Angel."

With Carol still tucked in his embrace, he looked down at her mother's stunned face and her father's silent expression. "You may not care, but know this. I'll take care of her. She's the most important person in the world to me. She is precious, and I'll always treat her as such."

With that, the two of them walked out of the room, out of the house, drove back to their house, and entered smiling. The small living room, warmly decorated, beckoned them. Carol had added her photographs to the walls along with Tom's. Some of her possessions now mingled with his, creating a home that was theirs. Blended. Together. As One.

Carol, eyes twinkling, ran up the stairs toward the bedroom with Tom right on her heels. Squealing as he caught her, she whirled around in his arms, pulling his face down for a kiss. Passionate. Hard. Wet. Long. Needy. Tongues dueling.

Slowly, the kiss became less desperate. She felt his lips moving gently over hers as though to memorize their shape and feel. Slow. Gentle. Full of promise. Love. Acceptance.

That night, they made love with all the feelings and emotions that the day had brought. Resting in the knowledge that they were truly as one, they worshiped each other's bodies long into the night.

Lying naked, curled tightly together, she drifted off to sleep with her head tucked safely against his broad chest. His arms encircled her, holding her as though she would slip away if he let her go.

"I hear your heartbeat," she said as she slipped into sleep.

"It beats for you," came the promise.

Chapter 23

Tom, on the phone with Shane, was listening to his friend's long, continuous flow of cursing. Holding the phone away from his ear momentarily, he caught Jake's look of irritation, knowing they were all pissed.

"How'n the hell did that judge let that asshole out on bail? If ever there was a fuckin' flight risk, it's Cal Penski. Fuck!"

Tom finally cut in. "Shane, not a damn thing we can do. Just wanted you to know he'll probably be headin' your way. Figure he's not gonna hang out in Fairfield very long, so he'll get back to his business in Richland."

"Can you tail him? Can you keep a man on him?" Shane barked out.

"Legally, no. You know that. But we do know he headed to his mom's house. Got someone watchin' the house to see if anyone suspicious shows up. He's not stupid, though. He's gotta know we are watchin' so he's not gonna try to run his business outta his mom's kitchen."

With Shane's cursing and thanks ringing in his ears, Tom hung up the phone. Resting his elbows on his desk, he rubbed one hand over his face while tossing his cell down.

Jake didn't say anything. He didn't have to. As friends and now partners for several years, they knew each other well enough to know when words weren't necessary. Both were pissed. Both were tired.

The chief walked over, seeing his two best detectives and reading their mood. "Men, you keep working the case with the Richland police. Make it airtight, and when he goes to trial, we'll have him."

Jake looked over at Tom. "You think we can get Bert to keep an eye on him for us. He may be willin' to be an informant if he dislikes his brother so much."

Tom snorted. "You think that weasel's gonna help us out. After I threatened him to stay away from Carol? No way."

Jake's cell rang, and he recognized the PI he put on as a tail for Cal. "Campbell. Got something?"

"Been quiet all morning. Just lettin' you know that Cal and his mom just got in her car. I tailed them, and it looks like they are at the Lo-

Foods grocery store over in the Stop and Shop Center. You want me to keep an eye on their car and tail 'em when they get out?"

"Yeah. Just let me know if they don't go back home. Was Bert with them?"

"Nah. Just Cal and his mom."

"Got it. Thanks." Jake hung up then relayed the conversation to Tom.

Tom nodded then leaned back in his chair, stretching his muscular frame, trying to ease some of the tension out of his body. Looking back down at the stack of files on his desk, he sighed as he and Jake continued working, secure in the knowledge that Cal was being watched.

∾

Carol and Jon were just finishing their shift when Sofia came in. The three friends had not worked simultaneous shifts in several weeks, and Carol found that she missed their company. Sofia passed them in the hallway, saying, "Got here early. I'll meet you in the break room when you're finished."

Jon nodded and waved her on as Carol was coming out of one of the ER examining room. "You done?" he asked her.

Smiling up at him, she said, "Yeah. Kid needed stitches. Fell off the monkey bars at the elementary school. I asked him who his teacher was. Thought it might be Laurie, but it wasn't."

"That's good, though," Jon added. "Laurie's had enough excitement for the year." Earlier the elementary school's kitchen had caught on fire and Laurie had to assist in the rescue of her students.

"Oh my God, yes! I'm so glad this little tyke wasn't in her class. Wasn't a bad cut, but boy, did it bleed! And what a talker. He couldn't hold still long enough for me to numb him, and he talked the whole time. How she deals with twenty-six of those little guys every day – I don't know how she does it!"

Jon laughed as they headed toward the nursing lounge saying, "Yeah, but I bet she says the same thing about our jobs."

Walking into the break room, they saw Sofia sitting with her feet on a chair and drinking flavored water instead of coffee.

"Damn, girl," Jon accused. "You look like you just got off shift, but you haven't even started. Carol and I are the tired ones around here."

"Yeah, well, you slugs don't have two kids at home and another one on the way."

The words hung in the air for a moment before Carol shrieked and launched herself toward

Sofia, grabbing her in a huge hug. "Oh my God, you're pregnant!"

Grinning, Jon walked over putting his arms around both women, joining in the hug.

They all talked for just a few minutes before Sofia had to go on duty. "We'll get together soon," she promised. "I can do virgin drinks at Smokey's. I'll even let you bring Mr. Sexy Ass Dick so I can have some eye candy to drool over!"

Carol blushed once again, knowing she would have another name to warn Tom about as she wrapped Sofia in another embrace, using one hand to pat Sofia's tummy.

Jon walked Carol to her car, making sure it was all clear. Hugging her goodbye, he trotted off to his truck.

Carol was on cloud nine. *Another baby for Sofia. Perfect.* She couldn't help the direction that took her mind, to Tom. The man who stole her heart but gave her back her life. She couldn't help but grin to herself as she settled into her car, remembering how he wouldn't let her be clueless. Glancing in the rear view mirror, she thought, *He helped me see me. I like who looks back at me. I like the image I see.*

A tapping on her car window snapped Carol out of her musings. Jumping, she turned her head around sharply to see Bert standing next to her car. He appeared nervous and stepped back to give her some space.

"Bert, what do you want?" she asked sharply, hating the tone of her voice. *Ugh, Tom has me suspicious of everyone around.*

"Miss Carol, I'm so sorry to disturb you. I know your boyfriend don't want me around, but I don't know who else to ask for," Bert said, anxiously glancing around.

Lordy, he's looking around to see if Tom is going to jump out and arrest him. Carol rolled down her window, feeling safe in the daylight. "Bert, what do you need?"

"It's momma. She's doing poorly today and refuses to go to the doctor. She doesn't have good insurance, doesn't have a family doctor, and refuses to go into the hospital. You're the only nurse I know, and I just hoped you would come, real quick like, and check her out. I promise if you think she needs help, I'll force her to go in myself."

"Is she at home?" Carol asked, not wanting to drive to Bert's house alone.

"Oh, no. I got her over there in my car. She just don't want to go in, but I saw you and thought that you could help. Can you come over, please?" he begged, twisting his hands together.

Sighing, Carol rolled up her window and got out of the car. "Okay, Bert. I'll take a look at her, but if she is really that sick, I'll definitely be insisting that she go into the hospital. And they take patients without insurance, so she doesn't have to worry about that."

"Oh, Miss Carol. Thank you so much," Bert said, moving away to show her to his car. They walked from the employee parking lot to the next lot over, for visitors. Bert led her to an old green car that had seen better days. Opening the back door, he leaned in saying, "Momma. I have got a real nice nurse here to take a look at you. She's a friend, and her name is Carol. So, momma, you let her check you out, okay?"

Bert's mother was wrapped in a blanket in the back seat, and as he moved out of the door frame, Carol leaned in. "Mrs. Penski, my name is Carol and I'm a nurse here. I just want to see how you're feeling." Carol moved forward and placed her hands on the blanket to pull it back when she quickly realized that there was nothing but a pillow under the blanket.

"Bert, what are—" Carol felt a sting in her hip as she was turning to see what game Bert was playing. Then...blackness.

Jake answered his cell when the PI called back. "Yeah?"

"Man, you're not gonna like this. Bastard gave me the slip."

"How the hell did he do that?" Jake growled.

"Sat here watchin' their car when momma came out by herself with some groceries and she drove off. Cal must have planned this, slipped out the back and had a ride waiting."

"Follow her. Keep an eye on the house. Call if you see him."

Jake was explaining to Tom what the situation was with Cal when Tom's phone rang.

Tom looked down as he answered, seeing Laurie's number on the screen. "Hey Laurie, what's up?"

"Tom, I'm so sorry to call you at work, but I just wanted to know if you have heard from Carol? She got off work an hour ago, and we were supposed to meet up at Bernie's, but she never showed. She's also not answering her phone. I just...well, it's silly, but I was just worried."

Tom, feeling the cold prickle of fear slide down his back, tried to keep his voice calm. "I haven't heard from her. I'll check it out. Let me

know if you get ahold of her. Thanks, Laurie."
Hanging up, he relayed the information to Jake,
and they rose at the same time, grabbing their
jackets on their way out of the door.

Arriving at the hospital parking lot, Tom
immediately saw Carol's car. Looking in, he saw
her purse lying on the passenger seat. The cold
prickle now became a cold rush as the fear
washed over him.

"Security cameras," Jake growled while Tom
called Jon.

They hurried into the hospital, finding Marcus. He admitted that he saw Carol make it to
her car, but he did not see her drive away. Jake
filled in Marcus with their concerns and he
called the head of security. Marcus let them in
the security office, where the security adminis-
trator was already pulling up the security tapes.

Tom watched, dread filling his heart as he
saw Bert approach Carol's car. *No, angel. No.
Don't get out of your car.* The voices in his head
warred with what his eyes were watching. He
saw Carol walk away with Bert in the direction
of another parking lot. Growling, "Next camera," he ordered the security admin, as the man
was already pulling the next camera up on their
screen.

They watched in silence as Carol and Bert

approached his car and opened the door to the back. Tom saw Carol lean in, then what he saw next stopped his heart. "Noooo, Goddamn it!" he roared as they saw Bert's hand move forward, jabbing toward Carol's hip. She immediately slumped forward into the car, and Bert pushed her the rest of the way in before getting in the driver's seat and taking off.

Jake was already on the phone to the station, filling in the chief who was immediately putting out an APB on Bert's car. Flipping his phone shut, he looked over at Tom. Tom wasn't moving. Not a muscle. He was simply staring at the screen of the monitor, which showed the empty space where Bert's car had been. Jake knew Tom was staring at the place where Carol was last seen. He put his hand on Tom's shoulder, forcing him to turn away from the monitor and focus on Jake's face. "Get it together, man. We'll get her."

As though hit with a cold bucket of water, Tom's eyes cleared, and he suddenly snapped out of his stupor.

Neither man believed in coincidence, and the thought hit them both at the same time. *Where the hell are Bert and Cal?*

When Tom and Jake arrived at Mrs. Penski's house, Jake kept warning Tom to stay cool and keep his mouth shut. "Do not screw up this case. You can't officially investigate now because of Carol. Let me do my job. You got me, man?" Jake asked. Glad to see the other patrolmen there, Jake needed Tom to keep his focus.

Tom glared at Jake, not answering him as they knocked on the door announcing their presence. Mrs. Penski opened the door, looking surprisingly forlorn instead of her former defiance.

"Know why you're here. Don't know what I can tell you, though. Cal made me take him to the store and then leave without him. Don't know where he is. Don't care where he is. That's boy's been trouble since he was little."

"We need to know the whereabouts of Bert," Jake stated.

"My Bert?" she asked, eyes narrowing. "He ain't got nothin' to do with Cal leavin'." Her eyes jerked nervously toward Tom as she heard him growling.

"Mrs. Penski, we have video evidence of Bert kidnapping a woman from the hospital parking lot. We need to know where he is, and we need to know now. You helpin' us will help him," Jake calmly explained.

"Hospital? That pretty nurse Bert and Cal were interested in?" she asked, her eyes moving between Jake and Tom. She licked her lips nervously and began twisting her hands together. Shaking her head, she moaned to herself, "Oh, I told Bert to stop it. Ain't no way no pretty nurse was ever gonna wanna be with him. 'Bout had him convinced to finally leave her alone when Cal came here the other day and stirred Bert all up again."

Tom could hear the roar of his heart screaming in his ears. His training knew that witnesses sometimes have to be handled slowly. With care. Cautiously. Letting them tell their story in their own time. *But this is not one of those times,* he wanted to scream at Jake.

Jake, sensing that Tom was ready to explode, moved slightly in front of him, effectively blocking Mrs. Penski's view of Tom. Probing gently, he continued, "We know Bert was interested in Ms. Fletcher, but what was Cal's interest?"

Wrapping her arms around her waist as though to protect herself from what was to come, she began to rock back and forth. "Cal found some pictures of her that Bert had taken. Not bad pictures, mind you. Just some pictures that he took following her around town. It was all innocent like—he never meant no harm. He just kept saying she was so purdy and so nice. Sometimes people aren't so nice to Bert, him being kinda slow and all."

She hesitated, gathering her thoughts so Jake prodded her again. Looking up, she snarled, "It woulda been fine if Cal hadn't gotten involved. He recognized the pictures of the nurse from when he was in the hospital. I think he kinda fell for her too, but he didn't let on to Bert. He convinced Bert that if he had that nurse all by hisself, then she would have to fall in love with him, but I think Cal just wanted Bert to get that girl so Cal could have her."

Tom's pounding heart threatened to stop at that moment. It was one thing to think that Bert had gotten Carol. While Bert wasn't harmless, he didn't think that Bert would actually hurt Carol. But Cal? *Oh, God. If she gets in the hands of a notorious drug dealer and prostitution ring leader.* Tom could feel his breath leave his body all in one great whoosh, and his legs threatened to give out.

Encouraging her to keep talking, Jake said, "Mrs. Penski, you're doing great. You're helping Ms. Fletcher, and you're helping Bert." Knowing that Bert was the key to getting Mrs. Penski to talk, he prodded, "Where did they talk about going? Where do you think Bert was heading?"

"You'll take care of my Bert? You'll make sure he's okay? Don't care no more about Cal, but Bert's different."

"I'll do all I can for him," Jake promised. "Where are they going?"

"Not sure. I figure Cal is heading back to Richland. He told Bert that he'd meet up with him somewhere there, and he'd help him win the nurse over. Don't know where Cal's place is, though."

Thanking her for her help, he turned her over to the other officers and grabbed Tom's arm steering him back to the truck. Tom was already on the phone to Shane while Jake was on his phone to the chief.

The chief had already been in contact with the Chief of Police for Richland, and they were on the lookout for Cal to return. Now that there was a possible kidnapping involving Cal, the police could pick him up as soon as they found him.

Tom got Shane on the phone who reassured him that they were looking for Cal.

"Got more. You gotta find him. He and his brother kidnapped my girl." Tom couldn't keep the shaking from his voice, but couldn't seem to find the ability to maintain control.

"Hell, man. Hold on, chief's calling a briefing. It's 'bout your situation. Call you back in ten." Shane hung up, leaving Tom still holding the phone to his ear, not knowing what to do.

Jake threw open the door to the truck, pushing Tom toward the seat. "Get in. We're going to Richland."

The two men headed out of town, determined to make the three-hour drive in half that time. Tom coordinated the investigation from his phone while Jake drove, using his flashing lights to speed along where possible. The chief reported that Bert's car had been found abandoned on the side of the road about an hour outside of Fairfield. State police investigators were at the scene, but the assumption was that was where Cal met up with Bert. The good news was that it was on the road to Richland so their hunch that he was heading there was probably correct. The bad news was that there was no sign of Carol.

They still have her. Tom could feel the sick feeling in the pit of his stomach rise and threaten to choke him. His ability to think like a detective had left hours ago, leaving him adrift, helpless, and utterly lost.

Jake glanced over to see Tom sitting quietly with his eyes staring blankly ahead. "Tom," he said softly. "We're gonna get her. We have the state police and the Richland Police working this case as a priority. We're. Gonna. Find. Her."

"But what shape will she be in?" Tom asked, almost in a whisper, shaking his head. "She…struggles…stress gets to her. I just don't…"

"Don't go there, man. Don't go there. She's strong. She's tough. She's smart. But she needs you. She needs you to be strong and focused. Can you do that?"

Sucking in a deep breath, eyes refocusing, Tom looked over at Jake. "Yeah, man. I got it."

Nodding in Tom's direction, Jake turned back to his speeding down the road.

Chapter 24

Carol slowly woke to the feeling of movement. Hazy. Floating. A gentle rocking back and forth. Heavy eyelids that did not want to open. Licking her lips, they felt dry. A strange taste in her mouth. Voices far away. *Did I get sick? Am I in the hospital?* The fog in her mind slowly lifted, leaving her as confused as ever. Forcing her eyelids to open, she realized that she was lying in the back of a car. *Whose car am I in?*

"Tom?" she croaked, her voice sounding foreign to her. Wanting to sit up, she tried unsuccessfully to push up with her arms. *Why won't my arms move the way I want them to?*

The voices stopped, and a man's face appeared over the seat in front of her. *I recognize that face.* But she couldn't come up with a name. Confusion mingled with a dreaded sense that something was not right, began to slide through her mind.

"How much did you give her?"

"Whatever you put in that needle for me."

Who are these people? Why am I in their car? What is happening? Needles? Forcing her mind to clear faster, Carol's nursing training began to emerge. *Needle? Something was given to me? Drugs! I have been drugged!*

With all her strength, she pushed up again, and, this time, was successful in sitting partially up in the seat. Two heads were in front of her. *Driving. One of them is driving. Think, damn it!* Feeling her mind struggle to make sense of what her eyes were seeing, she re-focused on the heads in front of her. The one not driving turned around, looking at her with an anxious look on his face. *Bert. Oh my God. Bert. He tricked me. He drugged me.* The moments in the parking lot came rushing back into her mind as fear rushed into her heart.

"Bert?" she asked, her voice slurring. "Whadda you doing? Why'd you do this?"

"Oh, Miss Carol. I have wanted you for so long, but you were always with that policeman. Cal told me that if I took you, then you'd forget about that cop and would be with me."

The driver glanced back at her as well. *Cal. Oh Jesus, Cal.* The memory of what the guards said about him when she was treating him rushed through her mind. *I have got to get out of here.* Glancing out of the window, she saw the

scenery rushing by. Fighting nausea that threatened to overtake her, she knew that the drugs
were still very much in her system.

"We gotta get some gas, and I'm getting
hungry," Cal said. "You got more stuff to give
her?"

No! I can't let them give me more! Sliding back
down on the seat, moaning, she closed her eyes,
hoping they would not drug her more.

"I got something, but she's okay. You stop
up here, and she'll be fine," Bert assured his
brother.

Carol could feel the car move to the right
and come to a stop. From what she could see,
they were at a little mom & pop gas station.

"I gotta go to the bathroom," she told the
brothers. "I gotta go bad."

Bert looked nervously at his brother who
was scowling. "Maybe we better let her. Don't
want her gettin' sick."

Cal twisted around in the seat and looked at
Carol slumped in the back. "Gonna walk you in
and gonna wait right outside while you piss. You
do anything, you'll regret it, get me?"

Carol just nodded, agreeing to anything to
get out of the car. Bert got out first then opened
her door. Half helping, half dragging, he managed to get her on her feet.

How am I going to run when I can't even stand? Glancing at the small building in front of her, she wondered if there would be anyone there to help. With Bert on one side and Cal on the other, they walked inside the store. Forcing her to the bathroom in the back, Cal called out loudly, "Damn girl started drinkin' this mornin' and is totally wasted now."

Carol wanted to shout out to the person behind the counter, but couldn't seem to get the words out before she was shoved into the tiny bathroom.

"Do your business and no funny stuff. I'll be right here. You give me any trouble, and I'll shoot the old man in the front," Cal warned in a soft voice, before shutting the door.

Stumbling over, Carol used the toilet as quickly as she could, trying desperately to not fall on her face. Now that he had threatened another person, she had no idea what to do. Grabbing onto the sink, she turned on the water then splashed her face. The cold water helped clear her mind, but her legs were still wobbly. *I have got to try. I have got to do something.*

Unlocking the door, she was shoved backward when it opened quickly. Bert was there pulling her out gently, and she could see Cal up front, making his purchases. Forcing her legs to walk as steadily as she could, she looked at her feet hoping to lull Cal into thinking that she was compliant. Just as she got close to the counter, she raised her head up and shouted, "Help me! They're kidnapping me!" while pushing Bert into Cal, knocking them both off balance. Stumbling outside, she almost made it to the side of the building when she was grabbed by the arm and swung around.

"Oh no, pretty girl. You ain't getting away that easily," Cal spoke with deadly calm, pressing a gun to her side while dragging her back to the car. Opening the door, he shoved her inside.

"Cal, don't you hurt my girl," Bert yelled as he came running over. "You be nice to her."

Cal sneered at Bert. "You dumb shit. She ain't no girl of yours. That sweet piece is gonna be mine. Been thinking about her since I first laid eyes on her."

Carol turned to see Cal point the gun at Bert. She could feel the shaking overtake her as she watched with horror the scene play out in front of her.

"In fact, brother, I don't need your sorry ass no more. You got the girl for me and got Ma to help get me outta that shithole town."

Bert looked at Cal, eyes wide as he stared at the gun. "You gonna shoot me, Cal? Your brother?"

Carol watched as Cal brought the gun up holding it directly at Bert. Just as Cal was taking a shot, he was knocked off balance by Carol's door opening into his side. Bert jumped out of the line of fire, as Cal rounded on Carol, slamming the door shut again.

Cal ran around the car, climbing into the driver's seat and gunning the car out of the parking lot. "You stupid bitch. Don't you get it? I'm makin' you my number one girl and you're trying to throw it away?"

Number one girl. What the hell is he talking about?

Cal jerked the car to the side of the road and came to a quick stop. Carol was thrown into the floorboard of the back seat. Crawling back into the seat, she was just turning around when she felt a stabbing pain in her arm. Screaming out, she tried to scramble around to see Cal when the darkness began to descend again. *No, not again...*

Jake's phone rang. "Yeah," he barked into the cell. "When? Shots fired? He still there? Got it."

Tom's heart dropped into his stomach once again at the questions he heard Jake asked. Twisting around in his seat so he could concentrate directly on his partner, he didn't even have to ask. Jake began talking as soon as he hung up.

"Cal and Bert have her. They stopped to get gas, and she tried to escape. The attendant said she was drunk, but I figure she is still drugged. Cal and Bert argued. Cal left Bert's ass there. 'Bout five minutes up ahead."

Tom, forcing his mind to think like a detective and not like a terrified boyfriend, called Shane and filled him in. "Gonna stop for just a minute to see what we can get outta Bert. Call you as soon as I can to give you an update."

Pulling into the gas station, they were met with a multitude of local police cars. Hopping out, flashing their badges, they approached Bert, who was cuffed and sitting in one of the cruisers. Before Jake could stop him, Tom hauled Bert out and slammed his back against the car.

"What the hell did you do with Carol?" he yelled.

"Tom," Jake ordered. "Stand down."

Tom let go of a shaking Bert but leaned down in his face. Speaking slow and even, he said, "I'll come back for you if she is hurt in any way. You got me?"

"I just wanted her to be my girlfriend. Cal told me that if I got her away from you, she would fall for me," Bert blubbered.

Jake, realizing how Cal manipulated Bert, tried to use that to gain information. "Bert, Cal really played you. Now he has Carol, and we gotta get to him to make sure she is safe. You want her safe, don't you?"

Bert's sad eyes looked up at Jake and then slid over to Tom's angry face. "I didn't mean for any of this to happen. I always knew she wasn't for me. Cal just made me feel that she could be mine."

Jake continued to probe softly. "Bert, you can't make someone like you. But now your brother has her, and you know he's not a nice person. He's not gonna be nice to her. You gotta tell us anything you know."

Bert nodded, eyes focused on a distant point past Jake's shoulder as though trying to work out a problem in his head. Looking back at Jake, he said, "Don't know anything about Cal's business, but he got a call the other day and I saw who was callin'. Cal was in the shower, so I looked at his phone when it rang. It didn't have a nice name."

Jake and Tom glanced at each other in question, then Jake prodded, "Not a nice name?"

"Yeah. I knew ma would be upset it she

knew he was taking calls like that in our home." Leaning in closer to whisper the name, Bert said, "Pussy Club."

Tom turned and stalked over to the truck, getting Shane on the phone. "What do you got on a place called the Pussy Club?"

Shane cursed. "Low-class strip joint. Been busted several times for prostitution. One of the places where the girls are always drugged out, usually against their will. Cal manages to stay clear, but we know he's involved. Place gets shut down then re-opens under new management. Real sleazy place. It's one that we keep trying to pin on Cal, but he manages to hide his involvements. Why?"

"Cal's brother just rolled on him. Said he got a call from them the other day."

"Could be where he's headed. At least it is a start. You're gonna hit Richland in about thirty minutes. I'll send you the GPS coordinates and tell you where we'll meet up. Getting my crew here ready to go. We've been after this guy for a couple of years."

"Shane, I don't give a shit about Cal right now. I just want Carol," Tom said, not embarrassed at the emotion in his shaking voice.

There was a brief silence as the words hung between the two men before Shane spoke. "Got it, man. I haven't found the right one yet, but when I do, I'd move heaven and earth. We'll do this. Promise." With that, he hung up, sending a text with the GPS information.

As Tom was climbing into the truck, he heard a small voice behind him. Turning, he saw Bert, still cuffed with a policeman at his side. "I know she's yours. Just get her safely back."

With a curt nod, Tom hauled himself up into the truck, and they headed down the homestretch toward Richland.

Once again, Carol slowly returned to consciousness, eyes blurry, eyelids heavy, strange taste in her mouth, and limbs that did not want to work. It took every effort to chase the fog away, not knowing where she was or how she got there. She had no idea how much time passed as she crept toward awareness. She finally realized that her eyes were opened but that the room she was in was very dark. She was no longer in the car but did not recognize the room that she was in. Minutes ticked by as she tried to raise herself up on weak limbs. A sense of déjà vu washed over her as she remembered the same feelings in the car.

Cal! He left Bert behind. Where did he bring me?

As her vision became more focused, she tried to look around. For what, she didn't know, but she had to do something. Tom would have no idea that she was missing. And when he did, he'd have no idea where she was. *Oh, Jesus. I have got to get out of this myself.*

She was lying on a bed in a small room. There were no windows. There was a chair in one corner. That was it. One bed. One chair. Carol pondered this in confusion. *This isn't someone's bedroom and it's not a hotel room.* She stood on shaky legs and made her way over to the door. Locked. Not wanting to fall down, she made her way back to the bed, sitting on the edge as she took deep breaths to try to clear her head.

She heard the doorknob jiggle before a young woman entered, carrying a tray of food. Carol stared at the girl, noting her unkempt appearance, sloppy clothes, but it was her face that grabbed her attention. Pale, dark circles under vacant eyes.

"Here's some food and a bottle of water," the girl said, setting the tray down on the bed. She looked up at Carol, rubbed her nose, and turned to move back toward the door. It was when she brought her arm up to rub her nose that Carol caught the signs. *Track marks on her arm. Jesus, she's high.*

Carol stood as quickly as she could, calling out, "Who are you? Where are we?"

The girl turned around, looking at Carol with a confused look on her face, answering, "Me? Why do you wanna know?"

Wanting to gain the girl's trust, Carol quickly answered, "So I'll know who to thank for the food."

The girl's gaze fell to the tray still sitting on the bed, and she looked back up at Carol, confusion changing to boredom. "Name's Sylvie. Not my real name, but 'round here, they call me Sylvie."

"Where's here? Where are we?" Carol asked cautiously.

Sylvie looked around the room for a moment, as though trying to come up with an answer. Her glazed, vacant eyes made their way back to Carol. "Huh?" was all she answered.

Oh my, God, she is wasted. Carol's ER training in dealing with intoxicated people kicked in, and she attempted to make her comfortable. "Here, you need to sit. How about we share the water?" Handing Sylvie the water bottle, she continued to slowly speak to her. "Sylvie, I don't know where we are. What city are we in?"

Sylvie, taking a pull on the cool water as though she were thirsty, looked up and said, "Richland. We're in Richland."

Carol pulled the sandwich apart, offering Sylvie half while continuing to speak. "What building are we in?"

Sylvie, taking the sandwich and greedily stuffing it into her mouth, said, "How come you don't know where we are?" Stopping and looking around again, she snorted. "Hell, all these rooms look the same at the Pussy Club. I guess one room for fuckin' is as good as another. Thought your room would be nicer, you being his woman an' all."

Fucking? Oh, Jesus, is this a whorehouse? His? Who is she talking about? Shit, don't let her be talking about Cal.

As if on cue, Cal came strolling into the room, eyes immediately falling to Sylvie holding the water bottle in one hand and the sandwich in the other. His eyes narrowed in anger as he stalked over, grabbing Sylvie by the arm and slapping her hard across the face. "I give you one simple job, you stupid cunt and you can't even do that?"

Blood spurted from Sylvie's nose and

dripped onto the floor.

Carol's protective instinct reared as she tried to stop him from shaking Sylvie. "No, no. It isn't her fault. I gave it to her."

Cal stopped shaking Sylvie, but his eyes cut over to Carol's. "What'd you do that for?"

Calm. Stay calm.

"I thought she looked hungry, and I just wanted to do something nice," Carol said quietly. "I'm sorry if I shouldn't have." Licking her dry lips, she looked him in the eyes.

Cal's face softened, and he let go of Sylvie's arm as he gave a head jerk toward the door. Sylvie stumbled out of the room. He turned to Carol, a smile replacing the anger from earlier. "You're as nice as I remember. That day in the hospital. You were nice. Spoke nice. Looked pretty. Fuckin' cops wanted to turn you against me, but you were still nice. I knew then I wanted you," he said, lifting his hand and running his finger down her cheek.

Fighting the revulsion, she continued to speak softly. "What happened to Bert?"

Cal choked out a guttural laugh. "My brother, Bert. What a waste! I was gonna take care of him, let him be part of my organization, but he wanted to stay with Ma. First time I go to prison, she turns me out, and he sided with that ole' bitch." Running his fingers back up her cheek to her hair, he continued. "Bert's been watchin' you for me. I had him think you'd be interested, so it was easy to get him to watch you, follow you, give you gifts. Even had one a' my men follow you when you were running. But gorgeous," he said, stepping closer as though to kiss her, "I was savin' you all for me. I'll get you outta here in a bit, but I gotta take care of business first."

"It was you. Doing all that stuff to me? The gifts, the runner?" *He's crazy. Oh my, God, he's crazy.*

Cal smirked as though to pat himself on the back. "You were so easy, doll-face. I sent one of my men down there to keep an eye on you. You ran the same path every day, so it was easy to have him scare the shit outta you. And he had the perfect viewpoint watchin' you and that policeman fuckin' by the door." Laughing, he just shook his head as he stepped back. "Who knows? I might just pay that asshole back by filming you and me fuckin' and send it to him."

Carol swayed, throwing her hand over her mouth, "I need a bathroom." Cal jumped back and yelled for Sylvie. She stumbled in looking at

Cal in confusion.

"Get her to the bathroom down the hall and try not to fuck up that simple job," he ordered. "Must be the Goddamn drugs makin' her sick."

Carol allowed Sylvie to take her arm and lead her out of the room and down the hall to the bathroom.

Cal followed them out, telling Sylvie, "I got shit to do. Make sure she gets back in that room and get her more food that you don't eat. Gonna send someone up to check on you in a bit." With that, Cal headed down the stairs at the end of the hall.

Walking into the bathroom, Carol continued to pretend to be sick, so she headed into the first stall. As she passed the sinks, she noticed a small window on the side of the room that appeared to be just wide enough for her to fit through. *Oh, thank Jesus.* Now to get rid of Sylvie.

Making gagging noises in the stall, she then came out and walked to the sink. "Sylvie, can you get some more water and food for me?"

Sylvie, standing at the sinks, had washed some blood off of her face but left the bloody paper towels in the sink. Sylvie, in her drugged state, just shrugged and sauntered out of the bathroom. Carol felt a quick pang of guilt, knowing that Sylvie would suffer the consequences of leaving her alone, but she had to think of herself first. *As soon as I can get out of here, I'm getting help for these girls. Jesus, he must keep them all drugged to stay in this dump.*

Running to the window, she found that it was the old fashioned type that opened from the top and the glass pane leaned back toward the room. She eyed the opening, then looked down at her body. *God, let me fit. Please, let me fit.*

Tom and Jake rendezvoused with Shane and the others from the Richland Police Department in a run-down, industrial area of Richland that had seen better days. A few bars, liquor stores, and stripper joints were mixed among the other shops trying to eke out a business with the economy down. By now, the evening was descending and the few street lights that were working gave off very little illumination for the rescuers.

Shane strolled over to Jake's truck as soon as they pulled into an empty parking lot down the street from the Pussy Club. Just at six feet tall, Shane was a large man, barreled chested with his Kevlar vest in place. His short dark hair was tipped in blond spikes and with his plain clothes on, he looked like he belonged in one of the seedier bars along the strip. Quickly shaking hands, Shane got down to business.

"We've been watching the building since you contacted us. We haven't seen the car that Cal was described as coming in, but he could have changed vehicles again. It has a garage in back with a metal gated door. Several cars have gone in or out so he could have been in one of those."

Another officer came jogging over with a piece of paper in his hand. "Got the search warrant."

The group gathered around, reviewing the plan for surrounding and entering the building. The police had a picture of Carol from her hospital ID that had been faxed over, but Tom had a more recent one on his phone. Shane glanced at Tom's phone, then looked back up at his friend's face.

"We'll get her, Tom," Shane said.

Tom found that once again, he couldn't speak. Anxious to get inside, he saw a look pass between Shane and Jake. Instantly, he knew that look. "Oh no. You're not leavin' me outta this. I'm cool. I got this."

Shane looked him over. "Puttin' my job on the line lettin' you go in. You stay focused. You look for your girl and leave Cal to us."

"Got it. All I want is Carol," Tom answered.

"All right. Let's do it." And with that, Shane led the others toward the club.

Chapter 25

Putting one foot up on the sink to gain height, Carol pulled her head up to the window and pushed the top half of her body through the narrow opening. Looking around quickly, she could see that she was on the third level of a four-story, brick building in what appeared to be a run-down industrial area. An old, rusty fire escape ladder ran down the side of the building, just a few feet from where she was. Using her hands, she grasped the outer edge of the window to continue to pull her hips as far as she could. *Goddamn it.* The metal sides of the window panes dug into her hips as she wiggled back and forth. The thin material of her hospital scrubs ripped on the sides as she continued to force her body through the opening.

Looking to the right, she realized the ladder was not as close as she thought. She was just going to be able to grasp it with her hands, but that was going to take a lot of strength to keep her from plunging down to the concrete below.

"Why the fuck did you leave her alone?" Cal's voice rang out from a distance.

Shit! He's coming back.

With her legs still dangling inside the bathroom, she stretched as far as she could, managing to grab hold of the ladder with her right hand. Just then she felt someone grab her foot.

"You fuckin' bitch, get back in here," Cal barked out, grabbing at her feet.

Carol kicked out as hard as she could, feeling her shoe come off in the process. Hanging on to the ladder with just her hands, she swung her body toward it, scraping her front across the brick wall. She felt her fingers slipping just as her feet found their way to one of the ladder rungs.

Catching her leg on a long metal spike that formerly helped anchor the ladder to the brick wall, Carol felt the stabbing pain as her leg was sliced.

"Where the fuck do you think you're going," Cal yelled, as he stuck his head through the window. "I'm just gonna get you on the ground, you stupid cunt, and then you'll wish you hadn't caused me this much trouble."

Carol looked at him, and his eyes locked onto hers. Cold. Dead. Serious. No sympathy.

Killer.

Oh, Jesus, help me. Her limbs still shaky with the effects of the drugs in her system, she began to descend. The metal was cold and rusty in places. She couldn't go as fast as she wanted...it was as though her hands and feet could not answer the call of her brain to hurry. *He's going to go down there. He's going to be there when I land. He's going to get me again.* She turned her eyes upward. *The roof.*

Shane led his team, along with Jake and Tom, through the front of the Pussy Club, with others surrounding all of the exits. Waving the search warrant, they fanned out through the front lobby and into the bar area. Several strippers stopped dancing and stood numbly on stage, not knowing what was expected. The few patrons left jumped up and attempted to escape, but were quickly stopped. The bartender, an enormous man with a shaved and tattooed head, glared out at the police. "Ain't doing nothin' wrong. Got a legit license."

"Shut the hell up," Shane growled. "Cal Penski here? He bring a woman here earlier?"

"Don't know no Cal," the bartender answered. His eyes shifted slightly, before landing back onto Shane's eyes.

If Shane hadn't been watching carefully, he would have missed the movement. *He's lying.*

Before Shane could react, Tom reached over the bar grabbing the bartender by the front of his shirt, jerking him halfway across the bar. Wrapping his other hand around the bartender's throat, he began slowly squeezing. "Not fuckin' around, asshole. Cal's here and he brought someone with him. Cough him up or you're gonna be suckin' your food through a straw for the rest of your life," Tom said with deadly calm.

The bartender tried to grab Tom's arms but found them pinned down by Jake. His eyes shot over to Shane, and he choked out, "You gonna...let...'em do...this?"

Shane, looking bored, just glanced at the bartender. "Do what, man? I don't see nothin'."

The bartender's face turned red, then purple, and he began gasping. "Up...stairs. Her...up...st." Tom let go suddenly, and the bartender's face landed heavily on the bar as he tried to breathe. Jake handed him off to one of the other officers and rounded the bar.

Shane looked up on stage at the girl closest to him. Thin with fake tits, she had the hollow-eyed look of a user. Speaking softly, he said,

"Can you show us where Cal took the girl? Which room?"

Confusion then fear showed on her face, as she shook her head. "He won't like it." Her eyes wide, she looked around desperately, as though to find someone to tell her what to do.

"Girl, he's not here to help you now. You know something about this girl he brought in, and you don't help us, that makes you a party to a kidnappin'. You want that?"

The dancer chewed her lip, still looking around. Her eyes finally fell back onto Shane's. Speaking softly, she mumbled, "She's on the third floor, back room."

Shane's eyes gentled momentarily. "Thanks, doll. You did good."

Tom was already pounding up the stairs with Jake right on his heels. Rounding the last landing to the third floor, he could feel his heart in his throat at what he might find. Several girls had come out of rooms to see what was going one. As more police followed Tom and Jake, they screamed and ran back into their rooms, pushing their clients in as they went.

Bursting through the stairwell door to the third floor, Tom plowed into Sylvie, knocking her to the floor. Jake grabbed her quickly, assisting her up as he scanned her bloody face.

"Where's the girl?" he asked her gently, seeing the signs of drug use on her arms.

Sylvie stared emptily at the men gathering around. "She was in there," she said pointing to the room at the end of the hall. As Tom sprinted off towards the room, she continued, "She ain't there anymore. She went out the bathroom window." Sylvie pointed to the door behind her and would have been knocked down again by Tom if Jake hadn't pulled her out of the way. Jake handed her off to one of the other policemen as he and Shane followed Tom into the bathroom.

By the sinks was a small, open window. The men saw blood in the sinks and Carol's tennis shoe on the floor. Tom's heart sank. *Oh Jesus, help her.*

Running to the window, he leaned out, glancing to the left and to the right. Seeing blood on the window, he noticed the ladder. "She went out here," he shouted back, looking down at the ground. "But I don't see her on the ladder."

Looking up, his heart nearly stopped. Carol was clinging to the rickety ladder trying to move upwards towards the roof. "The roof," he shouted. "She's going up." Turning, he and Jake ran out of the room towards the staircase.

Shane looked at Sylvie. "Where is he? Is he still after her?"

Sylvie barely nodded as her eyes raised upwards.

Shane nodded and headed after Tom and Jake, shouting for the rest of his men to follow. Radioing down to the men on the outside, he told them that Cal was up on the roof, and he wanted his men in place.

As the three men got to the top of the stairs leading to the roof, Shane grabbed Tom's arm, swinging him around. Tom reacted by advancing on Shane, anger and fear pouring off of him.

"What the hell, man?" Tom roared.

Jake, understanding both sides, stepped in between of the two men. "Tom," Jake spoke quietly.

Tom's eyes quickly shot over to his partner, friend, brother. Taking a shaky breath, he let it out slowly. "I got it." His eyes landed back on Shane's. "I got this."

Shane stared for just a second in Tom's eyes, then nodded his head toward the roof door. "Let's get your girl," he stated. "And that asshole."

Carol, sweating and shaking, managed to move

up one slow rung of the ladder at a time. Afraid of heights, she refused to look down, but she didn't have to look to know she was almost five floors above the hard concrete street.

Clinging to the ladder for fear of slipping, she was so weary she could only manage to hang on. The effects of the drugs had not worn off and with her leg bleeding, she realized that the effort of trying to move up the ladder was depleting what little energy she had left.

Looking up toward the roof, she knew she didn't have much farther to go. *Come on. You can do this. You're strong. You can do anything. You can do this.* Chanting this mantra over and over in her mind, she climbed up one more rung.

"Hey, Blondie. How's it going?"

Hearing that dreaded voice above her, Carol halted in her progress. *Oh, no. Cal went up and not down to the ground.* Glancing down, she realized she would never manage to get down before him. She was trapped. Trapped on a ladder clinging to the side of a building, five floors above the ground. With a killer just a few feet away.

Shaking, she wrapped her arms around the rusty metal as tight as she could, giving way to the tears threatening to fall.

"I was gonna give you everything, you stupid

cunt. You were gonna be my woman. My number one. Do you have any idea how many woman woulda wanted that, bitch?" Cal mocked. "So guess what I'm gonna do? I'm gonna sit right down and just wait. You'll either make it up here where you'll go in my stable— I'll make a killin' off of you, Blondie. Or you'll get tired and fall way, way, way down."

Carol couldn't stop the tears from falling. She wasn't going to make it. She couldn't hold on much longer, and she couldn't move up the ladder either.

Shaking, bleeding, clinging to the ladder. Holding on for her life. *Tom.* His face filled her memory. *I love him. I wish he were here. Will he ever even know what happened to me? He loved me for me. He loved me just as I'm. Not some image in his mind of who I should be. But he just loved ME. He saved me from the image in the mirror. If only I could tell him one last time.* Her arms began to shake as she felt her muscles weakening.

Tom, Jake, Shane and the other members of the police force quickly and silently crept onto the roof, revolvers drawn, ready for battle and rescue. Fanning out, shielding themselves with the large air conditioning units, they positioned themselves.

Hearing shouting and cursing to the left, Tom and Shane peered around the barrier. Cal. Alone. *Where's Carol? Jesus, is she still on the ladder?*

Shane signaled for his men to surround Cal, but warned them not to shoot. Creeping, they made their way closer to Cal without alerting him to their presence. They could now see that he is leaning over the ladder, waving a gun and shouting obscenities at Carol, still trapped on the ladder.

"Cal Penski. Drop your weapon," Shane's low growl rang out along the rooftop.

Cal whirled around, eyes narrowing as Shane walked out from behind a barrier with his revolver pointed directly at Cal's chest. Cal's eyes darted quickly around as Jake and Shane's men approached as well.

"You fuckers. You think you've won. This joint ain't nothin'. You want the man. You need me to get him. You shoot me now, you ain't never gonna get 'em." Looking Shane directly in the eyes, he grinned. "And I know you want the big man, you prick. I'm worth a lot more to you alive."

Tom rounded the corner of the barrier, holding his revolver at Cal's head. Cal's eyes widened at the sight of him and he licked his lips nervously.

"You ain't gonna shoot me over some piece of ass, are you, man? Nawh. You need me. You need me too much." Eyes darting back and forth between the guns trained on him, his mind raced.

Shane spoke up. "You think we need you to get to the top of this shithole chain? You think you're that Goddamn important? You're no more than a shit stain on the bottom of their shoes. I'll get them, asshole, and don't need you to do it."

Cal, sweating profusely, shook his head. "I know my rights. You can't just shoot me."

Shane jerked his head toward Tom. "Maybe I can't, but this here is just a man looking to get revenge on whoever's been fuckin' with his woman. And you happen to be that fucker, so I don't suppose there's anything stoppin' him."

Cal, still standing on the edge of the roof, lowered his gun down hoping it would look like he was surrendering while aiming it toward Carol.

Having heard shouting but unable to make out what was said, Carol continued to cling to the ladder. She spared a glance down just to look at her leg to see if she was still bleeding but was unable to do so without also seeing the ground five stories below.

Jerking her head back up, she clung to the ladder even tighter. *How long can I hold on?* Her muscles began to shake with the exertion and adrenaline. *Please, God. Save me.*

Glancing up, she saw Cal standing on the edge of the roof...with the gun pointing down...directly at her.

∾

Tom's hands were shaking as he held his revolver pointing directly toward Cal. *Focus. Hold it together for Carol's sake.* Impatient, knowing that Carol was clinging to the ladder, he knew that they had no more time to spare. "Shane," he said in a low growl.

"Got it, man," was the response.

Shane advanced a couple of steps toward Cal. "Step off the side, Cal, and drop the gun. We're through fuckin' around. Already told you, you're not needed. We'll shut down the drugs coming in with or without you. You got five seconds, or I give the order to shoot."

Cal knew his life wouldn't be worth living once he hit prison. Hell, if he even lived that long. *That Goddamn girl. If she had just come along willingly, he wouldn't be stuck up here on this fuckin' roof.* Sweat pouring, he made up his mind. Better to go out quick than be stuck in jail after rolling over on the bosses. *But I ain't going alone.* A shit-eating grin split his face as he whirled around firing off a round down at Carol before the bullets slammed into his body from all directions.

Hearing shots, Carol's eyes watched in horror as Cal's body flew passed her on its way down to the ground. *Oh, Jesus. Oh, Jesus. Oh, Jesus.* She began to shake violently as her body gave way to the adrenaline rush.

Tom ran to the edge of the roof with Jake and Shane right at his back. Peering over the edge, with his heart in his throat, he saw Carol still clinging to the ladder just out of his reach.

"Carol!" he shouted, his voice tight with emotion. "Angel, can you climb up?"

Carol's eyes shut tightly, she shook her head. In the distance, she heard Tom's voice. *He found me. He came for me.* It washed over her in relief, but her body would not move. She clung tighter to the ladder terrified of plummeting down as well.

Tom started to haul his body over the side to climb down the ladder to her, but Shane grabbed him back. "What the hell?" Tom roared out. "Let me get to her."

"Tom, that ladder may not hold both of

you," Shane answered, looking at the rusty ladder.

Tom turned to Jake with desperation in his eyes. "Jake?"

Jake looked at his best friend, knowing that he was at the end of his rope. "We'll get her. Stay here and keep talking to her. She needs to hear your voice. She needs to know you're close."

Shane was already on the radio, directing the police helicopter to the building site. "ETA is three minutes, Tom. Jake is right, talk to her."

Quickly laying down on the roof, with his head dangling over, Tom called to Carol. "Angel, it's me. Hold on. Help is coming. Can you hear me, babe?"

She managed to nod her head.

"You remember the first time I saw you? You were leaning over me, that golden hair like a halo. I coulda' sworn I'd died and gone to heaven. And I didn't even care. All I could think of what if you were what was waiting for me, then that was fine. From that moment on, all I have wanted is you. Never looked at another woman. Never looked back. Just wanted a future with you. I always thought I was in control. But the honest to God truth is that you've controlled my heart since I saw you. Can you still hear me?"

Another head jerk.

"I want us to get married. We can settle in my house or, if you want, we can buy a house of our own. Whatever you want. We can have kids. Watch 'em grow up. Little blonde angels, just like you. Only if they're half as beautiful as their momma, I'll have to lock 'em up just to keep the boys away."

Tom's voice cracked as the emotions overtook him. Jake, sitting right next to him, put his hand on Tom's shoulder to steady him. Tom sniffed and wiped his nose as tears fell freely.

"Just keep hanging on, sweetheart. Swear to God, I'm gonna get you."

The sound of a helicopter came upon them, drowning out their voices. Shane came running over as a rescue line was dropped. "Tom, gotta man who will be fastened into the harness and the chopper will lower him to her. He'll fasten a harness around her too and then it will pull both of them up and place them here on the roof. Already got the rescue team in place."

Tom standing to his full height took a deep breath. "It's gonna be me, Shane. Have them harness me."

"You're not trained in this, Tom. Let my men get her up here."

"We've got no time to argue, harness me up," Tom ordered.

Shane looked over at Jake, who just nodded. "Do it."

Tom was quickly harnessed in and lifted over the side of the building. Only needing to be lowered about ten feet, he quickly came upon Carol's trembling body. "Carol, it's me. You can keep your eyes closed if you want, but just know it is me that got's you. I'm the one touching you. Can you feel me?" his soft voice coaxed.

She nodded, keeping her eyes tightly shut. She could feel Tom's arms encircling her as something was wrapped around her waist and tightened.

"Carol, here comes the hard part. You have to trust me. I want you to let go of the ladder and hold on to me as tight as you can."

Carol shook her head, knowing there was no way she could let go.

"Angel, eyes on me," Tom softly ordered. Another shake.

"Angel. Eyes. On. Me."

Carol turned her head toward his voice, allowing his words to flow over her. Slowly, she opened her eyes, desperately seeking his. His face was inches from hers. His arms were wrapped around her. Blue eyes gazed at blue eyes.

"Ready?"

Nodding, she felt Tom's arms tighten even more. Suddenly she was flying through the air, being lifted. But all she felt was Tom wrapped around her body. *Protected. Safe. Cared for. Comforted. Accepted. Loved.*

Chapter 26

Carol lay in the Richland hospital bed, eyes closed in pain-drug induced slumber. Tom lay next to her, refusing to leave her side. Her leg was stitched, her cuts and bruises taken care of. She had answered all of the police questions about Cal's operation that she might know as well as her ordeal. Calmly. Quietly. Rote answers. To anyone else, it would look as though she had come through the last couple of days mentally unscathed. But Tom knew better. She had shut down, shut him out, shut out everyone. One of the hospital shrinks had come by, but she politely refused to talk or to take any antidepressants.

One more day, then they could head home. Jake and Rob had been burning up his phone, wanting to know what was going on. It seemed as though all of Fairfield was concerned about Carol.

Shane stopped by the day after the rescue. Tom slipped out of her bed, walking over to grasp him tightly. Tears shining in his eyes, Tom admitted, "Shane. I owe you. If we hadn't had you, I don't know…"

Shane, wrapping his arms around his old colleague, shook his head. "No man. She did it all. Her will was strong to get back to you, to stay alive. Hell, maybe one day we can all be that lucky."

"Gotta ring on her finger, plan on getting married as soon as we can. You better be at the wedding."

Looking down at his booted feet for a moment, Shane looked back up into Tom's eyes. Taking a deep breath, he shook his head. "Sorry, man. But, I'm going in. It's the only way to get these fuckers. Cal, he was someone we wanted, but he's not the top of the chain. So, I'm going."

Not the life he wanted, Tom nonetheless respected the men who went undercover. "Damn, Shane. Are you sure?"

Looking over at Carol resting in the bed, Shane gave a short laugh. "About as sure as any of us can be. Been thinking about it for a while. I'm ready. But I'm sorry I'll miss the wedding."

Clasping hands again, the two men said goodbye, not knowing when they might meet again. Turning quickly, Shane left the room, leaving Tom suddenly exhausted.

Moving silently across the floor, he slid back into her bed, pulling her close before falling asleep.

ॐ

Waking near dusk, Tom looked at her face, gently brushing her hair back from her forehead. Planting a gentle kiss there, he turned as he heard a noise at the door.

Standing in the hospital doorway was Carol's father, looking out of place in the hospital corridor. Glancing back down at Carol, seeing her still asleep, Tom slid out of the bed and walked over to the door.

"Mr. Fletcher," he acknowledged.

Carol's father glanced at his daughter lying still in the hospital bed. His eyes cut back to Tom's. "Is she all right?"

"She will be. Is there something I can help you with?" Tom looked behind her father to see if he was alone.

Looking uncomfortable, Mr. Fletcher said, "I came by myself. Her mother couldn't...well, it's been all over the news and...well, she..." Looking down at his shoes momentarily, he signed heavily. "She is embarrassed by the publicity." Looking back to Carol lying still in her bed, he said, "I just wanted to come by myself to see if she is all right."

Tom, angry at the pitiful show of parental concern, just replied, "She'll be fine. Nothin' that won't heal or I won't take care of."

Carol's father jerked his gaze back to Tom's eyes. "I know you don't approve of me."

"It's not my place to approve or disapprove. I just know that you've never understood her or been there for her. But I am. And I'm not going anywhere. We're not waiting to get married. As soon as she's healed, we're going through with the wedding."

Silence ensued as both men took measure of each other, gazes not faltering.

Cutting his eyes back to his daughter once more, Mr. Fletcher just nodded. He turned to leave but stopped just short of the door. Looking back, he spoke softly, "Take care of her."

Nodding, Tom replied, "Always planned on it."

With that, Carol's father left the room. Tom stood staring after him for a long minute. Trying to reconcile his warm, supportive upbringing compared to her cold one left him first angry, then sad. Sighing deeply, he turned back to her bed. Large, blue eyes were staring back at him, tears sliding down her cheeks. Blue eyes gazed at blue eyes.

Rushing to her side, he slid in the bed wrapping his arms around her small body. Pulling her in close, he cradled her head to his chest.

"I'm so sorry. So sorry."

"He came," she whispered. "That was hard for him, but at least, he came." Sniffling, she continued, "Tom, I want to talk to my counselor when we get back. I'm ready to talk."

Letting out the breath that he had been holding, he pulled her in even tighter. "Thank God. Anything you need, you got it. I'm here just for you, babe. I'll call her right now and set things up."

"Later is fine. Right now, I just want you."

Holding her close, knowing that she was going to be alright, he willed her to feel his love. *I got you, Angel. I'll always have you.*

Carol snuggled in, breathing him in. *Warm. Comfort. Safe. Here. Forever.*

"I hear your heartbeat."

"It beats for you."

∾

Pulling into the driveway two days later, Tom glanced over at a still-recovering Carol in the seat next to him. Pale, with dark circles under her luminescent blue eyes, there was a hint of a smile curving her lips. And her breathing had been easier since they had crossed into Fairfield.

Looking up at their house, he saw Laurie, Rob, Jake, Sofia, and Jon on the front porch waiting for them. Sighing deeply, he was glad their friends were so concerned but he worried about Carol. She was better, both physically and mentally, but he would be glad when she talked to her counselor.

Looking back at the friends walking from the porch to the truck, he hoped it wasn't too much. "Stay right there, sweetheart." He hopped out, rounded the front giving a quick head nod to their friends and opened her door. Carefully he scooped her out and carried her toward the house.

"I can walk, you know," she said softly.

Looking down into her blue eyes, he grinned. "Yeah, but this is so much more fun."

Their friends surrounded them, accompanying them inside the house. Tom placed her gently on the sofa, then settled in next to her back, pulling her tightly to his side. Sofia and Jon quickly checked her leg.

"I'm sure it's fine, guys," Carol admonished.

"Honey, nobody does stitches like I do," claimed Jon, as he carefully pulled back her bandage to see the handiwork.

"I don't trust those big-city doctors. Nothing like having your friends sew you back together," Sofia chimed in. "But I guess they took one look of your Mr. Hunka Don't Mess Up My Woman Detective, and they did you up good!"

Hearing Sofia's newest name for him had Tom's eyebrow raised in surprise. Carol couldn't help but giggle, and the sound was music to his ears. She hadn't laughed in two days.

Laurie brought in refreshments from Bernie's Bakery and the friends settled in for a short visit, keeping the conversation light. Everyone danced around the topic of the kidnapping, not wanting to say anything to upset Carol. Smiling, she seemed genuinely pleased to be with their friends.

After a while, Carol's eyes began to close, the pain medications working.

"What have they got her on?" Jon asked.

Tom nodded toward Carol's purse saying, "They're in there."

Sofia pulled open Carol's purse and pulled out the prescription bottles. "This is just pain meds. Do they have her on any anti-anxiety meds?"

Still holding a sleeping Carol in his arms, he just shook his head. "Hospital shrink came by twice, but she wouldn't talk. She also refused any medicines other than for pain." He looked down at the fragile beauty in his arms, cradling her close to his heart. "Almost lost her," he spoke in a whisper, his voice raspy with emotion.

Rob pulled Laurie in tightly, as tears fell from her eyes. Jake, still shaken by the events on the roof as well, walked over and placed his hand on Tom's shoulder.

"Honey," Sofia whispered to Tom. "You need to get her to her counselor and you need to go as well."

Tom just nodded. "Yeah. Already put a call in. We're going in the morning."

Jake squeezed his shoulder, "Good man." Looking around the room, he announced, "We need to leave so Carol can get some rest."

They all stood to leave, saying their goodbyes, as Jon checked with Tom to see if he knew how to take care of the leg wound. Receiving Tom's assurances, he left as well.

With Carol in his arms, he carried her upstairs to their bedroom. Laurie had already turned the bed down, so he just laid her gently on the sheets. Carefully sliding her yoga pants off her body, he looked at the neat stitches running down her thigh. His hands tightened into fists as he thought about that fucker with her. Drugging her. Terrorizing her. Chasing her. Taunting her. Shaking his head, he headed into the bathroom to shower.

Climbing in bed with her later, he gently pulled her body tightly in next to him, knowing the only way he would ever be able to sleep again was if she were wrapped in his arms.

∾

"You ready, dearie?" Jon asked Carol as Sofia fussed over her.

"You'd better be ready to go meet Mr. I'm Gonna Give You Some Loving Detective waiting at the alter," Sofia chimed in.

A smile lighting her face, Carol beamed, "Oh yeah. I have been ready!"

They watched as Laurie and Sofia walked down the aisle first, then the music began the bridal march. "Then let's get the show on the road."

Floating down the aisle, Carol made her way to the front of the church where Tom waited. Jake and Rob stood with him, creating a wall of masculine gorgeousness, but she only had eyes for Tom. Tall, blonde, handsome, his chiseled face in a panty-melting grin, he was her Viking.

The last two months had been difficult as

she alone and then with Tom, went through counseling with Ronda. Reliving her nightmares and fears had been traumatic, but day by day she was getting stronger. Glancing to the side, she saw Ronda in the church smiling at her. Returning her smile, she was so proud that she had not binged or purged throughout the ordeal. Looking back to Tom, she realized once again that she had what she had always wanted. *Trust. Companionship. Care. Comfort. Love.* She made her way to his side, placing her small hand in his much larger one.

Tom watched the beauty as she made her way to him. Heart near bursting, he felt the sting of tears. Blinking them back, not wanting to miss a moment of her journey down the aisle, he smiled as she approached his side. Taking her hand, they turned toward the minister.

Minutes later they were pronounced man and wife. Tom lifted her up in his massive embrace, kissing her the way he had wanted ever since he saw her at the back of the church. A kiss filled with love, promise, passion, hope. *Forever.* Slowly letting her slide down his body as the kiss ended, blue eyes gazed at blue eyes.

"I hear your heartbeat, Mr. Rivers," she said

with a smile.

"It beats for you, Mrs. Rivers," came the heartfelt reply.

Chapter 27

Epilogue

(5 years later)

"Angel, we're gonna be late," Tom called up the stairs.

"We're hurrying," came the reply.

Tommy looked up at his dad. "Why does mommy always say that?"

Hoisting his four-year-old son up in his arms carrying him outside to the truck, he replied, "Son, it just takes women longer to get ready than men. We don't fuss with our hair and clothes like your momma and sister do. But when they come out, make sure you tell them how pretty they are. Remember, we take care of our women."

Carol and two-year-old Joanna came running out of the house, hustling to get to the car. Tom looked over at his beautiful wife and little girl, but before he could say anything, Tommy piped up, "You two look beautiful. Daddy says we have to say that and take care of you."

Rolling her eyes, Carol just laughed. "Oh he did, did he? Well, I guess your daddy is right," she declared as she leaned up for a quick kiss.

"Ew, mommy's kissin' daddy," Tommy proclaimed.

"Son, that's the good stuff," his father said while buckling him in the car seat.

Arriving at Bernie and Mac's place for the Thanksgiving meal, the kids ran over to play with Richie and Sarah, Jakes' children with his wife Emma, and Brock and Caroline, Laurie and Rob's children. As the adults tried to settle the children down for the meal, they couldn't help but laugh at how far they had come in recent years. The boys didn't want to sit with the girls, but their dad's managed to convince them that girl cooties wouldn't jump on them.

Tom stood looking at Jake and Rob, saying, "You know, it won't be too many more years before these kids start pairing off. And I'm, telling you right now, your boys start sniffin' around my Joanna, I'm gonna have my eye on them."

Jake spoke quietly, "You think I'd let either one of your boys anywhere near my Sarah?"

Before Rob could retort, the women walked

over. "Down cavemen," Carol said. "The boys'll be fine and so will the girls. We just raise the boys to respect women and the women to respect themselves, and they'll be just fine."

Nodding at her wisdom, the adults made their way over to the food-laden tables. Bernie and Mac still presided over the table of family and friends. Jake's mother, Mary, sat with Tom's parents, Charles, and Nancy, at the other end of the table. Caroline toddled over to her parents, and Rob picked up his daughter, cradling her as he leaned over to kiss Laurie. Jake and his wife Emma were sharing a look that only lovers and partners can know. Carol recognized it because it was the same look she and Tom gave each other.

She continued to look around, appreciating the simple concept of family and friends gathered around a table. The food no longer bothered her. Eating was for nourishment and enjoyment, but not for stress relief. When she looked in the mirror, she saw the image of a strong woman and was determined to raise her daughter that way. *Healthy. Happy. Accepted. Loved. Family.* Tom leaned down for a kiss before the meal began, still amazed at the beautiful woman at his side.

As the meal was ending, Tommy and Joanna

crawled into their parents' laps, feeling nap time coming on.

"Daddy, I hear your heartbeat," came Tommy's small voice as he hugged his dad.

"Me too," came Joanna's sleepy voice with her cheek pressed up against her mother's chest.

Over the heads of their children, Tom and Carol looked at each other. Blue eyes gazing at blue eyes.

Together they said, "It beats for you," hugging their children close to their hearts.

If you enjoyed Carol's Image, please leave a review! Next up is Laurie's Time.

Keep up with the latest news and never miss another release by Maryann Jordan. Sign up for her newsletter here!

goo.gl/forms/ydMTe0iz8L

Other books by Maryann Jordan

(all standalone books)

All of my books are stand-alone, each with their own HEA!! You can read them in any order!

Saints Protection & Investigation

(an elite group, assigned to the cases no one else wants…or can solve)

Serial Love

Healing Love

Revealing Love

Seeing Love

Honor Love

Sacrifice Love

Protecting Love

Remember Love

Alvarez Security Series

(a group of former Special Forces brothers-in-arms now working to provide security in the southern city of Richland)

Gabe

Tony

Vinny

Jobe

Love's Series

(detectives solving crimes while protecting the women they love)

Love's Taming

Love's Tempting

Love's Trusting

The Fairfield Series

(small town detectives and the women they love)

Laurie's Time

Emma's Home

Fireworks Over Fairfield

I love to hear from readers, so please email me!

Email

authormaryannjordan@gmail.com

Website

www.maryannjordanauthor.com

Facebook

facebook.com/authormaryannjordan

Twitter

@authorMAJordan

Information on Bulimia Nervosa

"Bulimia Nervosa, commonly called bulimia, is a serious, potentially life-threatening eating disorder. People with bulimia may secretly binge – eating large amounts of food – and then purge, trying to get rid of the extra calories in an unhealthy way. For example, someone with bulimia may force vomiting or do excessive exercise.

If you have bulimia, you're probably preoccupied with your weight and body shape, and may judge yourself severely and harshly for your self-perceived flaws. Because it's related to self-image – and not just about food – bulimia can be difficult to overcome.

The exact cause of bulimia is unknown. There are many possible factors that could play a role in the development of eating disorders. But biology, emotional health, societal expectations and other factors increase your risk.

If you have any bulimia symptoms, seek medical help as soon as possible."

—Mayo Clinic, Diseases and Conditions,
Bulimia Nervosa

Acknowledgements

First and foremost, I have to thank my husband, Michael. Always believing in me and wanting me to pursue my dreams, this book would not be possible without his support. To my daughters, MaryBeth and Nicole, I taught you to follow your dreams and now it is time for me to take my own advice. You two are my inspiration!

My best friend, Tammie, who for eighteen years has been with me through thick and thin. You've filled the role of confidant, supporter, and sister.

My dear friend, Myckel Anne, who keeps me on track, keeps me grounded, and most of all – keeps my secrets. Thank you for not only being my proofreader, but my friend.

Going from blogger to author has allowed me to have the friendship and advice of several wonderful authors who always answered my questions, helped me over rough spots, and cheered me on. To Kristine Raymond, you gave me the green light when I wondered if I was crazy and you never let me give up. MJ Nightingale and Andrea Michelle – you two have made a huge impact on my life. EJ Shorthall, Victoria Brock, Jen Andrews, Andrea Long, A.d. Ellis,

ML Steinbrunn, Sandee Love, and all of the amazing authors of the Indie Round Table – thank you from the bottom of my heart.

My beta readers kept me sane, cheered me on, made me correct all my silly errors, and often helped me understand my characters through their eyes. A huge thank you to Denise, Sandi, Christina, Christy, Barbara, Tera, Vanessa, Jennifer, Myckel Anne, Danielle, Shannon, Angela, and Tracey for being my beta girls who love alphas!

Shannon Brandee Eversoll as my editor and Myckel Anne Phillips as my proofreader gave their time and talents to making Carol's Image as well written as it can be.

My street team, The Ladies of Fairfield, you all are amazing! You volunteer your time to promote my books and I cannot thank you enough! I hope you will stay with me, because I have lots more stories inside, just waiting to be written!

As the owner of the blog, Lost in Romance Books, I know the selflessness of bloggers. We promote indie authors on our own time because we believe fully in the indie author community. I want to thank the many bloggers that I have served with, and who are assisting in promoting my series.

Most importantly, thank you readers. You allow me into your home for a few hours as you disappear into my characters and you support me as I follow my indie author dreams.

More About Maryann Jordan

As an Amazon Best Selling Author, I have always been an avid reader. I joke that I "cut my romance teeth" on the historical romance books from the 1970's. In 2013 I started a blog to showcase wonderful writers. In 2014, I finally gave in to the characters in my head pleading for their story to be told. Thus, Emma's Home was created.

My first novel, Emma's Home became an Amazon Best Seller in 3 categories within the first month of publishing. Its success was followed by the rest of the Fairfield Series and then led into the Love's Series. From there I have continued with the romantic suspense Alvarez Security Series and now the Saints Protection & Investigation Series, all bestsellers.

My books are filled with sweet romance and hot sex; mystery, suspense, real life characters and situations. My heroes are alphas, take charge men who love the strong, independent women they fall in love with.

I worked as a counselor in a high school and have been involved in education for the past 30 years. I recently retired and now can spend more time devoted to my writing.

I have been married to a wonderfully patient man for 34 years and have 2 adult very supportive daughters and 1 grandson.

When writing, my dog or one of my cats will usually be found in my lap!